M000205122

About the Author

One of Stella's favourite memories is sitting around a log fire under the African sky sharing stories with family and friends – the sound of laughter and chatter. She grew up in beautiful, rural Zimbabwe, where she lived through a terrorist war, then moved to South Africa and now lives in Australia. Her life journey has been eventful with its highs and lows.

Stella's characters portray strong-minded women and close friendships. Even when all seems lost the determination to endure. To Stella, family and friends are everything.

Dedication

To my late husband John.

Our beautiful daughters, Toni and Rachel, whose reassurance and support has never waived.

My granddaughters, Emma, Joy, Anna, and Jessica, for keeping me young.

Stella Perrott

THE SKY IS BLUER

AUSTIN MACAULEY PUBLISHERS™

LONDON • CAMBRIDGE • NEW YORK • SHARJAH

Copyright © Stella Perrott 2021

The right of Stella Perrott to be identified as author of this work has been asserted by the author in accordance with section 77 and 78 of the Copyright, Designs and Patents Act 1988.

All rights reserved. No part of this publication may be reproduced, stored in a retrieval system, or transmitted in any form or by any means, electronic, mechanical, photocopying, recording, or otherwise, without the prior permission of the publishers.

Any person who commits any unauthorized act in relation to this publication may be liable to criminal prosecution and civil claims for damages.

This is a work of fiction. Names, characters, businesses, places, events, locales, and incidents are either the products of the author's imagination or used in a fictitious manner. Any resemblance to actual persons, living or dead, or actual events is purely coincidental.

A CIP catalogue record for this title is available from the British Library.

ISBN 9781398445147 (Paperback)
ISBN 9781398445154 (ePub-e-book)

www.austinmacauley.com

First Published 2021
Austin Macauley Publishers Ltd
25 Canada Square
Canary Wharf
London
E14 5LQ

Acknowledgements

Thank you to Gary Myers for the use of his painting as the front cover to my book. I first saw Gary's work at a Maleny gallery in the Queensland hinterland. I have always been passionate about blue trees and I have one of Gary's paintings hanging on my wall. You can see his work on his website. garymyers.net.au

My deepest appreciation to Judy Rostedt for editing my book and helping to improve my writing in so many ways. To John Jukes I am grateful for his wisdom in helping me complete my book.

Thank you, to Sharon Harte for proof reading and helping with the final touches.

Val Smetheram for her never-failing belief in me. Jan Human for assisting with the South African police ranks in the 1960/70's. A special thanks to Alan Hadfield for sharing his knowledge of military convoy timeframes, during the Rhodesian bush war.

I am also grateful to my dear friend Yvonne Gillot for her assistance with nursing and medical-procedures. Will Keys for assisting with legal advice and for his support.

My two daughters Toni Symmonds and Rachel Gerber who travelled this journey with me. Thank you for your love and encouragement.

Chapter 1

'Good afternoon, sir, what is your destination?'

The young man leant through the window, a police cap and badge elevating his authority.

'Good afternoon, officer. My wife and I are travelling to Beit Bridge, then on to South Africa.'

'You've left it a little late, sir, have you driven this road before?'

'No. This is our first trip South of the border.' Rick admitted.

The policeman frowned. His dark skin moist from the heat of the day.

'It would be advisable to spend the night in Fort Victoria and leave first thing in the morning.'

He stepped back from the car.

'I must caution you, sir. Should you decide to continue your journey you will be driving through an isolated area and we suggest you do not stop for any reason.' He held Rick's gaze through the car window. 'Make sure you have enough fuel and water. Do you have a weapon, sir?'

'No. I was told weapons aren't permitted across the border.'

Rick had left his 9mm calibre *Llama* handgun in his father's gun safe.

'You're correct, sir, but you could have left it at Beit Bridge police station to be collected on your return journey.'

'I wish I had known. How long is the travelling time to the border, officer?'

'It's about three and a half hours.' he reiterated a previous comment. 'We highly recommend you spend the night and leave first thing in the morning, sir.'

Rick turned to his wife.

'What do you think, Kath, should we spend the night in Fort Victoria?'

She considered this for a moment. The two cars travelling ahead of them had been cautioned, then continued their journey.

'I'll leave it up to you, lovey.'

She felt confident her husband would make the right decision.

'It'll still be daylight when we get there, I think we'll be okay, let's carry on, Kath.'

He turned to the policeman.

'We've decided to continue, thank you, officer.'

The young policeman saluted and waved the honeymooners through.

'Have a safe journey sir, madam.'

They were taking a risk. Rhodesians were living through a terrorist war and had become accustomed to the threat of terrorist attacks. In some ways they had become desensitised.

Rick and Kathy had the additional burden of a time restraint and a limited budget. Their plan was to cross the border into South Africa that day.

Kathy pushed a tape into the tape-deck keeping her thoughts to herself. *We have no form of communication if we break down or get ambushed.*

Rick exceeded the speed limit along the narrow tarred road.

'The sooner we get there, the better,' he muttered.

Kathy clapped her hands as she sang along with the tape. "Country Road, take me home to the place I belong."

The long stretch of road was mainly uninhabited apart from large game-ranches and a few native villages. They passed occasional military checkpoints and an odd car travelling in the opposite direction.

Forty minutes into their journey, they emerged from a cluster of granite hills bedecked with red and orange Masasa trees onto a long and open straight stretch of road. In the distance they noticed three figures dash across the road and disappear as quickly as they had appeared.

'Did you see that, Rick?'

Kathy tensed, sensing her husband's indecision. He slowed for a moment, then increased speed.

'I didn't like the look of them, Kath. They were too far away for us to see much, but they were in a hurry. Let's hope they didn't see us and they weren't terrorists.'

He clenched his jaw and gripped the steering wheel putting the little Datsun bluebird to the test, travelling faster than she had ever done before. The few minutes it took to reach the crossing place felt like an eternity.

Kathy glanced at her husband. The strained concentration on his face made her wonder what he was thinking. She gripped the sides of her seat and focused on the left-hand side of the road where they had seen the figures disappear into the bush. Her subconscious prepared for a burst of gunfire, the fatal result of an ambush. Her eyes flashed searching the rough terrain, not daring to breath until they were past the danger zone, but there was no sign of the men.

'Can we slow down a bit please, Rick.'

Kathy felt unsafe travelling at this speed in their little car.

'I'll slow down after we're...' his foot hit the brake as a Kudu[1] bull leapt across the bonnet.

Kathy screamed and cradled her skull as she propelled towards the dashboard, bracing for the imminent impact. Hooves flashed millimetres from the windscreen. It all happened so quickly - the majestic animal was safely across, but Rick had lost control of the car and struggled against the odds to keep the tyres on the tarred surface. The vehicle sashayed from one side to the other putting his driving skill to the test.

Eventually the little car straddled the centre line and settled down.

'Are you okay, Kath?' Rick's voice trembled as he sunk back into the seat with a sigh of relief.

'Oh, God, Rick, that was close.'

She placed her hand over her mouth as a wave of nausea subsided.

'Thank you, God.' she whispered into her praying hands.

'Bloody hell!' he laughed nervously. 'We avoid two hundred kilograms of Kudu and nearly lost control of the car. My heart's beating like a drum.' He chuckled nervously to himself. 'I'll have to thank my skid-pan instructor for that one.'

The adrenaline rush had them chattering and laughing as they dissected the frightening incident.

'I wish we'd stayed the night in Fort Vic now.' Kathy confessed.

'Yeah, me too, I'm sorry, Kath, I possibly made the wrong decision.'

He patted her on the thigh.

'That was scary, but we're almost half way and should be in Beit Bridge by five. Put on that new Neil Diamond tape will you, lovey?'

Half an hour later they stopped at a roadside military encampment.

'I'm going to tell them what we saw, are you coming with me, Kath?'

'No. I'm going to see if that little shop over there has any cold cokes. I'll meet you back in the car.'

---

[1] Large antelope

Her nerves were shot and she rubbed her bruised shoulder where the safety belt held tight during their close encounter.

Rick followed a uniformed man into the tented encampment. He was gone for some time. When he reappeared, he was followed by several camouflage clad men who scrambled into vehicles and drove off at speed, back in the direction the couple had come.

Kathy was waiting for her husband, propped up under the shade of a baobab tree.

'Did you get the Cokes?' he asked.

'No. Their cooler isn't working.'

She walked towards her husband.

'They were terrorists weren't they, Rick?'

'I think so, Kath. I showed the police where we saw the men crossing on their map.'

He started the engine.

'Let's not talk about it. We'll cross the border in a few hours and put all this behind us for the next few weeks.'

Kathy's intuition told her something nasty had happened that he didn't want to share with her. She gazed out the window at the changing scenery. The earth was parched and cracked, offering up little grass, stunted thorn bushes and the occasional enormous Baobab tree. The heat was stifling, even with the windows wound down.

Her mother's words preyed on her mind. "You came with us to South Africa, when you were six years old, Kathy. Don't you remember *anything* about that holiday?" She knew she should remember something, but try as she may, nothing looked familiar.

The formalities at the border post took forever and the sun was dipping as they crossed the Limpopo River bridge into South Africa. There was plenty of water under the bridge but nothing attractive about its murky green colour. The excitement of the day left them exhausted and they spent that night at Leopard Hotel outside Louis Trichardt.

The following morning, they entered the city of Johannesburg. Neither of them had driven through a large city before. Rick drove while Kathy navigated. The road signs were in Afrikaans and English which was confusing and she struggled to read the map book.

'What are "Slegs[2]"?' she muttered. 'Left, Rick, no right, no left. Oh hell, these street signs don't match the *map* book. I think we're lost.'

'I wish you'd make up your mind, Kath.' Rick grumbled as he swerved to miss a truck.

'Don't get snappy with me, I'm doing my best,' She shook the map book. 'Maybe we should pull over and try to make sense of the map or ask directions at a service station.'

'We don't need to ask people directions. I'll pull over so we can look at the map book together.'

He soon realised it was not as easy as he thought and even with his help, they got lost several times. The city spat them out the other side several hours later.

Kathy broke the tension.

'I'm sorry, lovey, my map reading skills are pathetic,' She started to giggle.

'Did you see the look on that lady's face when we nearly went up that one-way street the wrong way? I mean really! Who builds a road that goes only one way?'

Rick joined in her laughter.

'We're real country bumpkins when it comes to driving through a big city like Johannesburg. I think we should fly next time.'

They stopped for fuel and Kathy was relieved after speaking to a helpful African fuel attendant.

'Yes, madam, this *is* the road to Cape Town.' he grinned broadly at receiving a tip. 'Thank you, madam, have a good journey.'

Later when she calculated the exchange rate, she realised why he was so pleased.

The next night they spent at a run-down hotel outside Bloemfontein. The bath water was tepid and the bed lumpy.

'I hope Ocean-View hotel is a little more, classy than this.' Kathy grumbled after a sleepless night and cold egg on soggy toast for breakfast.

They would be at their destination by the end of the day and enjoyed the final leg of their journey through the Orange Free State.

Fields of golden sunflowers with happy faces nodding in the wind. Kathy was now pleased they had chosen to drive instead of fly. Newly ploughed fields and changing fauna and flora introduced candle-like red Aloes nestled on rocky cliffs and livestock grazing in pastures. They continued down towards the

---

2 Slegs:- only

Eastern Cape, rows of pineapples and wind-swept trees lined the way. Eventually, glimpses of sea and sand along the rugged coastline emerged.

The *"Ocean*-View *Hotel"* sign flickered as the car lights swept into the parking lot. They had barely stopped before Kathy leapt from the car.

'Catch me if you can,' she called to Rick, running down the steps towards the tumbling waves leaving foaming sheets of water up the beach.

She kicked off her shoes and chased a retreating wave, misjudged the returning deluge and was swept off her feet.

She shrieked with laughter. 'I'm soaked to the skin.'

Rick caught her hand, and they ran back and forth frolicking in the waves.

Two wet bedraggled new-arrivals rang the reception bell.

'Welcome, Mr and Mrs Barron, I trust you had a safe journey.' The receptionist smiled sweetly and without waiting for a reply continued, 'I'm sorry, you've missed dinner, but we could arrange for sandwiches to be sent to your room.'

They sat on their balcony overlooking the warm waters of the Indian ocean, Kathy asked herself, *how could I have forgotten something as magical as the sea*?

Their first week was spent taking long walks along the beach, swimming in the sea or hotel pool and eating far too much. They left their worries behind at the border, living in a magical world of no television, radio or newspapers. The second week they explored up and down the coastline savouring every moment. On their second last day the hotel supplied a blanket and picnic basket so they could picnic on the beach near the Great Kei River mouth.

They meandered through coastal bushland. A pair of Cape Spur-fowl took flight squawking noisily and Kathy jumped with fright.

'I didn't expect so much noise from such little birds.' she giggled at her silly reaction.

They spread a blanket over the sand and Kathy lay with her head on Rick's lap gazing into his green eyes.

'Thank you for making me the happiest woman in the world, my darling.'

He lifted her chin and kissed her.

On the return journey, Rick suggested they stop at a roadside café where they chose a table for two next to an open window.

Tuin kafee[3] lived up to its name with floral curtains tied back at the windows and fresh bowls of flowers on each hand-embroidered table cloth. A pretty young Xhosa waitress wearing a frilly apron delivered a chocolate milk shake and Coca-Cola to the young couple.

Kathy was distracted as she poured Coca-Cola into Rick's glass, her eyes fixed on the blond stranger near the counter. The fizzing liquid spilt over the rim of the glass, flowed across the tablecloth and dripped onto Rick's trousers.

He leapt to his feet and snatched the bottle from her.

'Kath, are you okay? What's wrong with you, lovey?'

She ignored his question and stared past him. He reached for her hand and squeezed it.

'Kathy, can you hear me?'

She didn't respond.

'Speak to me.'

His eyes followed her gaze.

The man at the counter was possibly in his mid-thirties, but there was nothing remarkable about him. He was reasonably good looking and wore long trousers with an open-neck shirt.

Rick lowered his voice to almost a whisper. 'Do you know him, Kath?'

Her gaze didn't falter.

'Stop that gawking, Kathy, you're frightening me!'

He moved around and crouched beside her.

With his hands on her shoulders, he attempted to gently twist her body to face him. She gritted her teeth and resisted.

He examined the stranger again.

'What is it about this man that frightens you? For goodness' sake, Kathy, tell me what's wrong?'

Blinking for the first time, her eyes met his. She looked down and picked up the hem of the tablecloth tracing the embroidery with her fingertip.

'Yes, I *know* him.' she muttered.

Her eyes lifted again as she watched a blonde lady with two little girls approach the man. The family left the café together.

'Rick, I'm going to be sick.'

Kathy ran from the room.

---

[3] 'Tuin kafee:-   Garden café

Chapter 2

Seven years earlier; the year is 1965 and the winds of change are sweeping Africa. The British Empire was granting its African territories their independence, but self-governance and majority rule is causing uncertainty. Especially amongst the inhabitants of the small landlocked country of Rhodesia.

Kathy's parents Ben and Frances Parker had bought their farm Huchi[4] in Rhodesia, shortly after they married. The crumbling brick farmhouse was over a hundred years old and badly in need of repair, but their limited budget only allowed for planting, reaping, feeding livestock and paying wages, these had to take precedence over everything else.

The grubby exterior of the rambling home with its wrap-around veranda had a penny vine creeper clinging to its walls. In the rainy season, strategically placed buckets caught water that leaked through its corrugated iron roof. Kathy loved the stone fireplace with its wooden mantelpiece. It was the heart of an enormous living area with chunky furniture draped in brightly woven throws. Patterned rugs and paintings of African wildlife provided a stark contrast against the whitewashed walls and grey concrete floors. Her favorite room was the kitchen with its old Angus wood-stove against the back wall. Each week after church, the aroma of a Sunday roast and vegetables would fill the house, reminding her of the treat in store. She loved Huchi; it was not just a house it was her home.

She knew her father would not have sold Huchi because of political unrest and he would have fought and died for the land he loved. He was dying of cancer. The biopsy taken from a bleeding melanoma nestled in his armpit was malignant. He had only a year to live; barely enough time to get his affairs in order.

Her father planted the "sold" sign at the farm gate and arranged for twelve-year-old Kathy and her mother to stay with his widowed sister Linda, in the city

---

[4] Huchi:-   Honey

of Salisbury. Kathy would continue attending boarding school, returning home for the weekends and school holidays, as she had done for the last five years.

Just six months after they moved to Salisbury, Aunt Linda collected Kathy from boarding school and drove her to the Salisbury General Hospital to join her mother at her father's bedside. Ben was deteriorating rapidly.

'Forget the farm, Franny. Make a home for you and Kathy in Salisbury. There's enough money from the sale of Huchi to buy a small house and pay for Kathy's education.'

Kathy knew her parents were devoted to each other; she watched her mother gaze at the once tall good-looking man she'd fallen in love with. He was now only a shadow of his former self. He uttered his final wishes in a rasping voice.

'Promise me, you'll look for a job, Fran... you're a talented writer; keep yourself busy and don't look back.'

Frances lifted his frail hand, rubbed it against her cheek and kissed his fingertips.

His eyes closed and he whispered, 'Kathy, you're our special girl; promise me, you'll take care of your mother. I want to think of my two girls together, always.'

Ben died in the annex of Salisbury General Hospital on the 3rd of June 1965. His funeral passed in a blur of heartache and tears for Kathy and her mother. Later, she recalled bowls of flowers, chicken casseroles, family and friends who came and went; then gradually they drifted back to their own busy lives.

She felt deep anger towards God. *Why my dad? He was a wonderful man. Why couldn't you take some horrible person?* At night her mother sobbed in the privacy of her bedroom. In the morning Frances would appear with a brave smile, but Kathy knew better – her mother was keeping up appearances for her sake. They were both hiding their true feelings.

The third school term arrived and Kathy returned to her weekly boarding school. It was too soon; she was depressed. She appreciated her school friends' support but each night she cried herself to sleep.

Her weekends in the city were boring. She would stay at Aunt Linda's house while her mother was house hunting for a home of their own. Then her friend Tanya Wisper invited her to spend her weekends on the farm with the Wisper family.

'Would it be okay, for me to go home with Tanya for the weekends, Mum?' she asked. 'There isn't much for me to do at Aunt Linda's house.'

Her mother agreed, promising to phone her at boarding school during the week, and keep her updated on the house-hunting.

'So far, every place the agent has shown me is too urbanised, sweetie. I'll phone you as soon as I find something suitable. I miss you, Kath. I'm hoping to have our own home by Christmas.'

On the 11th of November 1965, Rhodesia declared UDI[5]. Unilateral declaration of independence. Rhodesia was no longer a part of the British Empire. Frances commented that it was a brave step. To Kathy it meant very little. She was desperately unhappy and longed to return to her life at the farm.

It was weeks later that she received a positive call from her mother. 'It's a smaller house than our house on the farm, sweetie, but it has a similar wrap-around veranda with screened wrought-iron railings. There's a magnificent flamboyant tree in the back garden that reminds me of the trees we had on the farm. I hope you will like it, Kathy?' she rushed on. 'We'll be close to the city center and not far from the hospital if you still want to go nursing when you leave school. I've made them an offer.'

She paused trying to pluck up enough courage to mention the subject she had been avoiding.

'We'll have to find a new home for the dogs. It would be cruel to move large dogs onto such a small property.'

Kathy fired up.

'We *can't* give Dallas and Luger away. We've had them since they were puppies!'

She gripped the phone.

'They'll think we've *abandoned* them, Mum.' she muttered a polite goodbye, before she burst into tears and replaced the receiver.

Frances purchased the house at 66 Bakestone Street in the Avenues. After the sale was complete, she arranged delivery of their belongings. The furniture looked out of place in the smaller rooms, it was too bulky and dated, but she decided it would have to do.

Kathy saw the house for the first time when she arrived home for the Christmas holidays. It would not have mattered which property her mother had bought. For her nothing could replace Huchi. The new house with its large veranda and scarlet flowering flamboyant tree did nothing for her.

---

[5] UDI:-   Unilateral declaration of independence

'I know you've done your best, Mum, but apart from the furniture, it's nothing like our house on the farm. I wish we could go back to Huchi. I miss the dogs and I couldn't sleep last night with the traffic noise. I'm used to the quiet sounds of the African bush,' She was tearful.

Frances sighed. 'I've thought the same thing many times, sweetie. You'll eventually grow used to it, just give it a chance. Remember, darling, this was daddy's dying wish. He wanted us to make a life for ourselves here in Salisbury.'

She remembered something positive she hadn't told her daughter.

'The people who bought Huchi farm from us have agreed to keep the dogs and give them a permanent home.'

Kathy remained at boarding school for the next three years. She often spent the weekends and school holidays at her second home, with Tanya and her family on their farm. She didn't enjoy city life, but this all changed the year she turned sixteen. Charlotte moved into the house next door to 66 Bakestone Street.

Charlotte was only six months older than Kathy, but years older in confidence and maturity. She was a bronzed goddess with flawless skin and sizable breasts. It was Charlotte who suggested Kathy use an oil and vinegar sun potion.

'I guarantee you'll look amazing with a tan, Kathy. It'll get rid of that boarding school anaemic look. Don't they allow you outside at that place?'

'Of course, they do, it isn't a prison, Charlotte. I play a lot of sport, but I have a fair skin and burn easily; are you sure I won't get sunburnt if I use your suntan concoction?'

'Not unless you're silly enough to fall asleep in the sun.'

Kathy was home for the Christmas school holidays and had found a secluded sunny spot in the back garden where none of the neighbours could see her in her bikini. She opened her diary to read the last entry for 1969.

This is my fourth Christmas at 66 Bakestone Street, in the Avenues. I'm getting used to living in the city and have a new neighbour called Charlotte. She's quite nice.

I turned sixteen this year and have never been kissed. Nothing sweet about being sixteen!

I still miss Huchi farm, but Mum and I are safer living in the city. There have been several farm attacks.

Since declaring UDI four years earlier, the Rhodesian war had escalated and like many Rhodesians, Kathy hadn't fully understood the implications of UDI. She closed the diary, laid a towel on the lawn then shook a bottle of oil and vinegar vigorously. She unscrewed the lid and poured a little liquid into her cupped hand, smeared it over her body and lay belly down with her back exposed to the sun.

With a floppy hat to shield her face she closed her eyes and dozed in the warm sun. Her thoughts wandered back to Huchi, the anchor she had returned to all her life.

She was a little girl, home on the farm. Her mother lounged in her favourite wicker chair, staring through the screened alcove on the veranda.

'Is it time for lunch yet, Mummy?' her seven-year-old voice piped.

'We'll have lunch shortly, sweetie, come and sit here.' Her mother tapped the seat beside her. 'I need to tell you something first.' Kathy squeezed into the gap next to her and snuggled close.

'You've completed two years of home-schooling and you're going into standard one next year. You're too old for me to teach now, so you'll be going to a proper school with other children.'

She wrinkled her nose and waited for her mother to explain.

'It's a boarding school, sweetie. Do you know what that means?'

Kathy looked uneasy as her mother continued.

'It's a place where you live in a dormitory with other children during the week. A matron will take care of you when you're not doing lessons, and instead of coming home each day you'll stay in a hostel where you'll sleep and have your meals.'

'Why? Why can't I go to school and come back to Huchi afterwards?'

'It's too far to travel every day, my love. The nearest school is two hours away on a dirt road.'

Her mother took time to consider before she spoke again.

'You'll be going to Stanford Brown school as a weekly boarder. Of course, you'll come home every weekend and during school holidays.' Her tone implied this would be a fantastic opportunity.

'I don't want to go,' The little girl was adamant.

'And *we* don't *want* to send you *away*.' Frances reached to cuddle her, but Kathy shrank back.

'You'll make friends with other children the same age as you; most of them live on farms like ours.'

Frances searched for a way to persuade her daughter.

'Mummy isn't a teacher, Sweetie. You're a bright little girl who needs a good education.'

By nature, Kathy was stubborn, she found it hard to adapt to the strict rules and routine of the school and saw the boarding hostel as a bed away from home, nothing more. Sometimes she would refuse to finish the food on her plate and be left sitting alone at the long dining table. One evening a member of staff forgot about her.

She was missing at the eight o'clock bed check and the matron raised the alarm. Eventually, a staff member found her asleep on the bench next to the dining table, her food still unfinished. Kathy didn't have a large appetite and no one could force her to eat more than she wanted.

Mr and Mrs Parker visited the headmistress the following day. Kathy wasn't present at the meeting, but she knew her parents had supported her because she was never left sitting at the dining table again.

Over the years she learned to accept boarding school as her lot in life, but only because she could return home to Huchi every weekend and during the holidays. She was happiest on the farm. Her thoughts moved forward through the years as she remembered Christmas on the farm - throwing the ball for the dogs, learning to ride her bike and picnics at the dam. It didn't cross her mind that one day she would leave Hutchi to live in a city.

Kathy woke from her dream with a start. She propped herself up on one elbow, then glanced at her watch – she had fallen asleep.

'Drat.'

She twisted to look at the back of her arms and legs and moaned.

A crimson strip ran down one side of her body confirming her fears; instead of suntan she had sunburn. She dropped the oily mixture into the garbage bin.

The last person Kathy wanted to see was Charlotte who had assured her she would not get sunburnt, "unless you're *silly enough* to fall asleep in the sun". She hurried to her room with the intention of covering herself before anyone could see how burnt she was.

'Oops!' she exclaimed at finding Charlotte sitting on her bed reading a magazine.

'Oh, there you are, Kath. Where have you been? I've been waiting for you for *ages*.'

She looked a little put-out and then sat upright staring at Kathy.

'What, have you done to yourself?'

There was a hint of amusement in her voice.

'You look like a half-ripe tomato.'

Kathy glared. 'I fell asleep after spreading *your* oil and vinegar mixture over myself,' She sounded annoyed. 'Luckily, it's only the back-half of my arms and legs.'

She twisted to examine them and grimaced.

'Ouch, my back too; I do look like a partly boiled lobster and I'll probably shed my skin like one too.'

Suddenly she saw the absurdity in the situation. She pulled a silly face and they both laughed.

'Go and get some calamine lotion, Kathy, and I'll dab it on you. If you're careful your skin might not peel.'

Kathy stretched out on the bed still wearing her bikini while Charlotte obligingly dabbed her raw skin. They had only known each other for a few weeks but were already sharing secrets as teenagers do.

'I was four when my dad left home,' offered Charlotte. 'Mum has raised me as a single parent.'

'Do you remember anything about your father?'

'Oh yes, I remember *everything* about him. My dad's lovely. Neither Mum nor Dad wanted children. I was a mistake and Mum drew the short straw – *she* ended up raising me,' Charlotte sniggered. 'I've only seen my dad briefly a couple of times when I was small, but he's got plenty of money. He pays my private school fees and sends me money and a birthday card every year. When I leave school, I'm going to visit him in South Africa.'

Kathy was surprised that her friend displayed no resentment towards either of her parents.

'You're so clever, Char, I've got this terrible memory. I can't remember much before I was seven and went to boarding school.'

She looked thoughtful.

'Maybe it's because I've had a sheltered life on the farm, so there was no need to remember.'

Her friend had finished dabbing and Kathy sat up.

'I've got a secret, Charlotte. Do you promise not to tell anyone if I tell you something interesting about me?'

Her blue eyes watched her friend's reaction.

'Do you promise?'

Charlotte didn't enjoy games so her reply was half-hearted.

'Yeah, yeah I promise.'

'No, Charlotte! Not just *any* promise, you have to mean it. Do you cross your heart and hope to *die* if you *ever* tell anyone?'

'Okay.' she gave a resigned sigh. 'I cross my heart and hope to die.'

Kathy was still doubtful.

'Hmmm, I hope I can trust you… the thing is, I'm psychic. There's this boy who I talk to and I'm the only person who can see or hear him.'

Charlotte's eyes widened.

'Oooh a boy, tell me more, Kath. What's he like, is he good looking?' she smiled encouragingly.

Her reaction irritated Kathy.

'He's not a *real* boy, Charlotte, he's sort of… a *spirit* boy. I call him my Buddy. He's about fifteen and well, he's…' she thought for a second 'just normal. He's friendly and really nice – the thing is that I'm the only person who can see him or speak to him.'

She felt sure her friend was interested, now.

'I made the mistake of telling mum about me being psychic. She said it was un-Godly to dabble in the supernatural so I've never told anyone else.'

She looked down at her hands and became suddenly serious.

'I don't think Buddy likes the city. I haven't seen him since we left the farm.'

Charlotte looked at her incredulously.

'You're freaking me out, Kathy… you can't remember anything before you started boarding school and now you say you communicate with spooks!'

She pursed her lips.

'Tell me, Kathy, have you ever been on a date with a real boy? Not a *spirit* boy, I'm talking about the male species of the *human* race?'

Kathy thought for a moment.

'I met a boy called Ronnie when I was staying with my friend Tanya on their farm in Bindura. He liked me and wrote to me at boarding school, but when mum bought this house in Salisbury, I thought I wouldn't see him again, so I didn't write back to him.'

She showed no regrets at losing touch with the only boy who had ever shown an interest in her.

Charlotte looked at her askance.

'Gee, Kath, you've really been left behind at that girls' boarding school of yours – time you get with it, girl! My boyfriend Zach is *so* cool… wait till you meet him. He's handsome with jet black hair, he rides a 500cc motorbike and he's the lead singer in a band called "The Bandits".'

Kathy was impressed. To her, being a lead singer in a rock band lifted him to celebrity status.

Charlotte grinned.

'He's my mum's worst nightmare. She's told me I'm forbidden to ride on his bike.' she chuckled mischievously. 'Fat chance!'

Her infectious giggle made Kathy laugh too.

'Got to go, Kath,' Suddenly her uninvited friend jumped to her feet.

'Zach's phoning to tell me where the band's playing tonight. You should come with me sometime.'

She didn't even close the door as she was in such a hurry.

Kathy found her mother lounging on the veranda in her favourite wicker chair. She had bought it with her from the farm. There were only a few weeks left before the school term started.

'Take a seat, Kathy.'

Unsure if what she was about to hear, Kathy perched on the arm of a chair.

'How would you like to leave boarding school and spend your final two years of schooling as a day-scholar living here with me, sweetie?'

'Which school would I go to, Mum?'

'There are two girl's high schools within walking distance of here.'

Frances had done her homework before she bought a house in the Avenues.

'Can I go to the private school where Charlotte goes?'

'No!' Frances answered abruptly. 'Sorry, but we can't afford such luxuries. A government school will give you an excellent education anyway.'

Kathy agreed – anything was better than boarding school, even if she had to live in this horrid little house in the Avenues. For the first time in her life, she would be a day scholar and come home each day.

Starting at a new school, was not the only thing that happened that January. Frances was contacted by Woman's Weekly magazine and offered the position of Assistant Editor.

She was beaming from ear to ear when she told Kathy about her new job prospect.

'I went for an interview before Christmas. I didn't mention it to you, because I didn't think I stood a chance. I'm fifty-two years old and haven't worked for a magazine publishing company for thirty years.'

She hugged her daughter.

'Oh, Kathy, I'm excited and terrified all at the same time.'

Kathy hugged her back, thrilled to see her mother looking genuinely happy for a change. She was proud to have a mother who led by example, expecting no more from others than she gave of herself. Ben and Frances Parker had met at a sports club, where they both played tennis. They would tell anyone who would listen how they had fallen in love at first sight and married just ten months later.

Over the years Frances had often submitted short stories to magazine editors and Kathy remembered how the family would celebrate each time a cheque arrived, signalling that one of her articles was to be published. Her mother was still a strikingly good-looking woman, her red hair and flawless skin making her unforgettable.

At seventeen and a half, Kathy was a blonde version of her mother and had blossomed into a natural beauty, oblivious to the heads that turned whenever she entered a room. In contrast, her sophisticated friend Charlotte, expected everyone to acknowledge her beauty.

Kathy sometimes accompanied Charlotte to gigs when Zach was rehearsing with The Bandits rock band and this is where she met Rick Barron, the group's spectacled lead guitarist.

Rick was not conventionally good looking, but he was smart, funny and caring. He was older than the other band members and the only one who could read and write music. He was a second-year law student, studying at university. Kathy took a fancy to the tall guy with smiling green eyes and started regularly attending the Bandit's gigs with Charlotte. He eventually asked her out and they had been dating ever since.

Kathy was in her last year of school. Charlotte would do another year because she wanted to be a doctor and needed to complete her 'A levels' to enter Medicine.

Prudence Pistorius, Charlotte's mother and Frances weren't friends, but as they lived next door to each other, they sometimes met for a tete-a-tete. Prudence was a large formidable woman with a no-nonsense attitude.

'The girls are in their final years of school, Frances, and I'm sure you agree their studies come first. I propose that we ban friends from visiting during the week. They can see their boyfriends over the weekend and in school holidays.'

Prudence had a way of rubbing Frances up the wrong way, but on this occasion she agreed.

'I'll have a word with Kathy and tell her that no boys can visit during the school week.'

'It's a stupid rule,' grumbled Charlotte. 'Our grades are good; what difference does it make if we meet up with the boys for half an hour once or twice a week?'

Kathy sided with her friend and it wasn't difficult to put a plan into action. On Tuesday and Thursdays at an agreed time, Charlotte would tell her mother she was visiting Kathy to help with her homework. At the same time Kathy would leave her home to visit Charlotte. They met under the flamboyant tree then made their way out the back gate to a rendezvous around the corner where Zach and Rick were waiting. Half an hour later, they returned home, their mothers none the wiser, and no harm done.

'You see,' Charlotte boasted after a few weeks, 'I told you our plan would work; anyway, Kathy's psychic, so she'll warn us of pending danger.'

'Don't mock me, Charlotte, it's a bad omen.' Kathy cautioned her.

The following week their luck ran out. Prudence visited Francis while the two girls were allegedly in each other's company and the fool-proof plan was busted wide-open.

'You, bloody little hot pants!' shrieked Mrs Pistorius, as both men vanished into the darkness, unwilling to face her wrath.

What had seemed a mere prank, hours earlier, now assumed gigantic proportions. Charlotte's punishment was to be sent away to boarding school for her final year of schooling. She never forgave her mother for overreacting to this school girl prank.

Kathy got away scot-free.

Her mother claimed, 'My daughter would never do such a thing. 'It's the influence of that delinquent girl next door.'

'Oh, please, Mum!'

Kathy was so embarrassed.

'Don't be ridiculous, I'm just as much to blame!'

Chapter 3

Several years had passed since the death of Kathy's father and their move to the city of Salisbury.

Kathy had completed her nursing training and was now a state registered nurse. She was passionate about her nursing career and studying further to become a theatre sister.

A terrorist war was raging due to Rhodesia's declaration of independence and she found herself working long hours nursing men, women and children of all races, many with brutal war-related injuries. She joined others praying for an end to the terrible conflict.

One morning she was checking the admissions list when she noticed a Mrs Wisper had been admitted to the intensive care unit during the night. She hurried down the passage where she found her good friend from boarding school days, in a state of shock. Tanya sobbed in Kathy's arms, too distressed to speak.

Kathy later learned that terrorists had attacked the farmhouse shortly before Tanya and her brother had arrived at the homestead. Mr Whisper was already dead, Mrs Wisper barely alive, and in a critical condition. Tanya and her brother had rushed her to hospital.

Kathy held her friend tightly.

'Don't try to talk, Tanya. I'll get you something to help you cope with what you're going through.'

She gave her friend a glass of water and a mild sedative.

'Oh, Kath, please don't let Mum die.'

Heartbroken, Tanya fell to her knees and prayed at her mother's bedside.

Matron allowed Kathy to spend her shift in ICU where she did her best to comfort Tanya and other family members as they arrived during the day.

She remained late into the night, long after her shift was over. Mrs Wisper had always been so kind to her. She was a petite, kind-hearted lady who loved to bake and sew. She was well known for her exquisite homemade creations.

'I talked to Mum all the way here in the back of the car,' Tanya wept brokenly 'I kept hoping she'd regain consciousness and say something.'

Tanya kissed her mother's cheek.

'Please, Mum, wake up and speak to me.' Intermittent choking sobs disrupted her words. 'Oh God, please bring her back to us.'

Kathy had read the notes. The surgical team had drilled a small burr hole in Mrs Wisper's skull to relieve pressure on the brain. She was on life support and the prognosis was not good. Shortly after midnight, she sadly passed away without regaining consciousness. Tanya and her brother were in a state of shock.

'I can't believe this has happened. Please tell me it's all a bad dream, Kathy.'

'I'm so sorry, Tanya.'

There was little more Kathy could say or do as she watched the grief-stricken family walk out the front door of the hospital. After they had gone, she sat alone in the dark, feeling emotionally drained.

What a dreadful day it had been. She had hidden her personal feelings and the love she felt for this family, wanting to be strong to support them during their hour of need.

The emotions she had filed away after her father's death resurfaced. *I miss you so much, Daddy. I felt safe when I was a little girl holding your hand, walking through the rows of citrus trees. I never dreamt the world could be this cruel. I'll always be thankful for the wonderful years we had together.*

She turned her thoughts to Tanya and the Wisper family. She had loved going home with Tanya to their farm during her last few years at boarding school and tried to recall the fun and laughter, but it was overshadowed by this terrible tragedy. Kathy wept for the loss of life and a family torn apart, then fell to her knees and prayed.

'Please, God, find a solution and let peace return to Rhodesia.'

When she arrived home, she woke her mother to tell her the heart-breaking news. She could not remember the last time she had held her mother or told her she loved her.

'I love you, Mum. I don't know what I would do without you.'

They clung to each other and for the first time since leaving the farm, they both shared their innermost feeling.

"I miss daddy and I don't think I'll ever be as happy as I was when we lived on the farm.'

She allowed the tears to flow freely.

'I'm glad he's not here to see the pain and suffering. Never in my wildest dreams did I imagine the country would change so quickly. Perhaps, daddy had a premonition of what was to come and that is why he was in such a hurry to sell Huchi and move us into the city?'

Her mother gazed out the window.

'He was a wise man, Sweetie, he just wanted us to be safe.'

They talked for hours, exhausted, but too upset to sleep.

Later that day, Kathy phoned Rick to tell him the tragic news. He had heard about the farm attack on the radio, not realising it was Tanya Wisper's parents who had been killed. A lump rose in Kathy's throat as she told him the tragic details of the attack.

'It was awful, Rick, I felt so helpless, there was nothing I could do or say to console Tanya, but she didn't give up hope that her mother would regain consciousness. I cannot imagine what it must be like to lose both parents like that.'

The war was intensifying and the tragedies reported on the airwaves were on the increase. Somehow, because Kathy was close to Tanya and her family, it seemed much worse.

A few days later, Rick and Kathy attended Mr and Mrs Wisper's funeral, along with hundreds of other mourners who stared dumbly at the head stones. So many shattered lives in a community searching for solutions.

Rick and Kathy were very much in love and saving hard for their future; they planned to marry as soon as Rick was qualified. All able-bodied men were required to do call-up duties with armed services and Rick was seconded to the police reserve. Every three months he did a stint of bright-light duties in a remote area offering protection to farming families experiencing continued attacks. She dreaded his call ups and suffered many sleepless nights until he was back in the city with her.

Kathy led a busy life and now seldom had time to reminisce about her life on the farm or her spirit friend Buddy. He had faded away and she convinced herself he was just a figment of her imagination, but her subconscious would not let her completely forget him.

Charlotte and Kathy remained close friends, but Charlotte had never forgiven her mother for sending her to boarding school during her final year of schooling.

Being sent to boarding school had signalled the end of her relationship with Zach. He did visit her at the boarding school hostel a few times, but she had refused to see him.

She had told Kathy, 'I look stupid in my school uniform without any makeup. Zach sings in a rock band – he won't stay faithful to me when the girls throw themselves at him. I want us to stay friends. My dad once told me; if you love someone set them free; if they come back, it's meant to be.'

Charlotte completed her final year and received straight A's. The following year she entered the Faculty of Medicine.

'I'm too busy studying to be a doctor to have time for a boyfriend,' she told Kathy.

Zach did have a string of girlfriends after their break-up, but they hadn't lasted very long and Kathy often wondered if he was still in love with Charlotte.

Charlotte and Kathy celebrated their twenty-first birthdays with a joint party at Meikles Hotel. Charlotte's father paid for the party although he could not attend. The girls met with friends and family to let down their hair and dance to the Bandits' music until the early hours. Even if only for one night, they wanted to forget the political situation and enjoy a celebration they would always remember.

A few die-hard stragglers crossed the road to Rhodes Central Park where white-lights beamed through the water fountain, triggering Charlotte's sense of fun.

'Come on, Kath, let's strip off and swim in the fountain.'

Kathy laughed.

'I'll race you - the last in is a sissy.'

She kicked off her shoes and started unbuttoning her dress.

Rick hadn't drunk enough to stand by and watch his girlfriend strip in public.

'Stop that, Kathy! I know you've had a bit to drink, but think what you're doing?'

She pulled her dress back up around her shoulders and ran towards him linking her arm through his.

'Come on, Honey, lighten-up and have some fun.'

He pulled his arm away.

'If you take your clothes off and get into that fountain, then we're finished!'

His jaw set rigid.

'Stop being such a boring geek, Ricky,' she teased, 'I'm only twenty-one once. Strip off and join us.'

Off came her dress.

'Whoo-hoo, here I come.'

She jumped into the fountain.

Rick shook his head in disbelief as Charlotte splashed Kathy and they chased each other around the fountain.

'I can't believe you did that, Kath, you're nothing but a vulgar bimbo!'

'Lighten up, Lovey. I'm having fun, come and join us.'

She still thought she could persuade him.

'Come on, my macho man, are you jealous of your bimbo showing off her stunning body?'

The girls continued splashing each other and shrieking with laughter.

Rick was livid. 'You don't know when to stop, do you? I don't want to ever see you again.'

He turned to leave and she felt a wave of panic.

'You have to be kidding. Why are you being such a bore?'

Surely, he's joking, he wouldn't really leave me… would he?

'I don't appreciate my girlfriend making a spectacle of herself by running around naked for the world to see.'

With these words he stormed off into the night.

'Wait, Rick, don't go.'

She started to run after him and then stopped.

He's being unreasonable. I'm just having fun. She had always been stubborn and since her boarding school days she hated being ordered around. *If he cannot accept me as I am, then perhaps it's better he goes.* Her half-naked frolic in the fountain had just torpedoed her dreams of spending the rest of her life with Rick.

Each blamed the other for the break-up. Despite efforts from both sides to bring them back together, their own stubbornness and feeling of injustice kept them apart. Kathy convinced herself that Rick didn't love her and had been looking for an excuse to dump her.

She was miserable and lost weight, her once fitting clothes now hung loosely on a bony body. To comfort herself she thought of everything except Rick. Her happiest memories were of life on Huchi. She recalled a particular incident when walking near the citrus trees with the dogs. A troop of baboons appeared from a rocky outcrop and crossed the road ahead of them.

The dominant male stood on his hind legs baring his sharp teeth and barking a warning. The baboons would tear the dogs to pieces if they didn't retreat immediately. She called to them then turned and ran into the grove of trees. There was a brief wrangle between the baboons and dogs. She wove in and out between the fruit trees following her imaginary friend back to the farm house. To her relief the dogs arrived unharmed about twenty minutes later. This was one of many memories causing her sleepless nights with strange dreams and she was beginning to have doubts about some of her memories.

Kathy accepted that she was partly to blame for their break up, but Rick had acted like a real jerk. Someone had seen him with another girl and she believed he had used this incident as a convenient way of dumping her.

A week before Christmas the front doorbell rang. Kathy opened the door a fraction and peered through the crack. Rick's green eyes looked back at her.

'Kathy,' he called.

She shut the door and shouted to her mother.

'Mum, please get the front door, it's Rick. I've got to change, I'm still in my pyjamas.'

She joined her mother and Rick on the veranda and chose the chair furthest from him.

'I'm sorry I shut the door. I wasn't properly dressed.' she explained.

Frances initiated small talk to ease the tension in the room. Then she remembered an urgent need for fresh bread and hurried out the back door to the shops.

Kathy scratched around for something to say.

'We're having good rains.'

She was furious with herself. *How corny to discuss the weather?*

'Some farming areas have been declared drought-stricken.' Rick reminded her.

'But Salisbury is having plenty of rain.'

'We *don't* grow crops in the city,' Rick quipped, his eyes twinkling.

He had irritated her. She folded her arms, waiting for him to initiate the next topic. He rose and walked across to her with a gift tied with a red bow.

'Merry Christmas, Kath.'

'Thank you. I'll open it on Christmas day. I'm sorry, I haven't bought you *anything* yet.'

She felt guilty.

'How have *you been,* Rick?'

He raised his eyebrows. 'About the same as you by the look of things. *God,* Kathy. You're the stubbornest woman I know. Why risk everything we had for a swim in a stupid fountain? I thought I meant more to you than that.'

She swallowed, trying to keep her tone playful.

'That's *priceles*s coming from you, Rick Barron. You of all people know how I hate being ordered around. I believe you have a new girl-friend and want an excuse to dump me.'

He shook his head and stood up. A wave of panic washed over her. She didn't want him to leave.

'You have obviously been listening to scandal. I have not even looked at another woman.'

I have to say something to keep him here.

'You mean the world to me, Rick.' She floundered. 'I've been so miserable... why did you spoil everything by stomping off like that?'

'Because you called me a boring geek when I asked you not to strip off and run around naked in a fountain with your friend Charlotte!'

'We weren't naked, we were in bra and pants. You didn't object when I wore my bikini which is far more revealing. It was after midnight, there was no one there to see us!'

She raised her eyes to the ceiling.

'You're an insufferable prude.'

She walked to the window and drew the curtain further back, then turned to face him.

'I had a bit too much to drink, but I was having fun and I wanted the man I love to join me. But no. He called *me* a vulgar bimbo and stomped off.'

She couldn't help herself and she giggled.

'Ahaa, *Did I?*'

His green eyes sparkled. She slowly walked towards him holding his gaze. He pulled her into his arms and kissed her, holding her tightly as if he was afraid, she might escape. He pulled her onto his lap as he sat on the chair, then lowered her to the rug.

'I love you, Kath, I've missed you so much.'

They clung to each other hungrily.

'I love you too. Oh, Rick, please don't ever leave me again.'

'Will you marry me, Kath?'

'Oh yes, let's get married right away, Rick.' she purred.

The slamming of the back door alerted them to Frances' return. They were seated next to each other on the couch holding hands when she entered.

Frances hesitated in the doorway, a tentative smile on her lips.

'Does this mean what I think it means?'

'We're getting married, Mum.' Kathy beamed.

'Will it be a long engagement?'

'No!' they answered simultaneously.

A date was set for Saturday, the 12th of April the following year. Three months wasn't much time to plan a wedding. Fortunately, Frances had put money aside for her daughter's wedding. Rick's parents were happy to pay for a marquee in their garden as the venue. His parents also gave Rick and Kathy a cheque for their honeymoon. They had not planned on a honeymoon. Money was tight and they needed to set up a home.

'We both have leave due to us, Kath, so let's explore the possibilities of having a holiday. Zach spent two weeks on the beach in Durban and said it wasn't that expensive.'

Kathy agreed to visit a travel agent and see if they could afford to honeymoon in South Africa.

She asked her mother about a holiday cottage.

'Mum, have you got contact details for that cottage where you and Dad stayed in the Eastern Cape? Rick and I are thinking of going to South Africa on our honeymoon.'

Frances stiffened and she looked uneasy.

'Kathy, *you* came with us when we stayed in that cottage in Kleinemonde. Don't you remember *anything* about that holiday?'

Kathy was embarrassed about her bad memory. '*No,* I don't. All I remember is you and daddy talking about a holiday cottage on the South Africa coast.'

Frances lit a cigarette, took a pull and exhaled.

'We stayed at Travellers Joy cottage in Kleinemonde. It's a lonely spot, miles from the shops and the accommodation's very basic.'

She tapped her cigarette on an ashtray.

'It's not what you and Rick are looking for. Why don't you ask Harwood Travel Agents about their package holidays to Durban? You could fly instead of spending four days travelling by car.'

She was sure her mother was about to tell her something when the doorbell rang. Charlotte had arrived to take her to the dressmaker for a bridal gown fitting.

Rick took three weeks leave and left the honeymoon arrangements up to Kathy. Money would be tight but she calculated they could afford a two-week holiday at Ocean-View hotel on the Eastern Cape coast.

'If we travel by car, it's a three-day journey there and back, so we'll see the South African countryside.' Kathy was excited even though there would be little money for luxuries. They both had jobs and agreed to wait a few more years before having children.

Wagner's wedding march announced the arrival of the bride. Kathy had asked her mother to give her away and she glided down the aisle a vision of antique lace and white satin, her hand on her mother's arm. Frances wore a sage green three-quarter length party dress and a white rose in her hair. Charlotte, was her bridesmaid and looked stunning in flowing yellow chiffon. Rick, and his best-man Clive Adair, both stood tall in matching grey suits, carnations on their lapels.

'You look beautiful.' Rick whispered to Kathy, his green eyes twinkling as he took her hand.

Pastor Smith pronounced them man and wife. Rick kissed his bride. Rose petals and the all-important photographs followed.

The reception passed in the flicker of candlelight on starched white tablecloths, speeches, ripples of laughter and a dash of Deja vu. The Bandits played and Zach arrived late, but just in time to sing the lyrics of Frankie Valli's *Can't Take My Eyes Off of You*. Kathy dodged Rick's clumsy feet as they danced the bridal waltz and then arm in arm, they circulated amongst their guests.

Frances was chatting with other Parker family members. She looked up and caught her daughter's eye, beckoning to Kathy to join them.

'I have a feeling Mum's gossiping about me.' Kathy muttered to herself, but it was loud enough for Rick to hear.

He hugged her.

'Kathy, I love you. Let's not spoil our special day with your psychic mumbo jumbo.'

She took his hand and walked towards her mother.

'We better go and say hello to Aunt Linda and my side of the family.'

'Congratulations, Kathy, you look beautiful.' Aunt Linda hugged her niece. 'What a shame your father and...'

She pursed her lips.

'Er… uncle Harold aren't here today.'

Kathy forced a smile. *What a strange thing to say… mentioning my father who I adored and Uncle Harold who died before I was born in the same sentence.* She brushed it off as too much champagne. Nothing was going to spoil her special day.

Just Married was written with white shoe polish across the back window of their Datsun Bluebird. If that wasn't embarrassing enough, empty cans clattered as they drove off to the hotel where they would spend their first night. One night in the Honeymoon Suite at the five-star Monomotapa Hotel was a wedding gift from Charlotte. Neither had stayed in a hotel before, so they were taken aback by the luxury of their room. Crimson swags and tails dressed the large sliding doors that led to a balcony overlooking a manicured park. An enormous four-poster bed with a heart-shaped headboard and satin sheets dominated the room.

'I've never seen anything like it!' Kathy gushed. 'Have you seen the bathroom, Rick? There must be a hundred candles. Look at this, and oh Champagne, look chocolates!'

Kathy rushed from one exciting discovery to the next, overwhelmed by the opulence.

Rick lay on the bed hands behind his head, watching her antics with amusement. He patted the bed beckoning her to join him.

'Just as well you're on the pill,' he whispered between kisses. 'We don't want the pitter-patter of little feet just yet.'

The following morning the honeymooners were reluctant to leave the luxury of their room and left a little later than planned. They collected a packed breakfast from the reception and travelled towards Beit Bridge trying to make up lost time. Their intention was to spend the next night across the border in Louis Trichardt.

Chapter 4

Rick and Kathy were excited about spending their honeymoon in South Africa.

'Oh look, Rick, warthogs. Did you see the three little ones following mama and papa with their tails held high?' Kathy giggled with delight. 'I'm going to make a list of the birds and wildlife we see on our journey.'

'Warthogs are cheeky little blighters,' Rick commented. 'Clive and I heard a piglet squealing when we were walking through the bush a few years ago. The tiny little thing had fallen into an old mineshaft. Clive tied a rope around his waist and I lowered him down to retrieve it.' Rick roared with laughter. 'You would have thought he was strangling it the way it screamed in the canvas bag he carried it up in. We let it loose in the bush and the little blighter did a u-turn, ran back and bit Clive on the ankle, then ran off again. That's gratitude for you.'

Kathy joined in the laughter as Rick continued the story.

'Fortunately, Clive was wearing army boots so its little teeth didn't bite through.'

The next two days were spent travelling through the Transvaal and Orange Free State. They arrived at the Ocean-View Hotel in the Eastern Cape on the third day of their journey

They left their worries behind at the border, living in a magical world of no television or newspapers. During their second week, they explored up and down the coastline and with only two days of their holiday left they spent the day at the Great Kei River mouth. Rick suggested they stop at a café on their way back to the hotel.

The couple found a table and placed their order. Kathy was pouring Coca-Cola into a glass when she was distracted by a man standing at the counter. She allowed the fizzing liquid to spill over the rim and flow across the tablecloth, dripping onto Rick's trousers.

He jumped to his feet and wrestled the bottle from her. 'What's wrong with you Kath?'

She ignored his question and continued to stare past him.

His eyes followed her gaze. The man at the counter was possibly in his mid-thirties, but there was nothing remarkable about him. He was reasonably good looking and wore long trousers with an open-neck shirt.

Rick lowered his voice to almost a whisper.

'Do you know him, Kath?'

She blinked for the first time and her eyes met his,

'Yes, I *know* him,' she muttered.

She continued watching as a blonde lady with two little girls approach the man, then they left the café together.

'Rick, I'm going to be sick.' Kathy ran from the room.

In the ladies' room she flushed the toilet, then sat on the closed lid. Her body trembled and perspiration ran down her face.

'Hello, are you okay?' a woman's voice inquired while she simultaneously knocked on the door. 'Your husband asked me to check on you.'

Kathy's reply was devoid of emotion.

'I'll be out shortly. Tell my husband I won't be long.'

She washed her hands, checked her face in the mirror and wiped the smudged mascara from her cheeks.

Rick was standing near the counter waiting for her. He hid the wet patch on his trousers behind his hands.

'Are you sick?' he asked tenderly.

'I'll be okay. Thanks for waiting, Lovey. Let's go.'

She took his arm and placed it around her waist.

'Quickly.' she added.

Back at the car, Rick pulled the picnic blanket from the back seat, shook off the sand and then wrapped it around Kathy's shoulders hugging her as he did so.

'You're in shock, my love, keep yourself warm.'

He started the car engine.

'Now, tell me what's upset you?'

Kathy raised her hand to silence him.

'Not now, please, Rick. I need to think.'

They travelled without speaking for several minutes.

'Kathy, I love you. What's going on? Has this got something to do with your being psychic?'

'No! It's more complicated than that…please don't ask. I've got a blinding headache,' she closed her eyes, gently massaging her temples.

'Should we stop at the chemist?' he smiled, trying to lighten the mood. 'You'll have to go in. I look like I've crapped my trousers.'

His attempt at humour failed.

'No, don't stop. I've got tablets in our room.'

They drove the rest of the way in silence. When they pulled into the hotel parking lot, she jumped from the car and retched distressingly into the garden bed, the bitter taste of gall lingering.

'Rick,' she called detesting her weakness, but she needed his help to get her to their room.

Kathy reappeared after a hot bath wearing her dressing gown and a towel wrapped around her wet hair. She lay on the bed next to her husband.

'Rick, I'm exhausted. I don't know where to start.'

He rolled onto his side and held her gaze.

'At the beginning, my love.'

He took her hand and gazed lovingly into her eyes.

'Thank you for being so patient with me,' she gazed back at him, then sat up and drank a glass of water with two dissolved disprins. She smoothed the pillow, lay back and closed her eyes speaking softly in short sentences punctuated with long pauses.

'I'm sorry… it's been such a shock… I'm not sure what's real or what I'm imagining.'

She brushed a tear from her cheek.

'One minute, I see vivid pictures in my mind and then I'm unsure of myself,' she breathed deeply trying to relax.

'It all goes back to when I was a little girl. I remember that holiday at the cottage now; it was somewhere near here, on this coast and I remember that man we saw today… well… I think I do. That's the problem; one minute I know, the next I'm not sure what's real.'

She pulled a blanket up over herself.

'It's about Trevor. It's Trevor I kept seeing on the farm... I called him Buddy but it was Trevor.'

Her eyes fluttered and she felt drowsy.

'I need to sleep Rick. I'll tell you everything when I wake up.'

When she woke up, Rick was lying next to her reading a book. He rolled over to face her.

'Hi, sweetie, how are you feeling? It's not like you, to sleep for so long during the day.'

She attempted a smile.

'I needed it. My mind feels a little clearer now.'

His eyes searched her strained face.

'Can I ask you something, Kath?'

She nodded.

'Who is Trevor?'

She propped herself against the headboard.

'Trevor was my older brother. He died when I was a little girl.'

'You had a brother... who died?' Rick repeated, astounded.

'Yes, I had forgotten about him.'

'You had forgotten you had a brother?' he sounded even more astounded.

'Stop *repeating* everything I say, Rick. I know it sounds crazy, that's why I didn't want to tell you.'

His tone softened.

'This is all new to me, Kath. I'm just surprised that you didn't tell me you had a brother. How old was he when he died?'

'I'm not sure. Let me think... he was a teenager and he must have been about sixteen.'

She rubbed her forehead.

'I can't *believe* Mum and Dad would keep this from me. It's as though Trevor vanished off the face of the earth. They didn't even mention his name. There were no photographs. And what happened to his bicycle and his clothes? I need to phone my mum. She's the *only* person who can explain these flashbacks I'm having.'

She cupped a hand over her mouth, breathing deeply through the gaps in her fingers, watching her husband's expression. *He doesn't believe me.* 'I know it's difficult to believe that I could forget I had a brother. I feel like I'm in the middle of a bad dream. All I can tell you, is... my brother Trevor died when we were here on holiday in the Eastern Cape. It was only when I saw that man earlier today, that it all came flooding back to me.'

She massaged her temples again. *Dear Lord, if this is all a dream, please wake me up.*

'It's okay, Kath. We'll go down to the reception and phone your mum. There must be a reason why you forgot and why your mum didn't mention him.'

Kathy felt fragile and was grateful that Rick did not ask any more questions.

At the reception, Rick gave the receptionist his mother-in-law's phone number and she contacted the international telephone exchange.

'Rhodesia, Salisbury, telefoon nommer [6] vyf' vyf sewe twee' twee asseblief[7],' the ladies spoke in Afrikaans.

'Dankie Marie' ek sal later weer prober,[8]' the receptionist translated.

'There is no reply, I told the operator we will try again later.'

Rick and Kathy thanked her and agreed to return later that evening. Rick placed his arm around his wife and shepherded her into the foyer.

'Let's go for a walk along the beach before dinner, Lovey… it'll help clear your mind.'

She laid her head on his shoulder as she walked beside him.

'I love you, Rick. I'm as confused as you are; please give me time to work through my thoughts.'

He squeezed her hand.

'I love you too, Kath… I'm here for you.'

They strolled along the shoreline carrying their shoes. A sea-breeze caught Kathy's long hair and tossed it in swirls behind her. The sun dipped, turning the horizon to shades of pink and gold.

It was some time before Kathy broke the silence.

'In my second year of nursing, I did a module on memory loss called psychogenic amnesia[9]. It's a field that interests me. It tells how the memory can lose the ability to recall personal information after a traumatic experience. It can last for hours and even years. I think that's what happened to me. I was so upset when my brother died that I couldn't cope emotionally, so I buried the trauma in my subconscious. What I don't understand is why my parents kept it from me? Why didn't they remind me?'

---

[6] telefoon nommer :-   telephone number – five five seven two two

[7] asseblief :-   please

[8] dankie Marie ek sal later weer probeer :-   Thank you Marie I'll try again later

[9] Psychogenic, amnesia :-   partial or whole loss of memory

She pushed a lock of hair back from her face before continuing, 'When we were at the café today, it was that man's voice that triggered my memory. I knew what he looked like before I saw him standing there.'

She shivered.

'I'm not psychic. It was my brother's spirit that I kept seeing. My mind must have conjured up a vision of him. He was very real to me and it's curious that he didn't looked ghostly or shadowy. He just looked like a regular young guy.'

She stopped to glance down at the wave rippling over her feet.

'When I was at boarding school, I overheard some girls talking about a game called glassy-glassy. They said it was about people with psychic powers who could speak to spirits that only they could see. That sounded like me. I thought I might be psychic and so I visited the school library to find out more. I didn't know how to spell the word and was looking under "*s*" instead of "*p*" until one of the librarians helped me. There was nothing suitable for a ten-year-old to read, so I convinced myself that I must be psychic.'

She waited for Rick to comment and when he didn't, she continued, 'I worshipped my big brother, but he found me a pest. I can hear him saying, "Go away, Kathy," because I was always asking silly questions.'

She giggled as she thought about her brother, and continued chatting away without paying much attention to what she was saying.

'Mum and Dad always insisted I took the dogs with me for protection when I wandered off on my own on the farm. I told them I didn't need the dogs because my buddy was with me. Only I could see him or believed in him, so I couldn't blame them for not having faith in an imaginary friend.'

Rick put his arm around her and hugged her as a way of encouraging her to carry on.

'One day, I was climbing the hill behind our farmhouse. The dogs had run ahead and I was about to jump down between two rocks when I heard this *Sssssss* sound. *There* was an enormous puff adder[10] lying between the rocks with its head drawn back ready to strike. It sounds far-fetched, but I believe that Trevor's spirit saved ...'

She stopped mid-sentence. *Why am I telling Rick this? He's a lawyer who deals in facts. He calls spirits - mumbo jumbo.* She shook her head and rubbed her eyes. Her thoughts were muddled and she went quiet.

---

[10] puff adder:- venomous snake

Rick noticed she had stopped speaking.

'Carry on, Kath. I'm listening,' his words were comforting but not convincing. She was beginning to doubt herself.

'Do you mind if I go for a jog? I want to clear my thoughts.'

She increased speed leaving footprints in the damp sand. The wind on her face felt refreshing and she held her head high.

'Aaaah!' her cry resonated above the roaring waves as she fell to the sand. 'Something's bitten me Rick, help me, ouch it's stinging,' she was holding her ankle when he reached her. A rusty nail, hammered through a piece of driftwood had penetrated the ball of her foot.

'Keep still, I'll get it out for you,' he pulled at the plank of wood and dislodged the nail.

She screamed in pain.

'Sorry, Kath, but the nail's out now. Come on, Lovey, let's get you back to the hotel.'

He lifted her under the arms onto her uninjured foot.

'Hold on to me and hop… we don't want to get sand in that wound.'

Two ladies appeared out of the twilight.

'Can we help? We heard you cry out – have you hurt yourself badly?' the taller of the two asked.

Kathy regretted her scream. She wanted to be alone with her thoughts. *Oh no. I can't make small-talk with strangers when my head's spinning.*

'Hi. Thanks for offering. I stood on a nail, but I'll be fine. I'm a nurse, so I know what to do. My husband will help me back to the hotel,' she hoped she didn't sound too ungrateful.

The tall lady ignored her and wrapped Kathy's arm around her shoulder.

'Two crutches are better than one. We're also nurses and we outnumber you two to one, so don't argue.'

Kathy had little choice but to thank them.

'Hold tight, and we'll swing you between us,' the taller woman told her.

Her companion carried Kathy's sandals and made the introductions.

'I'm Fron and the lady helping you is my older sister, Indi. She's always been bossy, so get used to it.'

'Really?' Kathy sounded curious. 'Fron and Indi?'

'Yep, or Saffron and Indigo if you want our full names. That's what happens when you grow up in a hippy household.'

Saffron had a delightful laugh which rang above the sound of the waves.

'Every year we come to Ocean View for a sister only, holiday. We're both nonconformists, so don't be too shocked by our repartee.'

Kathy and Rick didn't mention anything about the happenings of their day to the ladies, who turned out to be great fun. Kathy found herself laughing as she swung her way home. The four of them got along famously.

'Where do you nurse?' Kathy asked.

'We're both theatre nurses at Groote Schuur Hospital in Cape Town.'

After helping Kathy to her room, Indi suggested Rick contact a doctor.

'That nail was possibly rusty and Kathy will need antibiotics, I'm sure the doc will give her a prescription.'

The ladies made sure she was comfortable before agreeing to meet up for dinner-theatre the following evening.

When the doctor arrived, Rick accompanied the elderly gentleman from the reception to their room and briefed him on the return of Kathy's memory and her distress over remembering her deceased brother. He also told him about the rusty nail that had penetrated her foot. Doctor De Beer dressed the wound, pleased to hear that Kathy had recently renewed her tetanus vaccination.

'I hear you've had quite a shock today, my dear. Your husband tells me you remembered an upsetting incident from your childhood?'

She pinched her lips

'It's upset me badly.'

'I'm sorry to hear that. You're possibly still in a state of shock. I'm going to give you a prescription for a course of antibiotics. I have a sample with me. Take this now and then continue following the directions given to you by the chemist and drink plenty of fluids,' he placed two tablets beside a glass of water on her bedside table.

'I want you to take both these tablets now; the second one is a sleeping-pill and will give you a good night's rest. Ask the hotel to call me again if you don't improve.'

'We're leaving for Rhodesia the day after tomorrow,' Rick explained.

'In that case, here are some dressings and a tube of antiseptic ointment. Keep the wound clean and dry and remember to complete the full course of antibiotics.'

Kathy was almost asleep by the time he left the room.

Rick would dine alone. They would have to phone Frances in the morning.

Chapter 5

Rick woke Kathy with a kiss the following morning.

'You slept well, Lovey. How are you feeling this morning?'

'I'm still half asleep. I had this dream about travelling in a big black Dodge with Mum, Dad and my brother Trevor. We were on the road from Rhodesia to South Africa, and I couldn't see out the windows of the car unless I stood up on the seat.'

She yawned.

'Whatever that Doctor gave me, really zonked me out… I'm still half asleep.'

'Better get up and dressed now if you want to go downstairs and call your mum before breakfast.'

Kathy dressed at a snail's pace, fighting to keep her eyes open.

They held hands walking down the stairs.

'What are you going to say to your mother, Kathy?'

'I'll keep an open mind until I've heard her side of the story. *Honestly!* It doesn't make sense. I mean, what kind of mother denies the existence of her own son?'

Rick realised she was fragile and did not ask any more questions.

The receptionist handed Kathy the receiver.

'Your mother is on the line, Mrs Barron.'

Kathy tried to speak, but the words wouldn't come.

All she could utter was one strangled word. 'Trevor!'

She thrust the receiver into Rick's hand, covered her mouth and streaked towards the restroom.

Rick could hear his mother-in-law's concern.

'Kathy, what's happened… are you all right, Sweetie?'

He spoke into the receiver.

'Frances, it's Rick. I'm sorry, but Kathy's gone to the bathroom.'

'Oh, Rick, what's happened? When did she remember about Trevor?'

She didn't allow him time to answer.

Her voice trembled. 'I should have told her, my poor little girl.'

'Frances, can you tell me what happened to Trevor?'

'What did Kathy tell you?'

She sounded a little guarded.

'That she had a brother called Trevor who died when she was a little girl.'

'Is that *all s*he told you?'

'She hasn't said what happened to him, only that he died when you were on holiday, here in South Africa.'

There was a lapse before she spoke again.

'Trevor was murdered, Rick!'

He was stunned.

'Oh, my God!' I had no idea... no wonder she reacted the way she did. I thought maybe he was ill or had an accident. Does Kathy know *how* he died?'

'It's difficult speaking about this over the phone, Rick... you say, Kathy remembers she had a brother, but she doesn't know *how* he died?'

'No. I didn't say that. Kathy may know how he died, but she hasn't told me. She's very shaken and I'm afraid to ask questions.'

'When did she remember about Trevor?'

'Yesterday afternoon. We tried to phone you, but there was no reply. We intended calling you again after a walk on the beach, but Kathy stood on a rusty nail. I had to call the doctor who gave her a sedative to help her sleep through the night.'

'Oh my God, oh my God!'

He heard Frances catch her breath, but she recovered quickly.

'I'll tell you very briefly what happened, Rick, we can discuss the detail when you get back home.'

'Go ahead, Frances. I'm listening.'

'The holiday cottage in Kleinemonde where we stayed was fairly isolated. One night, Kathy's father hadn't return home from a fishing trip, so we walked up the beach to look for him. He'd caught an enormous fish and it had taken hours to carry it home.'

She cleared her throat.

'We helped him carry the monster fish until we reached the estuary. The cottage stood on a cliff overlooking the inlet and Trevor ran ahead to light the gas lamp and prepare the kitchen table for filleting the fish. We could see the cottage in the moonlight and when we got close enough, we allowed Kathy to run after her brother. It took Ben and myself some time to climb up the bank carrying the fish. When we reached the front door, we found Kathy sitting on the step.'

The phone began to crackle, making it difficult for Rick to hear her.

'It was dark… the lamp… fish… table. Then I tripped over something.'

The crackling suddenly cleared.

'Trevor was lying on the floor. God, Rick, we tried so hard to save him.'

Rick could hear the pain in her voice.

'He was already dead.'

Thick choking sobs echoed down the line.

'It was the *worst* moment of my life.'

Her voice became muffled and he guessed she had cupped her hand over the receiver.

'Frances, are you okay, would you like to phone me back?'

There was silence for a moment and then she spoke again.

'No, no, I'm *not* okay, but I want to finish, Rick. We phoned the police and then the doctor. Afterwards we checked on Kathy who was still sitting on the front steps staring into the dark.'

The line started to break up again.

'She was covered… blood… dazed.'

He was missing more than he was hearing.

'It's hopeless, Frances. The line keeps breaking up I can't hear you. If we get cut off, can you phone me back? I'll give you the number.'

'I've got a pen, go ahead.'

Once she had written down the number, she continued,

'Kathy didn't speak for three weeks. Not a word. Then on the way back to Rhodesia when we were crossing the Limpopo River, she looked up and said, "*Look, the sky is bluer.*" Those were the first words she had spoken since her brother's death. From then on, it was as though nothing terrible had happened and Trevor didn't exist.'

Rick's thoughts were racing. *Kathy might have witnessed her brother's murder. We'll have to visit the police station so she can give a statement. I wonder where the man we saw at Tuin kafee fits into all this?* He needed to know more.

'Frances, do you think Kathy witnessed her brother's murder?'

'We don't know, Rick. We often wondered about that. She had blood all over her, so we know she tried to help him.'

'Was the killer ever arrested?'

'No. The police did arrest a local African man squatting in the area, but they released him when witnesses confirmed his alibi.'

'Did the police question Kathy?'

She sounded agitated.

'I've *told* you, Rick, Kathy didn't speak at all until we returned to Rhodesia. When we got back, we took her to our GP who sent her to a paediatrician in Salisbury. He didn't want her labelled as having mental problems and suggested we remove all reminders of her brother and allow her to remember him in her own time. We didn't think that would take, fifteen years.'

Rick understood the need to explain her side of the story, but he wanted the facts surrounding the homicide if he was to take Kathy to the police station.

'Frances, this call is costing a fortune. Can you phone me back with the docket details the police gave you?'

He listed what he thought was important.

'Please phone us back in about an hour.'

He wanted her to know he was aware of her pain.

'I'm sorry, Frances, it must be awful for you to dredge up this tragedy. We'll be home by the weekend and you can explain everything to Kathy.'

He replaced the receiver and only then, remembered, he hadn't told her about the man in the café who had triggered her daughter's memory.

He felt a hand on his arm. It was Kathy who looked pale and flustered.

'I'll speak to Mum now, Rick.'

'Sorry, Kath, I didn't realise you were back. I've hung up, but your mum's phoning us in an hour.'

He kissed her cheek.

'Where have you been all this time? I've been speaking to her for ages.'

She side-stepped his question.

'What did Mum say about Trevor?'

'She's concerned about *you, Kath.*'

He guided her out to the garden.

'Are you *okay,* Lovey?'

'Sort of. I wanted to talk to Mum, but when I heard her voice, I couldn't breathe and knew I was going to be sick.'

'Are you okay now?'

'Not really. I fell asleep on the toilet; that sleeping pill the doc gave me has really zonked me. Can we have breakfast and a cup of tea now? Then we'll talk.'

She fidgeted at the table, reading the breakfast menu several times before placing her order.

'Kathy…' Rick hesitated at her haunting stare as it reminded him of her fragile state. 'Lovey, we need to talk about what has happened.'

He wavered when his gaze fell on her trembling hands; he was eager to get answers and took a chance.

'Kath, do you remember *how* your brother died?'

She glared at him, pushed back her chair and fled out the door. He assured the waiter he'd soon be back, then hurried after her.

'Wait, Kathy,' he caught up with her.

'I'm sorry, please come back. You didn't have dinner last night, so you must have something to eat now. We've got a long day ahead of us. I promise I won't mention anything about your brother until we're back in our room.'

Back in their room, Kathy sat propped against the bed-headboard.

'Yes, Rick, *I do* know what happened to my brother. I was there. I saw that man kill him.'

'*What* man?'

'The man we saw at Tuin kafee yesterday. He's the man who killed my brother! He looked younger back then.'

She drew her knees up to her chest and wrapped her arms around them.

'Did Mum tell you if they had arrested Trevor's killer?'

Rick shook his head.

'No. The African squatter the police arrested had an alibi, so they released him.'

He caught her eye.

'So, you know the man we saw yesterday?'

'I don't know who he is, but I recognised him and I'm positive he's the man I saw that night.'

Kathy stood up and began to pace the room. *Good. At least the wrong man hasn't been in prison all these years. That sneaky bastard thinks he's got away with it.'*

There was no easy way for Rick to broach the subject.

'Kath, I know you're upset and angry, but please come and sit down here next to me.'

He patted the side of the bed.

'I need to talk to you.'

He drew her close.

'We must visit the police station so you can give them a statement.' he lowered his voice and added cautiously, 'It won't be easy, but it's important to tell them everything you've remembered.'

She drummed her feet hoping to sidestep the issue.

'Aah *please,* Lovey, can't this wait? In *my* mind Trevor only died *yesterday,*' she fought back the tears.

'I feel helpless, just like I did the night he died. I'll never forget the look in his eyes, the way he just stared at me… as if he was pleading for help. I kept asking, what should I do? Of course, he didn't answer.'

A shiver ran down her spine.

'I don't want to talk about it now.'

He put his arms around her and hugged her tightly.

'I wish we could stay on a few more days, Kath. Unfortunately, we haven't got the money or the time. We must go to the police station today and record everything you remember while it's still fresh in your mind. You don't need to be afraid. I'll be with you and make sure that no one hassles you.'

She wiped a tear from her cheek.

'My memory of that night is crystal clear. It's as if it's been frozen in time.' She changed her mind. 'You're right, we should get it over with.'

The phone rang. Rick reached for it and wrote down the details Frances had found for him, then passed the phone to Kathy. He could only hear one side of the conversation.

'Hello, Mum. Hmm, okay, let's do that. We were at a café… there was a stranger, a man, at the counter. It was his voice that bought everything back to me… everything about Trevor's death.'

She didn't elaborate, just told her mother the bones of what had happened.

'I'm not feeling great Mum. We're going to the police station now. Hmm, we'll talk about that when we get back to Rhodesia.'

Rick parked the Datsun outside the entrance to the police station. There was not much time for him to prepare Kathy before she gave her statement.

'When you were a little girl, Kath, do you remember if the police spoke to you after the incident?'

'I don't know, Rick. I couldn't even remember the *incident*, as you call it, until yesterday when I saw that man at Tuin kafee. I'm so angry with everyone for hiding this from me. I could have told them what I saw, long ago.'

Rick was thinking like a lawyer now. He needed to coach his client.

'Try to stay focused on the main point and concentrate on what you're going to tell the police. They are only interested in facts, not emotions or your *personal* thoughts. You're about to accuse a man of murder… you were six years old and only saw him by the light of a gas lamp. You *have* to make *sure* they see you as a credible witness.'

She tossed her head, her eyes blazed.

'*So!* What do you *expect* me to say, Rick? I'm not making this up. I *saw* that man kill my brother. I'm sorry if it's *inconvenient* for you.'

Rick remained calm, but his tone was authoritative.

'Cool it, Kath! Lower your voice. I'm only trying to help you. The police are likely to ask you this same question. Just give them the *facts,* not smart answers. And try not to get emotional, we need to make *sure* they take you seriously.'

She muttered through clenched teeth, 'It's easy for you to say stick to the *facts,* don't get *emotional.*'

She took a deep breath.

'I know you're only trying to help me, Lovey. I'll do my best, but I'm not making any promises.'

'I'm your husband, Kath, and your lawyer. I know how the police think.'

He kissed her.

'I love you. You're a smart lady. You can *do* this, just stay focused.'

When they entered the police station, two young uniformed policemen greeted them in Afrikaans. Rick tried his limited Afrikaans, but quickly reverted back to English.

'My wife and I are on holiday from Rhodesia and would like to see a senior officer about a homicide that took place in Kleinemonde fourteen years ago.'

'Fifteen.' Kathy corrected.

The two constables spoke English at the same level as Rick's Afrikaans. Rick and Kathy sat on a wooden bench waiting for someone who spoke English to arrive and help them.

'Good morning, my name is Constable Pienaar.'

He was a short, stocky man and had it not been for his uniform he could have been mistaken for a professional boxer.

'Come through to the charge office, Mr Barron and I'll record your complaint. Captain Oberholster will be here shortly.'

His English wasn't wonderful, but at least they understood each other.

Rick corrected him.

'We're not here to make a complaint, Constable Pienaar. We need to speak to Captain Oberholster about the murder of Trevor Parker that took place in 1958.'

He placed a piece of paper with the details Frances had given him on the desk.

'You'll find the original docket number and dates listed here.'

Rick watched the constable transfer the information onto a docket sheet.

'This is my wife, Kathy. She would like to give a full statement. Kathy's been suffering from memory loss and only remembered her brother's murder when she saw a man at the Tuin kafee, yesterday.'

Rick took charge while Kathy remained silent.

Chapter 6

A booming voice alerted them to the arrival of Captain Oberholster.

'Bring a tray of tea to my office, Mrs Brits.'

Captain Oberholster lifted his head and indicated the two chairs facing his desk as Constable Pienaar escorted Rick and Kathy into his office,

'Good morning, Mr Barron take a seat.'

He was a big man who exuded self-confidence. He sat upright - golden lapels stretched across broad shoulders, chin held high and muscular arms resting on the armrest of his chair.

'Thank you for your patience, Mr Barron. Constable Pienaar has already requested a copy of the murder docket for eh…'

He checked the docket in front of him.

'Trevor Parker.'

His guttural accent was pleasant enough and his command of English good.

'I see you claim to have new evidence. Can you tell me what has happened?'

Up until now, he had ignored Kathy who was sitting next to Rick.

'Thank you for seeing us, Captain Oberholster; this is my wife, Kathy.'

The captain nodded dismissively in her direction.

'Give me a minute to read Constable Pienaar's report, Mr Barron.'

Rick squeezed his wife's hand to reassure her. The captain didn't take long to glance through the report.

'I see that Mrs Barron claims to have recognised her brother's killer. When did this crime occur?'

It was a rhetorical question. He again referred to the docket.

'Oh, I see… nineteen fifty-eight. That's some time ago.'

Kathy frowned. *Is he insinuating that I won't remember because of the date?* She felt the need to set him straight.

'I wish to make a formal statement, please, Captain Oberholster. I have only just remembered that my brother was murdered, but everything is clear in my mind. I know what I saw.'

He peered down his nose at her, as though she was a petulant child.

'Go ahead, Mrs Barron.'

Kathy had briefly rehearsed what she would say.

'I was six years old when I saw my brother murdered. For fifteen years I buried the memory in my subconscious. No one was aware that I had witnessed the crime. Then yesterday, I saw a man at a café. Initially, his voice caught my attention, but when I saw what he looked like it triggered my memory. I know he is the man who killed my brother.'

The captain avoided eye contact. He made no attempt to record her statement, instead, he shuffled through the papers on his desk.

She was annoyed by his dismissive attitude towards her.

'Captain Oberholster, please could you record my statement in writing?'

He lifted his head.

'I have the details in front of me, Mrs Barron.'

He turned to Rick.

'It's amazing that your wife should recognise this man after fifteen years, Mr Barron. She must have a good memory. Does she have any idea who this man is?'

Rick pointed to the last entry on Constable Pienaar's notes.

'While my wife was in the bathroom, I recorded the registration number of the car the man and his family were driving. We were...' Kathy cut him off.

'Please, let *me* explain. The sub-conscious can instantly block a traumatic experience from the memory. In some cases it is lost forever. In my case, it has returned with crystal clarity, fifteen years later. It's as if everything that happened back then has been frozen in time and I remember it very clearly. I'm ready to give a statement now.'

While she spoke, Captain Oberholster rested his jaw in his hand, staring into space. When he spoke again, he ignored her speaking again directly to Rick.

'I haven't heard of a case like this. I'll ask my secretary to come in and type her statement?'

'Salamina!' he raised his voice. 'Come to my office and take a statement.'

Mrs Brits hurried in and settled at a small desk pushed against the wall, her back to them. She rolled a sheet of paper into her typewriter and began to type.

The captain sat back into his chair.

'Mrs Barron, will you tell us what you witnessed fifteen years ago on the night your brother died?'

She kept to the facts, as Rick had instructed.

'I climbed up the steep bank to our holiday cottage and then sat on the front step to catch my breath. That's when I heard two voices coming from the kitchen. My brother Trevor was speaking. I didn't recognise the other voice.'

She breathed deeply to relieve the tension.

'I wanted to surprise them, so I tiptoed to the kitchen doorway. There was a gas lamp on the kitchen table and Trevor was leaning against the table facing a stranger who had his back to the sink.'

She closed her eyes.

'I can't remember what they were saying, but their conversation was friendly… they were smiling at each other.'

She stared straight ahead as she recalled the details.

'The stranger was a nice-looking young man with blonde hair and possibly eighteen or nineteen. I was about to show myself when he lunged forward towards my brother. I didn't understand what was happening, but… Trevor's eyes told me something was wrong. His arms went stiff and his face looked strange… sort of contorted. Then he made a loud growling sound or maybe more of a gurgling sound. I thought he was fooling around.'

Her breathing quickened.

'I don't think he knew what was happening either. He didn't try to protect himself. He didn't scream; he just made that strange noise.' her voice trembled. 'It all happened so fast.'

Salamina stopped typing and turned to look at Kathy, who blinked away the tears and forced herself to smile, indicating her appreciation of this sympathetic gesture.

Kathy continued, 'When the stranger stepped back from Trevor, I saw the long blade in his right hand. I was terrified! Trevor slumped to the floor landing in the shadow of the table.'

She chewed her bottom lip.

'I didn't see the stranger leave… I must have been in shock. The slamming of the back door startled me and I crawled across the kitchen floor to where Trevor lay.'

Kathy cheeks were wet with tears. She searched her purse for a tissue.

Rick passed her his handkerchief.

'Are you all right, Lovey?'

She was struggling to control her emotions, but she was determined to tell the whole story.

'I knelt beside him, his eyes were wide open and I thought he was teasing me. Dead people are supposed to close their eyes. I punched him in the arm.'

She looked at her husband.

'I was just a little girl, Rick; I expected him to jump up, so when he didn't, I punched him again. That's when the light caught my hands and I noticed blood all over them. There was blood on my clothes, my legs and it was everywhere. I was kneeling in it.'

She turned her dull wet eyes towards Rick and sobbed into his shoulder. He pulled her closer to comfort her.

'It's okay, my love; it's okay, you can stop now.'

The tap, tap of the typewriter stopped. Mrs Brits poured a glass of water from the jug on a side table and handed it to Kathy.

Kathy dried her eyes and drank the water while the others in the room looked on.

'Ahem!'

Captain Oberholster had spent most of the time while she was speaking shaking his head or writing notes. Now he rapped for their attention, speaking directly to Rick.

'I can see Mrs Barron is traumatised by the memory of this event… what a terrible thing for a small child to witness.'

His words were kind, but his tone was cavalier. He gave Kathy a quick glance.

'Would Mrs Barron be up to answering a few questions?' he asked Rick.

Captain Oberholster was beginning to annoy Kathy and she snapped.

'Yes, Captain Oberholster. I *will* answer your questions, and please speak directly to me and not through my husband.'

He offered a small smile and then again searched through his papers. Kathy wondered if he was deliberately avoiding eye contact with her.

When he next spoke, he didn't look up.

'Mrs Barron, can you describe the man you saw in the kitchen at the cottage that night?'

She replied with confidence.

'The stranger was fairly tall with an average build and blonde hair. He had a South African, Afrikaans accent, but spoke English to my brother. He was wearing khaki shorts and shirt.' She then added, 'He was the same man I saw at Tuin kafee yesterday.'

'Please answer *only* the question asked, Mrs Barron!'

His steely eyes bored into hers. She sensed that her directness had angered him.

'What time of night did the attack take place?'

'It was late at night, I can't remember. You can check when you receive the criminal docket.'

'And what lights were on in the kitchen at that time of night?'

'The house was not wired for electricity. There was a gas lamp burning and my eyes had adjusted to the light. I could see clearly. I have good eyesight.'

Captain Oberholster rubbed his chin.

'Did the man you saw at Tuin kafee yesterday resemble the man you saw kill your brother?'

'Yes. I'm sure of it.'

She pressed her lips together, resolute.

Captain Oberholster turned and thanked Mrs Brits.

'Close the door behind you.' he asked as she left the room.

His eyes swung to Rick.

'I assure you, Mr Barron, that unsolved homicides are high on the priority list of our murder and robbery squad. We will investigate this new information. Could you bring your wife back in two days to sign her statement?'

'I'm sorry, but we're leaving to return to Rhodesia tomorrow morning, Captain Oberholster.'

'I see, I didn't know. I'll find out how quickly we can complete the statement.'

He left the room and returned a few minutes later.

'Our forensic sketch artist is available at three-thirty this afternoon. Can you bring Mrs Barron back to do an identity sketch of the man she saw yesterday?'

Kathy answered for herself, 'Yes, we will come back after lunch.'

Rick and Kathy had lunch at the hotel and then packed their bags ready for an early start on their return journey to Rhodesia the following morning. They then headed back to the station.

The forensic sketch artist had already set up when Rick and Kathy arrived. He explained the technique he used to create a facial composite and Kathy wasted no time describing the stranger to him.

'Round eyes… a little further apart… a little rounder. *Yes,* those are his eyes. Longer hair… slightly bushier, perfect.'

Every feature was clearly defined, until she saw the man at café appeared before her.

'That's him!' her voice rang with conviction. 'That's what he looked like when I saw him in the kitchen at Travellers Joy. He looks older now, but he hasn't changed much.'

She was pleased with herself.

Rick was amazed at her accuracy. The first stencil off the Roneo machine[11] was smudged and discarded in the waste-paper basket. As Kathy left the room she reached for the stencil and put it in her handbag. *I'll show it to Mum.*

Captain Oberholster was even stiffer than he was at their first meeting. He scowled at the identity sketch lying on his desk. Kathy sensed that something had annoyed him.

'Mrs Barron, is this a *true* likeness of the man you saw at Tuin kafee yesterday?'

His tone was gruff and almost offish.

'Yes. That's the man,' she replied confidently.

What have I done wrong? Why is he suddenly so grumpy?

Rick took another look at the sketch. 'I think it's a very good likeness, except he looks twenty years younger in the sketch.'

The captain glanced from the sketch to Kathy this time he held her gaze.

'Mrs Barron. We have no doubt you witnessed your brother's murder. Everything you've told us is plausible. However, fifteen years is a long time and you were *very* young. The lighting was poor. You saw this man for only for a few minutes – maybe seconds. The memory can play tricks under such circumstances.'

Rick had warned her the police might raise these doubts and she sensed the captain was trying to discredit her statement. She stabbed a finger at the sketch on his desk.

---

[11] Roneo machine: - apparatus that makes copies

'Find this man and you'll find my brother's killer. I know what I saw. I'm *not* going to change my statement.'

Captain Oberholster's face flushed with anger.

'Mrs Barron. Your sketch and your statement raise more questions than answers. How would this man get to the cottage at that time of night without using a vehicle and what would his motive be for killing a young boy he didn't even know?'

He's calling me a liar! Kathy was furious.

'Isn't that what the *police* should be doing? Investigating the new suspects alibi and motive!'

Oberholster folded his arms and scoffed. She could see he was mocking her. *How dare he.* She sprang to her feet.

'Oh, that's *right*... *y*our famous murder and robbery squad don't even *have* a suspect, do they?'

'*That's enough,* Mrs Barron!' he bellowed, towering over her as he stood. 'There's a good chance you've identified the wrong man.'

A purple vein throbbed in his neck. He was not used to being challenged.

A deep rage burned inside and she erupted, 'Are you calling me *a liar?*'

Rick intervened, catching her hand. He knew she could be strong-willed and stubborn, but he was astounded that she had the courage to take on this giant of a man. Their raised voices reverberated throughout the police station.

Rick pleaded with her to stop.

'Calm down, Kathy! No one is accusing *you* of lying.'

He moved between them, leaning across the desk to shake the officer's hand while keeping a tight grip on Kathy's wrist.

'Thank you for your time, Captain Oberholster. My wife has suffered a severe shock. She's upset and exhausted, I must get her home.'

He pulled her towards the open door.

She turned as they reached the doorway.

'You *know* the man in that sketch, don't you? You're *protecting* him and that's why all of a sudden you're hostile towards *me.*'

She didn't care if the entire police station heard her. Rick wrapped his arm around her waist and guided her out of the building.

Kathy sat in the passenger seat of the car, trembling. She had no idea where she had found the strength to stand up to Captain Oberholster. Rick wrapped a shawl around her shoulders and rubbed her arms to stop her shivering.

'Are you okay now, Kath?'

'I'm sorry, Rick. I don't know what came over me. I blew it, didn't I?'

Her emotions were mixed.

She gave an awkward giggle. 'Did you see the veins throbbing in his neck? I thought he was going to have a stroke.'

Tears streamed down her face even as she laughed.

'Calm down, Kath!'

He hugged her.

'Captain Oberholster is a bully. It took courage to stand up to him. Even I'm scared of that man.'

He started the engine.

'I love you, Kath. I'm glad we're returning home to Rhodesia tomorrow.'

Chapter 7

Ocean-View hotel was hosting a dinner and variety show that night. Rick suggested that they give it a miss.

'We're already packed up for an early start tomorrow morning and we've had an exhausting day. Perhaps we should have an early night.'

Kathy wouldn't hear of it.

'It's because we've had an awful day that I want to go. Tonight, is the last night of our honeymoon and I don't want to explain our reasons for not going to Indi and Fron. Let's forget about the return of my memory for one last night and have some fun.'

Indi and Fron, the sisters they had met the previous night, had booked a table for four. It was an excellent show with plenty of humour and entertainment. Kathy let her hair down and had a few drinks.

She woke up the following morning feeling ill.

'The glare is awful. Aaaw. it must be something I ate last night… or I might have gastro.' Kathy complained as she staggered into the bathroom.

Rick heard her retching; she reappeared white-faced and flopped onto the bed.

'You've got a hangover, Lovey.'

She bristled.

'I have not! I know the difference between a hangover and gastro… besides, I don't drink… well, not usually.'

He grinned and handed her a glass of fizzing ENO's.

'Exactly, that's why I know it's a hangover, here… drink this, it'll make you feel better.'

Rick helped her sit up and drink from the glass.

'Try to keep it down.'

She sank back into the pillow, her face the colour of chalk. He pulled the cover over her.

'Go back to sleep, Lovey. I'll see you after breakfast.'

When Rick returned, he woke her with bad news.

'I asked if we could have the room until mid-day, but we have to vacate by ten o'clock.'

Kathy groaned as she dragged herself into a sitting position. Originally, they had planned to have breakfast at six and leave by seven that morning, but it was ten-thirty when they eventually left the hotel parking lot. There was little chance of making up time as the South African Traffic Police were notorious for their speed-traps and there was no money to pay a fine.

Rick drove the first day while Kathy slept. She lifted her head occasionally when Rick braked or mentioned something of interest. They found a motel shortly after sunset and retired for the night

The next day Kathy felt physically better, but had very little to say – she was grieving the loss of her brother. Rick pushed one tape after the other into the car cassette player singing a long and allowing her time to reflect.

Driving through the city of Johannesburg at rush hour was again challenging. Rick negotiated his way through the traffic congestion with the aid of his trusty navigator. Kathy's map reading skills had improved slightly and there were no arguments. By the time they stopped for the night outside Potgietersrus, Rick had been driving for twelve hours.

Kathy took over the driving on the third day to give Rick a well-earned break. They wound their way up through the mountainous Louis Trichardt Pass towards Messina and the South African border with Rhodesia. They again left late and their progress was slow.

Kathy felt deflated. The excitement she had felt when they travelled toward the Eastern Cape a few weeks earlier was forgotten.

'I'm looking forward to getting home, but dreading facing Mum and finding out what happened after Trevor's death. There are so many questions running through my mind.'

'What sort of questions, Lovey?' Rick asked.

Kathy's mind was in turmoil. 'I'm wondering if I should have stayed behind to sign my statement and *flown* home. I don't trust Captain Oberholster. He didn't believe anything I said – he could try to change my statement. I'm not sure why my sketch should make him so angry?'

She was venting out loud, not expecting Rick to reply.

'Your sketch definitely caused quite a commotion, Kath. Perhaps, you identified the *local Mayor.*'

He grinned.

'Being challenged by a mere slip of a girl, nearly pushed the captain over the edge.'

Kathy found his words comforting. It was important to know she had his support.

They completed the formalities at the South African border post and drove across the Limpopo bridge into Rhodesia.

Kathy pointed upwards.

'Look, the sky is bluer.'

'No, it's not,' Rick countered. 'But your Mum says those were the first words you said three weeks after Trevor's death.'

She lifted her eyes to the sky and giggled.

'I can see the difference. You can only see it if you're a true blue Rhodie.'

Her husband shook his head and grinned.

'I remember dad stopping the car halfway across the Limpopo bridge and pointing back at Rhodesia. "I want you to look back and if you can see that the sky is bluer, then you are a true blue Rhodie." Of course, we all said we could see the sky was much bluer,' A shallow sigh escaped her.

Once they were back on Rhodesian soil, Kathy started to feel a little more excited. This was her home and the land she loved. Rick pushed a John Edmund tape into the cassette recorder and they listened to patriotic folk songs about Africa. They were encouraged by their belief that Rhodesia was a country where people of all colour and creed could live in harmony. They hadn't listened to the news or read a newspaper for three weeks and had no idea what was happening back home. Rick threw a copy of The Rhodesian Herald onto the back seat after reading only the headlines. He wasn't ready to face harsh reality, just yet.

They were stopped at a military roadblock outside Beit Bridge where they assured the camouflage clad soldier that they were only travelling as far as the Bubi River Lodge to spend the night.

A storm was threatening when they arrived at the lodge and during the night thunder and heavy rain rattled the roof. After months of drought, rivers and creeks flowed, restoring the life of Africa. Dusty leaves washed clean and the once-parched earth was soaked to the roots providing sustenance to all living creatures.

They were an hour into their journey when the steering wheel started to shudder.

'We've got a puncture, Kath. Oh, bugger, this is not a good place to stop,' Rick cursed.

No sooner had they pulled over and started to unpack the contents in the boot, when two other cars pulled over.

'Let me give you a hand. We need to get you back on the road, my mucker[12].'

A young, fresh-faced chap, travelling on his own started to help them off load.

The elderly couple in the second car were just as helpful.

'Have you got a weapon with you?' asked the older man.

'No.' admitted Rick as he retrieved the jack from the unpacked boot.

'Well, both my wife and I are armed, so we'll stay with you.'

'Thanks, that would make me feel a lot happier,' confessed Kathy.

The camaraderie between travellers was wonderful. After the spare tire was in place and the boot repacked, all three vehicles travelled together the rest of the journey, creating their own little convoy.

They arrived in Salisbury late afternoon. Rick unlocked the door to their bachelor pad and swept Kathy up into his arms to carry her over the threshold. He flicked the light switch and nothing happened. Back on her feet, Kathy made her way across the carpet and pulled back the wall of curtains to allow dwindling rays of sunlight to filter into the apartment. An unmade queen size bed was piled high with neatly wrapped, unopened wedding gifts.

'When did you arrange for the utilities to be connected, Rick?' They looked at each other in consternation.

Each thought that the other had contacted the council. It was Friday, and the municipal officers didn't open until Monday.

Fortunately, the phone was working, so Kathy picked up the receiver and phoned Frances, whose home was only a few streets away.

'Hello, Mum.'

'Kathy! How wonderful to hear your voice, where are you?'

'We're home, Mum, in our unit, but we don't have lights or water yet, can we spend the weekend with you?'

---

[12] Mucker::-   Good friend

The dark shadows under Frances's eyes told of sleepless nights and tearstained pillows as she relied the pain of losing her son all over again. She hugged her daughter and son-in-law warmly.

'How was your journey home? I hope you're not too tired, sweetie.'

She eyed Kathy critically.

'It's good to be home, Mum, but I'm exhausted. Nothing a hot bath and a good night's sleep won't cure. Would you mind if we have an early supper tonight and talk in the morning?'

Kathy climbed into bed and was asleep by eight o'clock.

Rick woke her with a kiss.

'Good morning, love. You've slept for twelve hours. You must have been exhausted.'

She sat up in bed and he handed her a cup of tea.

'I'm spending the day with my folks, Kath... they want to hear about our honeymoon... and I want to tell them about your brother and the return of your memory.'

Kathy and her mother spent the whole day discussing the events surrounding Trevor's murder. Frances was determined to have everything out in the open as soon as possible. Over breakfast, she assured Kathy she would hold nothing back.

'I feel guilty about letting you and your father down, sweetie. I promised him I would tell you about Trevor when you turned twenty-one. It's no excuse, but I didn't want to spoil your combined birthday party with Charlotte. Then you were depressed about your break up with Rick and the next thing you're getting married. There was never a right time to tell you,' She looked remorseful.

'I'm sorry I hurt you. I was about to tell you the day you asked me about our holiday in the Eastern Cape. Then Charlotte arrived and I saw how happy you were about going on your honeymoon,' she groaned. 'I simply kept putting it off.'

'I wish you had told me, Mum. It was a terrible shock when I remembered about Trevor. I doubted my own sanity. How could I have forgotten *my own* brother? How was I going to tell Rick? I was physically ill and threw up several times.'

She rubbed her arms in a self-soothing gesture.

'I know you had your reasons for waiting. You were following the advice of the paediatrician, but as soon as I was old enough to understand, I wish you'd told me.'

Kathy noticed how distraught her mother looked and softened her tone.

'Let's forget about how I found out, there's nothing we can do to change it. Will you tell me what happened after Trevor's death? What did you and Dad do?'

Frances lit a cigarette and took a puff before balancing it on an ashtray.

'Your father and I were in shock. We didn't know what to do. We left Trevor's body in the East London mortuary and drove back to Rhodesia with you. You hadn't said a word for weeks. We knew you understood what was going on but you didn't speak. Daddy and I prayed for you every day and when we were crossing the Limpopo bridge back to Rhodesia our prayers were answered. *"Look the sky is bluer."* Those were the first words you spoke.'

Frances's hand trembled and she took another puff of her cigarette.

Kathy giggled.

'I remember when we crossed the Limpopo River, daddy said the sky was bluer in Rhodesia.'

Frances eyes brightened as she recalled.

'Between the two borders, you chatted away as if nothing had happened. But there was still a problem; you didn't remember anything about your brother or your life before that day.'

She stroked Kathy's hair. Society was very unkind to anyone considered mentally unstable back in the nineteen-fifties. She stubbed her cigarette out.

'We took you to see a child specialist; a paediatrician called Doctor Hamilton. He spent hours assessing you and, in the end, he described you as a bright and happy little girl who just refused to remember a traumatic incident. He suggested we remove all traces of your brother from our home and allow you to remember him in your own time. It wasn't meant to take fifteen years,' she rubbed her weary eyes. 'People would sometimes mention Trevor's name, but you didn't react, it was as if you didn't want to hear.'

'What happened to Trevor's body, Mum?'

'We had his body flown back to Rhodesia and arranged a private family funeral. He's buried at the Salisbury Cemetery not far from Daddy's grave. We can visit Trevor's grave when you're ready, Kath.'

'I'd like that, Mum. Let's buy some flowers and visit the cemetery over the weekend.'

Kathy could only imagine the pain her parents had suffered. To give up the grieving process of their beloved son for her was the ultimate sacrifice. She squeezed into the wicker chair next to her mother and snuggled close as she had done as a child. They held each other and cried. These were the first of many tears shed that day.

'I'm so sorry, Mum. It must have been terrible for you and daddy.'

'It was the worst time of our lives. Your father and I removed all reminders of Trevor from the house and kept his belongings in the locked room. Do you remember you once asked what was in that room?'

Kathy did remember asking that.

'You told me all your memories were locked in that room,' she smiled, 'you told me the truth, Mum; perhaps that's why I didn't asked again. What happened to all of Trevor's belongings when we left the farm?'

'We gave everything away to the farmworkers' children. We thought Trevor would like that.'

Frances ran beautifully manicured fingernails through her red hair.

'Ask me whatever you like Kathy. I don't want any more secrets between us.'

Kathy remembered the few study modules on modern psychiatry she had done during her nursing training. She was aware of the out-dated methods used in the fifties. Fortunately, great progress had been made in the mental health field during the sixties and continued into the seventies. She could only guess that when doctor Hamilton recommended her parents allow her to remember in her own time, he had believed it would take only weeks or months.

Kathy told her mother how the stranger at Tuin Kafee had triggered her memory and repeated what she had told the police about the night Trevor was murdered. She showed Frances the smudged identity sketch taken from the waste paper basket.

Frances examined the drawing a baffled look on her face.

'He looks like any other young man. What was he doing at our cottage at that time of night?'

She had asked the same question Captain Oberholster had asked.

'Why would a stranger kill Trevor?'

The next few weeks were busy. Rick and Kathy worked long hours for little money. Rick was still doing his articles and Kathy didn't earn much as a nurse. They decorated their apartment as best they could and entertained small groups of friends in cramped conditions. Their reward for being married was to wake up in each other's arms every morning. Very few couples lived together before they married in the seventies, but the world was changing rapidly.

They had been back home in Rhodesia for ten weeks. Kathy was concerned as she had still not received her statement from the East London police.

She visited her doctor for what she told Rick, was a routine doctor's appointment and was shocked by his diagnosis.

'No, you're wrong, Doctor. I'm on the pill,' she was adamant and then she faltered.

'Well, most of the time.'

Most of the time wasn't good enough; she was pregnant and their plan to be financially stable before having children was a non-starter. She had continually forgotten to take her birth control tablets during their honeymoon. *Surely a few days wouldn't make any difference*, she had told herself. Now she knew she was wrong.

Unsure of how Rick would react to the news, she prepared a special dinner that night.

'Rick, we need to discuss something important.' she giggled nervously.

'What have you done?'

'You mean what have *we* done,' She countered.

She placed his hand on her stomach.

'Rick, I'm pregnant. Can you feel my little bump?'

He rubbed her stomach.

'Are you sure?'

'Of course, the doctor confirmed it today; he or she is a honeymoon baby!'

Rick took the safe option.

'That's wonderful news, Lovey.'

He kissed her.

'It's a bit sooner than planned, but we'll manage. When is our little fellow due?'

'I'm about eleven weeks pregnant, so he or she is due sometime in January.'

The phone rang. It was Frances.

'I've received a registered slip from South Africa addressed to Rick. I'll leave it under the mat so Rick can collect the item from the post office. I'm guessing it's your statement, Kathy.'

'I'm sure you're right. Captain Oberholster would have deliberately sent my statement to Rick, after all I'm a mere woman,' Kathy muttered sarcastically, before giggling nervously.

'We've got good news for you, Mum… I'm pregnant.'

Frances was delighted and they agreed to have dinner with her the following evening after Rick collected Kathy's statement.

A framed photograph of Trevor had joined other family members on the mantelpiece in Frances's lounge. Kathy stared at it, thinking. *He looks exactly how I remember him.* The early evening was devoted to baby talk. After dinner they turned to the serious business of Kathy's police statement.

Frances had also placed a copy of the original police report on the coffee table beside the unopened one. Kathy slit open the registered envelope and unfolded the pages.

'What the…'

She reddened angrily.

'How could he?'

She bit her lip.

'I had a hunch Captain Oberholster would do something like this – Salamina typed my statement in English and *he's* had it translated into *Afrikaans.*'

Rick took the statement from her.

'This is a delay tactic. Captain Oberholster did this on purpose. He knows we can get it translated, but it's inconvenient and will waste our time.'

Frances was giving Kathy's protests little attention. Instead, she was examining a notelet that had been attached to the statement with a paper-clip.

'The official stamp on this note says, Commandant Marais, Pretoria Head Quarters. I wonder if this is *Captain Marais* who has now been promoted. He was one of the policemen who headed the initial investigation into Trevor's murder?'

Kathy was furious. 'If you're right Mum and he's now a commandant, can you ask him to kick Captain Oberholster out of the police force?'

Frances chuckled at her daughter's cheeky comment.

'No seriously, Kath. Your father and I respected Captain Marais. He felt there were inconsistencies with the investigation and wondered why Trevor didn't try to defend himself. Also, why nothing was stolen from the cottage apart from a bread knife. They didn't find the knife and presumed it was the weapon used by the killer.'

Frances glanced at the note again.

'Captain Marais said a squatter would have stolen food and run.'

Something dawned on her.

'If this statement went via Pretoria *that* would explain why it took so long to *reach you*, Kath.'

Kathy placed the statement back in the envelope. None of them could read Afrikaans.

'I'm meeting Charlotte for lunch tomorrow to tell her about the baby. She speaks Afrikaans and I'll ask her to translate it for me.'

Rick and Kathy were already struggling financially and would soon be living on only Rick's salary. In Rhodesia, pregnant nurses left work as soon as their bellies started to show. The couple discussed their options and agreed to continue living in their bachelor apartment until it was too small for the three of them.

Charlotte was thrilled to hear her best friend was pregnant and couldn't wait to splash out on baby clothes. She agreed to translate the statement and return it in a few days.

'How many weeks along did you say you were, Kath?'

'The doc said about eleven or twelve. Why?'

'You're very big. I think you're having twins.'

Kathy protested, 'There are no twins in either Rick's or my family, so I doubt it.'

She found her friends comments strange. *What would Charlotte know about babies?*

When they met again a week later, Charlotte had been on a shopping spree and handed over a huge bag of baby clothes. Kathy was delighted. She 'oohd' and 'aahd'over the tiny garments.

'Thank you, Charlotte, they're so cute; these are the first baby clothes I've received for my little one.'

She then turned her attention to her translated statement.

'This isn't my statement. The wording has been *changed*. Why is no one taking me seriously?'

Her fist came down with a thump on the table and Charlotte jumped.

'*Stop it,* Kathy. *Your* memories are from fifteen years ago. I think it's time you switched your focus. – you're having a *real-life* living breathing baby who needs your full attention. Nothing will bring Trevor back.'

Kathy reflected for a moment.

'I can't forget what I saw, Char. It wasn't Trevor's fault that I lost my memory. If it wasn't for my amnesia, they might have caught his killer by now.'

'Okay, Kathy…let's agree on something – you check your statement and make the changes, then send it back to captain, whatever-his-name-is. Put your guilt back in the amnesia box and direct your energy towards the birth of healthy twins.'

She patted Kathy's baby bump.

'In return, I promise that one day, I'll help you put the bastard who killed your brother in prison and throw away the key.'

Kathy sighed. 'I'm not having twins. But you're right as usual. My baby deserves my full attention. One day I'll return to East London and find Trevor's killer, with or without your help.'

It was a few months later before the doctor detected the second heartbeat.

'It's twins, my dear, this could mean an early delivery.'

Twins changed everything. Their bachelor pad might have been big enough for one very tiny baby for a few months, but two babies made it impossible. When her mother returned from visiting Commandant Marais in Pretoria, Kathy would ask her if all four of them could move into 66 Bakestone Street and live with her.

Frances and Charlotte had left for Pretoria in South Africa a few days earlier. Frances had an appointment with Commandant Marais and Charlotte was to visit her father.

Chapter 8

Charlotte and Frances stopped at the police check point outside Fort Victoria. The area between Fort Victoria and Beit Bridge had become a hot spot, and after hearing Rick and Kathy's story about seeing what they thought were terrorists crossing the road, they would take no chances. It was mid-morning and the road was reasonably busy, making them feel a little safer. Frances had borrowed Rick's 9mm Llama handgun and would leave it with the Beit Bridge police station to be collected on their return.

It was a long drive and both ladies were perspiring profusely by the time they reached Beit Bridge. Frances was grouchy, standing in the sluggish queue inside the poorly ventilated Customs building.

'You'd think they could invest in a few ceiling fans,' she grumbled loud enough for those around her to hear.

Charlotte was embarrassed at her companion's outburst.

'We're nearly at the counter, Frances, it won't be much longer.'

It was Charlotte's turn to drive as they crossed the Limpopo River bridge. Frances hung out the window, clinging to fifteen-year-old memories.

'Kathy was six years old when we crossed this bridge. I had to hold onto her to make sure she didn't fall out the car window. My son, Trevor, was teasing her, pointing out hippos in the water. "Look, there, Kathy. Can you see that baby hippo with its cute, little ears?"

'"Oh! Yes," said Kathy, "I can see it." We all laughed. The river was in flood, there was nothing to see, but a fast, moving expanse of dark green water.'

Frances giggled and then turned thoughtful.

'Not for one moment did I imagine that only three of us would travel back across this bridge.'

'I'm so sorry, Frances. It must have been a terrible time for your family.'

Charlotte patted Frances shoulder, sympathetically.

The two ladies stopped for the night at Leopard Hotel outside Louis-Trichardt. The following morning, they drove through to the city of Pretoria and arrived at their destination in good time. It helped that Charlotte could speak and read Afrikaans. After they had checked into the Protea hotel, Frances caught a taxi to police headquarters, while Charlotte waited for her father to arrive.

'Good afternoon, Mrs Parker. It's good to see you, you're looking remarkably well. Please take a seat.'

'Please call me Frances, Commandant Marais. I must congratulate you on your promotion, you've done very well for yourself.'

She didn't think he'd changed much after fifteen years. His hair had thinned a little and he now wore a regent moustache. A row of service medals and braided epaulettes on his jacket elevated his position to a senior commissioned officer.

The commandant asked after her husband. She felt a twinge of sadness.

'Ben passed away some years ago. He was diagnosed with cancer and died in 1965.'

'I'm sorry to hear that, Mrs Parker, er, Frances; your husband was a *farmer,* wasn't he?'

She brought him up to date on her family situation and answered his questions about war-torn Rhodesia. He rested his elbow on the desk, chin in hand and appeared genuinely interested.

'Now tell me, Frances, how can I be of assistance to you?'

She steeled herself, determined to represent her deceased son to the best of her ability.

'I'm here to discuss new evidence in my son's homicide case.'

She was unsure of herself; butterflies fluttered in her stomach. He noticed her hesitation and nodded, encouraging her to continue.

'You will recall that my daughter Kathy was only six when her brother died. She didn't speak for weeks and when she finally did, she repressed the memory of my son's murder.

'She married earlier this year and while on honeymoon in the Eastern Cape, her memory was triggered by a man she saw. She says he's the man who killed Trevor. We didn't know she witnessed the murder you see.'

Frances explained how Kathy had witnessed the murder and given a statement to the police in East London.

'I believe you've seen her statement, so you're aware of what I'm telling you?'

'Remarkable,' he mumbled. 'I read your daughter's statement, but go ahead and fill me in on any gaps.'

'Did you also receive the forensic sketch she did of the culprit?' she raised her voice questioningly.

'Eh, yes, indeed. I kept a copy and then forwarded the original statement to you.'

'We didn't receive a copy of the sketch, just the statement. It didn't matter; Kathy kept a discarded copy of the sketch, so I know what he looks like.'

She felt a little more confident.

'The statement we received had been translated from English into Afrikaans. Is that standard practice? Do you translate everything into Afrikaans? We don't speak Afrikaans, so it was very inconvenient.'

He frowned.

'No. All statements should remain in the language they've been recorded in. I'll check what happened.'

Frances handed him a copy of Kathy's corrected statement in English.

'This is her corrected copy in English for your records, Commandant Marais.'

'Thank you, Frances, I'll read it later.'

A tea tray arrived on his desk.

'I'll do the honours.'

She reached for the pot and poured the tea.

The Commandant took a sip of tea and stroked his moustache before he spoke.

'Frances, I remember your son's case well. It happened shortly after my promotion to captain. There were...' he searched for a word, *"unexplained"* circumstances. I've read your daughter's statement and seen the sketch – it's remarkable that she can remember so clearly after fifteen years.'

He placed the tea cup on his desk and lifted his gaze.

'If only we had these facts at the time, there may have been a different result.'

He sat back comfortably in his chair and folded his arms.

'I'll be honest with you, Frances. Your daughter was six years old; she saw this man in poor light for only a few minutes and only came forward to make a statement after fifteen years.'

Frances intuitively knew she didn't want to hear what he was about to say.

'We've no doubt your daughter witnessed the attack. She saw a young white man who possibly resembles her sketch.'

He pinched at his chin, thoughtfully.

'That forensics sketch is too detailed for any small child to remember after fifteen years. She drew the man she saw at the café. There are possibly similarities, but we don't believe *this* man is your son's killer.'

Frances was stunned. She vacillated between confusion and anger as a flame flushed her cheeks.

'Are you saying… you don't believe my daughter's statement?'

He cleared his throat.

'Of course, we believe your daughter's statement; it's her *sketch* that has caused the doubt. That sketch resembles a prominent businessman who lives in East London. The vehicle registration number your son-in-law gave the police, confirmed it was this man.'

Frances clenched her teeth, trying to control her fury. *Kathy's right. Captain Oberholster did recognise the man in her sketch.*

'Was this man *even* questioned?' she quizzed.

'Yes, the police *did* interview the man your daughter saw. We also *want* to find your son's killer and will continue to search for the perpetrator.'

She felt deflated. She wanted to return home with something positive to tell Kathy.

'What makes you *so* sure the man my daughter identified is the *wrong* man, commandant?'

'Because we have no reason to *suspect* him. He has no priors and as far as we know, he's an exemplary citizen. Incidentally, he has an *alibi* for the night your son died. We believe the man in the café looks similar to the stranger your daughter saw attack your son. Her memory was triggered and she has unintentionally transposed the looks of the man in the café onto those of the killer.'

Frances was grasping at straws.

'So, you're telling me, the police don't believe my daughter, but they believe this man's fifteen-year-old alibi,' she knew she was possibly going too far.

'Frances. I'm on your side. This man has cooperated fully with our investigation. He's lived in East London all his life.'

He searched her face.

'I do understand your frustration – you came here in the hope that your daughter's evidence would result in the arrest of your son's killer.'

She acknowledged to herself, *that's right; that's precisely why I travelled all the way from Rhodesia.*

She took a chance.

'Commandant Marais, can you give me the name of this suspect?'

He gave an exasperated sigh.

'You know I can't do that. I've possibly told you more than I should have, already. And please don't refer to him as a *suspect*. We have no evidence to connect him to the crime.'

'So, my daughter's statement and her sketch, have made no difference to this enquiry.'

Frances gave him a hostile look.

'I'm angry with myself. I feel I've failed my son by allowing the police to forget about him. After all these years my daughter tells us what she saw happen, and *you* dismiss *her* eye-witness statement as a *mistake!'*

He worked to calm her.

'I'm sorry, Frances, I wish we had caught the killer. It would have given you some kind of closure. Please, believe me, we haven't forgotten your son and we are *not* dismissing your daughter's statement. Her sketch is very helpful and there's a good chance we'll find the killer because of this new information. Don't be disheartened. Please stay in touch, and I will do the same.'

They shook hands before she left police headquarters. She felt she had failed both her son and daughter. Her shoulders slumped as she made her way to the waiting taxi.

Frances sat stiffly on a wing-backed chair in the hotel lobby, turning the newspaper pages without reading the words. She re-examined every detail of her meeting with Commandant Marias. *It's ridiculous to suggest that Kathy transposed a stranger's identity onto that of the killer.* She was angry with him, but more so with herself. Now *she* was having doubts – *perhaps Kathy has identified the wrong man.*

'Hello, Frances.'

Charlotte arrived accompanied by a nice looking, older man.

'This is my father, Daniel Pistorius. Daddy, this is Frances Parker, Kathy's mum.'

He lifted her hand to his lips.

'Enchanté, mademoiselle, I had no idea Kathy's mother was so young.'

Daniel was CEO of a large financial company. He travelled the world, spoke several languages and his English was excellent. Frances could see from whom Charlotte had inherited her good looks.

'Daddy is paying for our drinks and dinner, so don't hold back!' she giggled hugging her father.

Daniel Pistorius was charming, and although Frances initially contributed little to the conversation, she enjoyed the banter between father and daughter.

'How was your visit to the commandant?' Charlotte asked.

'Hmm, it didn't go well.'

Frances didn't want to discuss the meeting but felt she couldn't be rude.

'There isn't much to tell. Commandant Marais thinks Kathy has identified the wrong man in her sketch. He mentioned something about transposing the face of a prominent businessman onto that of the killer.'

She didn't try to hide her scepticism.

'The police supposedly interviewed the suspect.' she corrected herself. 'Sorry, I'm *not allowed* to call him a *suspect.* Apparently, men of his calibre don't *commit* murder.'

She made light of her bitter sarcasm with a weak smile.

'I'm sorry, can we change the subject? I don't want to ruin the evening.'

'Not at all… you sound like a concerned mother.'

Daniel looked at her sympathetically.

'Do you believe this commandant fellow is taking your son's death seriously, Frances?'

'I have no way of knowing. He's very professional and I respect him. Although it's difficult to keep abreast of what is happening when I'm living in another country.'

Daniel indicated he understood.

'Charlotte told me about Kathy remembering her brother after a fifteen-year lapse. I travel a lot, but when I'm here, I'd be happy to visit Commandant Marais on your behalf.'

She liked Daniel and thanked him. Having a contact in Pretoria could be useful.

Chapter 9

When Kathy, Rick and the twins moved in to share her home, Frances was delighted. Shortly before the twin's birth, modifications had been made to the house, with a section of the veranda being converted into an additional bathroom. Both families found sharing the home to their advantage. The grandchildren loved their grandmother and Frances enjoyed having her daughter, son in law and grandchildren living with her.

Ben and Rebecca (Becky) celebrated their second birthday at 66 Bakestone Street. By now Kathy was back nursing at the hospital three nights a week and Rick was earning good money as a qualified criminal lawyer. Frances was the editor of two home and garden magazines and highly respected by her business associates. They appeared to be happy, living busy lives and financially stable, but beneath the surface simmered the awareness of a terrorist war raging around them.

Rick enjoyed his job and was ambitious. As part of the war effort, he was drafted into the police reserve and every few months he was conscripted to bright-light duties to protect farming families. Kathy was concerned that the children were seeing very little of their father. Rick's employers and the police reserve were demanding more and more of his time.

'I can't remember the last time you played with the children, lovey. You arrive home after they're in bed most nights and when you do have a weekend free, you're off on police reserve duties. The twins never see you. I think we should take time off and go away for a long weekend.'

'I know what you're saying, Kath. I miss spending time with you and the twins, but I'm snowed under with legal cases at the moment. I'll put in for a few days off next month.'

Their time away together was precious. Kathy enjoyed being a wife and mother and seldom had time to reminisce about the past, but she had not forgotten her brother's murder. At Christmas and Easter, she visited the

Salisbury cemetery to fill the vases on Trevor and her father's graves with flame lilies and country flowers. During these visits, she would gaze at Trevor's headstone. *I haven't forgotten, big brother; one day I'll return to East London and bring your killer to justice.*

Frances had a new man in her life. Tim Sharp had recently joined the publishing company where she worked. He was a widower with two married daughters and three grandchildren.

Kathy was not convinced. 'I cannot understand what you see in him, Mum. He's podgy and balding – can't he do something about his tobacco-stained teeth?' Kathy was exaggerating of course.

No one would ever be good enough to replace her father. Frances was wise enough to understand and ignore her daughter's bias comments.

'Tim's an intelligent and kind man whose company I enjoy. We're going to see a show at the REPS theatre tonight.'

All around them the old Rhodesian way of life was crumbling. Some referred to its decline as the 'boiled frog syndrome'; the premise being that if you put a frog into lukewarm water and bring it slowly to the boil, it will not sense danger until it's too late and the water boils. Atrocities were on the increase and Kathy spoke often of the possibility of leaving the country and moving to live in South Africa.

Rick did not agree.

'The Rhodesian spirit is still strong, Kath. It's premature to talk about leaving the country. All our family and friends are here and I believe there's a good chance a peaceful solution will be found.'

Without his support, there was nothing more to say. This all changed a few months later.

Kathy reached for the phone. It was Charlotte, and she was crying. Immediately she knew something was very wrong, her friend seldom cried.

'Charlotte what's wrong? Tell me what's happened?'

'He's dead; oh, Kath… he's *dead.*'

Heaving sobs choked her words.

'I held his hand… he was still alive… oh – Kathy, my Zach's *dead.*' Her voice trembled as she rushed on. 'His legs… it was awful… I can't talk.'

Her voice faded and Kathy heard her replace the receiver.

She left the twins with a neighbour and drove straight to the hospital where she found Charlotte locked behind a toilet door, weeping like her heart would break.

'I loved him, Kath. He was my dearest friend and he asked for me when he arrived in emergency.'

Her sobs were jagged.

'His legs had gone.'

She opened the door, and stumbled out. Kathy tried to break her fall and ended up on the floor beside her friend. They sat against the wall, arms entwined and sobbed.

'Come home with me, Char. The hospital will understand,' Kathy encouraged.

Her words triggered a bizarre reaction. Charlotte sprang to her feet.

'No, I can't, Kath. The emergency is full of casualties and my patients need me.'

She had to forget about her own personal feelings – she was *Doctor* Charlotte Pistorius again.

She washed her face.

'Quick, lend me your lipstick and hairbrush, Kath. I need to dolly myself up and look respectable.'

She hugged Kathy tightly.

'Thanks for coming. I don't know what I'd do without you.'

She hurried back to the emergency department. The hospital was short-staffed and nurses and doctors alike worked long hours. They dedicated their time to saving as many lives as they could.

Kathy phoned Rick to tell him the tragic news. She knew he would be heart-broken. *It always hits harder when the person is a close friend.* Rick found it difficult to speak.

'I think I'm in shock, Kath. I can't believe it... I don't know what to say.'

He blew a distorted whistle.

'Oh hell, I'm late. I'm due in court; we'll talk about it when I get home.'

Although Zach was younger than Rick, they knew each other from junior school. Zach was Italian, so family meant everything to him. His good looks and larger-than-life personality made him popular with everyone. Rick was an only child, more reserved, and happy to allow others to hold the limelight. The two shared a love of music and together had formed the Bandits rock group.

Rick spoke of his friendship with Zach that night as they sat on the veranda.

'I can't believe he's gone Kath.'

He gazed at the night sky.

'It was Zach who encouraged me to buy you that Christmas gift and visit you after our break up. I wanted him as a best-man at our wedding, but as you know, our wedding date clashed with *his* parents wedding anniversary. To him, family came first, but he left their party just long enough to sing "you're just too good to be true" at our wedding. That meant a lot to me.'

He closed his eyes as if trying to recall memories.

'Zach loved life and the ladies. I've often wondered if he was still in love with Charlotte; he would never hear a word against her after they broke up and none of his other girlfriends ever lasted very long.'

Charlotte joined them on the veranda later in the evening when she returned home from the hospital. She looked awful having worked eighteen hours straight.

'I didn't want to stop, because I'd have to face that Zach was gone.'

She looked exhausted. Rick poured her a Bacardi and Coke.

'Thanks, Rick, it's good to relax with you guys, it's been a terrible day.'

'I'm sorry, Char, we're devastated about Zach, we can talk about something else if you'd rather?'

Kathy didn't want her friend to feel pressured into reliving her painful memories.

'I'd like to talk about him, if you don't mind?'

'Go ahead, Charlotte, we're listening.'

Rick offered an understanding nod.

'Zach was on army call-up with the SAPPERS sweeping for land-mines when he stepped on an anti-personnel mine. His injuries were severe and both legs were gone.'

She rubbed at her forehead.

'When he arrived at the emergency, he asked for me. He must have been in such pain, but he gave a cheeky grin and said, "Hi, Char." I kissed him and he asked me to give him my hand. His grip was amazingly strong considering he'd lost so much blood. I was running beside him as we wheeled him towards the operating theatre. He pulled me towards him, "I've always loved you, Char, I always will,"' She started to cry. 'I love you too. You're going to be okay, Zach, we'll be together again.'

A grief-choked wail escaped her.

'He went into cardiac arrest – oh, God! We tried so hard to save him.'

She broke down and sobbed uncontrollably.

At Zach's funeral Rick spoke from the church lectern.

'Zach was my best friend. He liked fast cars and fast women.'

This caused a titter of laughter.

'The only things he loved more, was his folks, his family and his friends. I have so much to thank Zach for. The time the cops chased us through Salisbury central park – possibly the less said on that escapade the better. Our joint venture, starting the Bandits – man, we had a blast.'

Rick forced a smile.

'On a more serious note. Thanks, Zach for always being there when I needed a friend. Cheers, my mate; you'll be sadly missed, but never forgotten.'

Charlotte was emotional and kept her speech short.

'Zach was my first love and we were best friends. He was handsome, funny and talented. He was taken from us at the prime of his life. I'll miss you, good bye, my love.'

After the service proud Rhodesians huddled together, wondering where the future would lead and if the atrocities of war would ever end.

There was a noticeable change in Rick after Zach's funeral. He later confided in Kathy.

'Zach would have hated to live without his legs; perhaps it's better he didn't make it.'

Kathy gently placed her hand on Rick's shoulder.

'I'm sorry, my love, I know you're going to miss him.'

Charlotte phoned Rick at work a few days later and asked him to join her for coffee.

'Thanks for coming, Rick, I wanted to talk to you alone. You and Kathy mean the world to me; she's the sister I never had. Normally, I wouldn't meddle in your affairs, but Zach's death has changed my perspective in many ways.'

She clenched her hands into fists.

'Get your family out of Rhodesia, Rick. I see too much pain and suffering and the country is in a bad way. I'm asking you to talk to Kathy about moving to South Africa. It's not *fair* to risk leaving her a widow and your children without a father.'

Rick listened intently as he clenched and unclenched his jaw.

'Kathy has been wanting to investigate the option of moving south, but I haven't been keen until now. Thanks for your honesty, Charlotte. Would you consider moving?'

It was a fair question.

'I don't have children, Rick, and I'm gaining invaluable experience as a doctor, but I don't want to live like this for the rest of my life. If you and Kath move to South Africa, I'll follow.'

That night Rick and Kathy had a serious talk.

'I'm taking Zach's death as a sign to move on, Kath. If you agree, I'd like you to go ahead and start making enquiries about us emigrating to South Africa?'

Kathy gave a thoughtful sigh.

'I think it's a good idea. We'll speak to Mum after dinner.'

Kathy would not move without her mother. She had not forgotten her father's last words, "*I want my girls to be together always.*"

Rick, Kathy and Frances had to look past their good jobs and comfortable home.

'There'll *never* be a *right* time to leave, Mum. We love this country, but it's changed beyond recognition. I'm going to investigate the emigration process and see if we'll be accepted by South Africa.'

Kathy collected and completed the South African emigration forms ready to post. Frances half-heartedly agreed to move with them.

'There's no rush,' she assured them.

'Maybe not, Mum, but please sign your forms so I can send them off with ours.'

Much to Kathy's relief, Frances signed them.

That night, Kathy was restless and her mind was over-active. *Are we doing the right thing in leaving Rhodesia?* she asked herself. Just then, Trevor appeared at the end of the bed.

'Hello, Trevor,' she whispered as she reached towards him, their fingers touched and he was gone.

She knew it was all in her mind, but he looked so real. *It's strange that I should see Trevor's spirit after all these years. He still looks the same.* She thought back to her time on the farm when she had called him buddy, not recognising him as her brother. *I wonder if it's some kind of omen? If he knows we are planning to move to South Africa.* The next day she felt more positive about their move and posted the emigration forms.

Charlotte wrote to her father about Zach's death. She also mentioned that she had encouraged Rick and Kathy to emigrate to South Africa and Frances would move with them. A few weeks later she received a letter back. Enclosed was an envelope addressed to Frances and a note from Daniel.

"Hello, Frances. I hope you are well. This letter is from Maria and Eric Van Wyk, my good friends who live in East London, Eastern Cape. Fond regards, Daniel."

She opened the envelope and read aloud,

Dear Frances,

We have not met, but have a mutual friend in Daniel Pistorius. Daniel contacted us to say that due to the war in Rhodesia, you are planning to move to South Africa. We can only imagine what it must be like to have to leave the country you love.

Eric and I live in East London and should you decide to move to here, we would like to offer you and your daughter's family accommodation until you are settled in your own home. We have a large house and can easily accommodate a family of five.

Frances read on in silence.

'How amazing. These friends of Daniel's have never met us, yet they are offering to open their home in East London to our family until we have accommodation of our own.'

'Oh, Mum, that's wonderful. What a generous offer,' Kathy was thrilled.

Frances phoned Maria who was as charming on the phone as she was in her letter.

'We are rattling around in this huge house, Frances. Eric and I would like to help make your move as comfortable as possible. It will be difficult for you and your family to settle in a new country please consider our offer.'

'Thank you, Maria, we are so grateful to you. We haven't met and yet I feel I know you already. We've sent in our emigration papers and if we are accepted into South Africa, I'll contact you again.'

After speaking to Maria, the family had a brief discussion and agreed that if South Africa accepted their application, they would move to East London and stay with Maria and Eric until they were settled. Everything slowly fell into place. South Africa accepted their emigration application and Frances phoned Maria and Eric to formally accept their offer.

'Why East London, Frances?' Tim, Frances's boyfriend asked.

'Most people are moving to Durban in Natal; it's more English than the rest of South Africa.'

'There is no simple answer to that, Tim, I don't know. It was possibly the letter from Maria that helped us make the decision.'

She had answered him as best she could.

Once they received confirmation that the emigration process had been successful, Frances put the house on the market. She was asking a realistic price and the market was still fairly strong. It sold within six weeks, at the asking price.

With the deal done and dusted they started preparing to leave the country. The Rhodesian banks were restricting the amount of currency allowed to leave the country. This meant that only a small portion of the money received for the house could be transferred to South Africa.

Kathy did her homework.

'We can take our furniture with us, perhaps we should use some of the money we cannot take, to buy new beds and electrical appliances.'

Rick agreed. 'Let's do that. We can even buy the children clothes to grow into - go for it.' The bank would transfer money from the house sale to a South African bank account slowly over the next few years, but the family would need ready money for setting up costs.'

Kathy also learnt there were restrictions on vehicles.

'I have to sell my new Renault. We're only allowed to take vehicle older than two years out of the country. I'll get a good price, but of course we can't take the money with us.'

Fortunately, Rick and Frances's vehicles were over two years old. Rick's vehicle had a tow hitch and they could take the trailer with them.

All three family members resigned from their jobs and packing boxes littered the house. No one threw them a farewell party or offered support. Most friends and colleagues were blatantly hostile, accusing them of betraying their country and running away.

Rick's parents could hardly be civil to Kathy.

'How can you take Rick away from everything he loves? He's got a good job with great prospects. I hope you know what you're doing, Kathy.'

Rick's mother left no doubt about her feelings.

'We will possibly never *see* our grandchildren again.'

'Don't worry, dear, they'll be back.' Rick's father added. 'You'll see; everything will turn out well for Rhodesia and all those who ran away will return.'

'Why don't you and Mum emigrate to Cape Town? You'll only be a few hours away from where we are living and we'll see plenty of each other,' Rick suggested.

'We're not moving anywhere, Son. We're very happy where we are.'

They refused to even discuss the possibilities.

Charlotte, on the other hand, could not have been *more* supportive. She helped with the packing, then took the children to the park to give the adults a break.

'You're doing the right thing, Kath. I'll join you in South Africa after you're settled,' she promised. 'I wish our friends realised how difficult it is for you to leave everything you love and know, to start a new life. I think a lot of people are frightened. They don't know what the future holds.'

She hugged Kathy.

'Keep your chin up, girl.'

The last few days at 66 Bakestone Street were tense. The children could sense their parent's anxiety.

'Can we sleep in your bed, Mummy?'

Becky stood in the doorway holding her brother's hand.

'Come and climb into bed with Daddy; I'll go and sleep in the spare room.'

Kathy knew she would keep them all awake with her tossing and turning.

It was mid-November when the removal truck arrived to collect their furniture and belongings. It was an emotional time. Tim had agreed to accompany Frances in her car on the three-day journey to the Eastern Cape. Rick, Kathy and the twins would spend their last week in Rhodesia with Rick's parents.

Chapter 10

Since the sale of her house five weeks earlier Frances had been suffering from insomnia. She reclined in her wicker chair, chain-smoking between cups of tea and wrestling with troubling thoughts. The glow of morning brought relief from another sleepless night.

It was six months since she had agreed to move to East London in the Eastern Cape of South Africa. She knew she should have had the courage to say, "No! Not East London. That's the city that took my son from me."

Three years before, when she had visited Commandant Marais in Pretoria. He had told her that the man her daughter identified in her sketch resembled a business man who *lived* in East London. *What if he still lives there? I could meet Trevor's killer in the street. He could be sitting next to me at a restaurant or even be living next door.* In her heart she knew it was too late to change their plans. When the Van Wyk's had offered to open their East London home to her whole family, it was such a generous offer she didn't feel she could refuse.

She put on a brave face, and took a last look at her empty house at 66 Bakestone Street. She then locked the door and bid a silent farewell to the magnificent flamboyant tree in the back yard.

Tim had arrived to help with the last few packages.

'What happened, Fran, you're limping?'

She explained how a table leg had dropped on her foot during the move.

'It was painful when it happened, but it's a little easier now. Just a little bruising,' she assured him as she hooked her arm through his and used him as a crutch to help her hop to the car.

He had taken two weeks' leave from work to share the driving on the journey south. They would spend that night at his home and leave first thing in the morning.

Frances made sure she was alone before she eased her foot out of the shoe and sock. She quickly covered the unsightly swelling with a clean sock. An early night and painkillers helped her sleep soundly until the alarm woke her at 4 a.m.

Tim helped her hop to the car and suggested they visit the hospital outpatients before they left on their journey. Frances wouldn't hear of it.

'I'll be sitting in a car, resting it for three days. My foot's bruised, not broken!'

'How do you know that?' Tim asked, looking worried.

'Because we haven't got time for a broken foot,' she responded illogically. 'You'll possibly have to drive the first day.'

She noticed his sceptical look.

'It's *nothing* to worry about, Tim, really. I'll drive tomorrow.'

She smiled her famous Frances smile to assure him.

Tim had packed her car and secured the roof-rack the night before, ready for the three-day journey. He had thoughtfully prepared a flask of tea and sandwiches to avoid stopping until they reached Fort Victoria. He knew the Beit Bridge military convoy would not wait for them. Due to several recent incidents, it was now mandatory that all travellers joined the convoy. The war had escalated and even the convoy itself had been attacked on occasion. Frances's Peugeot sedan was one of the last vehicles to join the dozens of cars and trucks making their way to Beitbridge. Police reservists manned the Mazda pick-up trucks with M.A.G machine guns mounted on the turret on the open back. There was an armed vehicle positioned at the front, middle and rear of the convoy.

The convoy stopped at the Lion and Elephant hotel to allow travellers to stretch their legs and use the facilities. Frances was in too much pain to accompany Tim when he looked at the soapstone carvings. Native African artists had made a good living selling their artistic creations along the roadside until holiday makers were ambushed and killed while travelling this lonely stretch of road. Now there was no choice but to move their stalls and sell their creative work where they knew the convoy would stop.

'I've bought you this amazing sculptured head of an old man as a souvenir, Frances. What do you think?'

Frances held it gently.

'It's magnificent. Thank you, Timmy. Look at the character lines in his face and his gentle eyes. I'll always treasure it,' she hugged the carved head fondly, then wrapped it in a hand towel and placed it in the glove box.

The stifling dry-heat poured in through the open windows of the vehicles as they crept along. Frances took a last look at the granite outcrops and scrubby thorn-bushes lining the dusty roadside and then looked resolutely ahead.

Tim ended up having to drive all of the three days. When they arrived at the East London beachfront, the sun was dipping toward the horizon. Frances had not complained about her injured foot, but Tim could tell she was in a lot of pain. They watched as waves crept forward, lapping the sand and then sweeping away again. The shrill cry of a gull attracted Tim's attention.

'That's a sound we don't hear in Rhodesia, Franny.'

He placed his arm around her shoulder and hugged her. She nestled against him.

'Will you help me across the sand, Tim? I want to feel the waves wash over my feet.'

He carried her to the edge of the water. She curled her injured leg, at the knee, then remembered she was wearing bright pink and giggled.

'I must look like a flamingo.'

She unfurled her foot and gingerly allowed her toes to touch the sand. A searing pain shot up her leg and she cried out in agony. Her chin began to tremble and tears trickled down her face.

'I've made a terrible mistake, Tim. I shouldn't have moved here… I want to go back home to Rhodesia.'

She clung to him, stammering between sobs.

'This is… where I lost my beautiful boy.'

Tim held her tightly and spoke tenderly.

'You're depressed, Frances. Your son isn't here; he's at Huchi farm, running through paddocks, he's driving the tractor and doing all the things you told me he loved doing,' Tim continued speaking softly. 'Franny, you're in pain, you're just not thinking straight.'

He picked her up and placed her gently on a grassy bank. They sat side by side until Tim broke the silence.

'I think emigrating to South Africa is the right move, Fran. After I've sorted out my affairs, I hope to join you if you'll have me?'

She cuddled against him.

'Of course, I will. Thank you,' she whispered, looking up at him, her lashes heavy with tears.

'That's my Franny,' he encouraged. 'Kathy and family will be here in a few days and then all this darkness you're feeling will lift, my love.'

Maria Van Wyk answered the doorbell. She was a tiny lady with dark curly hair and a pretty oval face. Tim carried Frances up the front steps and seated her on the nearest chair. He peeled back her socks and saw her injury for the first time. Both Tim and Maria gasped in shock.

'Good heavens, Frances, what happened?' Maria asked, sinking to her knees and holding, Frances' throbbing foot with both hands. 'We must get you to the hospital immediately,' She called her husband; 'Eric!'

X-rays showed Frances had a broken bone in her foot and a fractured ankle. Two days in hospital and she was in a better state of mind. She had slept for nearly forty-eight hours and medication had her pain under control.

'I can't tell you how wonderful the nursing staff have been,' she told Maria. 'Thank you for the flowers and for everything you have done for me.'

Frances knew that she had a true friend in Maria.

Tim collected her from the hospital the following day and carefully walked beside her as she swung her way to the car.

'I'm becoming quite an expert swinging between these crutches.'

She seemed much happier and even laughed at Tim's corny jokes.

'It's good to be back home,' Frances commented, sitting at the lunch table chatting with her hosts.

She looked around the room.

'I'm admiring your Dutch décor, Maria. I love natural materials and the craftsmanship of your furniture is amazing. Did you make these pieces, Eric?' she asked.

He laughed. 'No, I'm not good with my hands. My grandfather was a carpenter and made this dining suite and the sideboard.'

Frances felt relaxed in this comfortable sprawling single-story home, full of character and charm.

When Tim mentioned he had enlisted Maria's help in sending out Frances's CV to a publishing company, Frances thought he was teasing.

'Please tell me your joking, Tim?'

It wasn't a joke.

'The stamped envelope is already in the post. This job is made for you, Franny. You have everything they're looking for.'

She looked at him in disbelief.

'I know you mean well, Tim, but I wish you'd asked me first.'

She didn't want to sound too ungracious, so she added, 'It doesn't matter. No one will contact me after they see how old I am.'

Three days later, Frances was attending an interview at the office of Rural Life magazine. The publishing company was looking for a mature qualified person with experience to assist their editor. She hobbled between crutches to the interview room and clumsily dropped a crutch when she attempted to shake hands. The kindly-looking white-haired gentleman's whole face creased into a smile as he retrieved it for her and helped her to a chair. There was an instant rapport between them. She was offered the position and had accepted it before the interview was over. She knew she would be happy working with this man.

Frances improved both mentally and physically during the following days. The happy bubbly person she had always been, started to re-emerge – Rhodesia was the land of her birth; where the sky was bluer. Her husband and son were buried there, but she had brought her memories with her and she knew it was time to stop looking back.

Chapter 11

December 1976

Kathy, Rick and the twins spent their last seven days in Rhodesia with Rick's parents at their home in Salisbury. Rick was an only child who as far as his parents were concerned, could do no wrong. They had always liked Kathy until she started filling their son's head with the idea of leaving the country and emigrating to South Africa.

Becky and Ben were almost three, and out of their comfort zone at Granny Barron's house. They had boundless energy, and much to Kathy's amusement, took turns in placing their tiny fingers on forbidden items around the house and reprimanding each other.

'Don't touch it, Ben, don't touch it!'

Kathy soon discovered her parents-in-law disapproved of everything she did or said. To avoid conflict, she spent as much time as she could outdoors with the children.

Rick received a phone call to say Clive Adair, who was best man at their wedding was in hospital. He had been shot in the foot during a skirmish. It didn't sound too serious, but Clive and Alice were close friends, and Rick and Kathy wanted to see them before leaving the country.

That evening, Rick's mum added another complaint to her growing list.

'Can you put the children to bed now, Kathy? It's after six and this is grown-up's time.'

Kathy had had enough.

'I thought you wanted to spend time getting to know your grandchildren better. Their routine has been disrupted and they're afraid to be left in the room on their own. They won't go to sleep until we go to bed.'

She held her mother-in-law's gaze.

'Why don't you take your grandchildren to the Lion Park tomorrow and spend real time with them? That'll give Rick and me a chance to visit Clive Adair in hospital.'

Rick knew about Kathy's inner strength, so he wasn't surprised by her outburst, but the senior Mrs Barron looked stunned. She had bullied Kathy shamelessly over the past few days, not dreaming her daughter-in-law would answer back in front of her husband and son.

Rick's father agreed, 'We would love to take the children on an outing. You're quite right, Kathy; we do want to get to know our grandchildren better.' He looked from his wife to the children. 'What do you think of that, Ben and Becky? Would you like us to take you to the Lion Park tomorrow? It'll be fun.'

'Yippee!'

Ben climbed onto grandad's knee, while Becky hugged grandma's legs.

Rick and Kathy visited Clive the following morning.

'I've just received bad news,' Clive told them, 'There are complications and they may have to amputate my whole foot.'

Kathy left the two men together, while she went in search of the matron, who she knew well from her nursing days.

'Hello, Kathy, my dear, it's good to see you. I'm sorry, but the prognosis for Clive Adair is not good. There's a good chance he'll lose his foot.'

When Kathy returned to Clive's room, his wife had arrived. Kathy had not seen Alice for months. The last time they met, Alice was *offish* with her and had said. "I hope you and Rick are happy in South Africa. We don't need people like you. If you can't take the heat, then *good riddance.*"

To Kathy's surprise, Alice seemed pleased to see her and hugged her warmly.

'It's so good to see you, Kathy. Rick tells me you only have one more day here before you move to the Eastern Cape. I hope it goes well for you.'

'Thanks, Alice,' Kathy soon discovered why there was a change in her attitude.

'When I heard Clive had been shot, it was such a shock,' She looked at him lovingly.

'One of the guys with him was killed, so I count myself lucky that he came home to me.'

She then asked Kathy about the emigration process.

'I made a list of everything I did. I'll send it to you, Alice.'

'Thanks, Kathy, but please don't tell anyone else that we're thinking of going.'

This was typical of many of Rick and Kathy's friends who would make enquiries about the emigration process, then ask them not to tell anyone else that they were thinking of leaving.

Rick's parents thoroughly enjoyed their time with the twins.

Rick's father was impressed with his grandson.

'Ben asked such mature questions. He wanted to know why we couldn't go into the enclosure to pat the lion cubs. I explained that the mother lion would eat us. He laughed at me.

"Oh, no, Grandad, don't be silly; they're just big, pussy-cats. Lions don't eat *people.*"' He roared with laughter.

Becky helped her, grandma lay the table for dinner that night, and Kathy overheard her ask,

'Gwanny, will you visit us in Souf Afwika.'

'Of course, Becky, we may even come to live near you.'

Kathy smiled to herself. She was pleased to know that Rick's parents were considering joining them.

The journey south was slow and tedious. Before the family reached the border, Ben had thrown up and Becky had come out in a severe heat rash. They ploughed on regardless.

After three days cramped in the car, the children were miserable and Rick and Kathy were exhausted. It was a huge relief to reach the Van Wyk's home in East London. Two grubby, tear-stained children threw themselves into Maria and Tim's arms. Grandma Frances balanced on her crutches in the doorway at the top of the front steps, eager to see her family.

'Oh, Mum, it's wonderful to be here.'

Kathy hugged her mother.

'What have you done to your foot?'

'It's a long story, sweetie. I'll tell you about it over dinner.'

Maria and Eric Van Wyke welcomed the young family into their home and into the South African way of life, the different currency, language and customs. Frances and Kathy found Maria's advice on the best brands and products to buy at the supermarket was invaluable.

Eric helped Rick with the legal requirements for registering their vehicles and applying for work. He learnt that Afrikaans lessons were a must. South Africa had a dual-language, English/Afrikaans system, but many people only spoke Afrikaans. One of the subjects Rick did at school was Afrikaans and he had spent the last few months, brushing up on his vocabulary with Charlotte's help.

Apartheid[13] was something Frances, Rick and Kathy knew little about.

Eric explained briefly. 'It's the segregation of different racial groups. For example, people of different race groups can only rent and purchase homes or attend schools in their own allocated areas.' Kathy soon learnt that women were also discriminated against.

She had always controlled the family finances and visited the local bank to open a bank account.

'Please ask your husband to come with you to open the account. We need his permission,' the teller advised her.

Kathy thought she had been misunderstood.

'Oh, no, this bank account isn't for my husband; it's for me.'

The teller sighed, '*I know* it's for you… but you *have* to have your husband's *permission!*'

Kathy's eyes widened – she was not used to being treated like this. In Rhodesia, women had the personal freedom to explore opportunities without being shackled to a man. She thought back to the way Captain Oberholster had treated her four years earlier and wondered if this was why he had been so angry, when she, as a mere female, dared to challenge him. In South Africa, the *man* was the head of the family and women were usually subservient.

Just ten days before Christmas, Frances, Rick and Kathy visited the East London Police station where Rick asked to speak to Captain Oberholster.

'I'm sorry, sir, Captain Oberholster was transferred a few years ago,' the young constable advised him. 'I'll check if Captain Botha can see you. Who can I say is here to see him?'

'Rick and Kathy Barron, and Mrs Parker.'

On hearing their names, Salamina Brits swung around on her chair and signalled her recognition to Kathy, who mouthed, "hello," back to her.

---

[13] Apartheid:- segregation by race

Kathy was relieved to hear that Captain Oberholster had been transferred. She had been dreading seeing him again after their last meeting ended so badly.

'Captain Botha has agreed to see you, but he can only spare a few minutes.' the constable advised them.

Captain Botha appeared a little stiff, but Kathy found his demeanour more approachable than Captain Oberholster. His square jaw, wide-set brown eyes and bushy eyebrows complimented a stocky masculine body.

Frances lay her crutches beside her chair and took the lead.

'Captain Botha, we're here to find out what progress you've made in my son's homicide.'

She pointed to the buff folder Rick had placed on his desk. 'All the details are in that folder.'

The captain read the first page and then lifted his head to indicate she should continue.

'My daughter Kathy visited Captain Oberholser and gave him a witness statement.'

'I see. Would you give me a moment please, Mrs Parker?'

He continued turning the pages of the folder.

Frances glanced out the window. A flowering Jacaranda tree in the courtyard brought back memories – this was the same office where she and her husband, had given their statements, twenty years earlier. Momentarily distracted, she hadn't realised Captain Botha was speaking again.

'I'll ask Mrs Brits to request a copy of the original document, Mrs Parker. It would be better if we meet after I've familiarised myself with the case. Where can you be contacted?'

She ignored the question, feeling a little name dropping wouldn't hurt.

'I visited Commandant Marais at police headquarters in Pretoria a few years ago. He was the original investigating officer in my son's homicide and he mentioned that a businessman living in East London resembled the sketch my daughter drew of her brother's killer.'

She paused for effect.

'We now *live* in East London, so there's every chance we'll discover this man's identity, sooner or later. This is one of the reasons we came to see you.'

Captain Botha stroked his chin.

'I can't comment without reading the docket, Mrs Parker. Thank you for bringing this to my attention. If you could leave your contact details with me, I'll be in touch in the New Year.'

The phone rang at that moment and he picked up the receiver.

'Captain Botha, hoe kan ek jou help[14]?'

He placed his hand over the receiver and apologised, 'I have to take this call. I'll see you again in a few weeks.'

The festive season came and went with a flurry of decorations, twinkling lights, Father Christmas and excited children. Family and friends filled the Van Wyk's household to overflowing.

Rick attended several interviews early in January and eventually accepted a position working for a small legal firm in their criminal division. It offered an excellent salary package, but few promotional prospects. He was ambitious, and had only taken the job because he needed to provide for his family.

Kathy found two night-shifts a week at the local hospital, and the children started nursery school.

Now that Frances, Rick and Kathy were employed, they signed a six-month lease for a house on the outskirts of town. The removal van delivered their furniture and squeals of delight were heard from Ben and Becky as they peddled up and down the wooden floorboards on the veranda. For the first time in two and a half months, they slept in their own beds that night.

The family would be forever grateful to Maria and Eric for their hospitality and friendship.

Rick surprised Kathy with a second-hand car.

'I thought that as we are living further out of town, you would need a car. I think I got a really good buy. It only has thirty thousand on the clock.'

Kathy was impressed. It looked very nice, although she knew nothing about cars.

Kathy made a routine visit to the doctor.

'I thought I might be. I forget to take my stupid contraceptive pills every time we travel.'

---

[14] hoe kan ek jou help:-   How can I help you

She had fallen pregnant with the twins when she forgot to take her birth control pills on honeymoon. Now, she had forgotten them again during the removal and journey to East London.

'You're possibly as far as thirteen weeks pregnant, my dear. I can hear a healthy heartbeat,' Doctor Kobus informed her. 'I'm quite sure you guessed you were pregnant.'

'Yes, I did know; I was hoping I was wrong. An unplanned baby shortly after arriving in a new country and starting a new job is a little overwhelming.' she admitted. 'But I'm delighted about the baby and the twins will be thrilled.

That night while they were having dinner, she told Rick she was pregnant.

'That's a bit of a shock when we've just settled into new jobs. I can guess what happened, you forgot to take your birth control pills during our move. Oh well! as long as he or she is healthy.'

Kathy learned something else new that week. The lady on the front page of the local newspaper looked familiar, so she bought the paper. Later that night when the children were in bed, she read the headlines – *tragic death of botanical artist.* Joan Erasmus, a mother of two young daughters, had fallen to her death while collecting plants on Morgan Bay cliffs. She turned to page six where the story continued and gasped.

It was the same family she had seen at Tuin kafee. The footnote under the photograph read, *Joan and Robert Erasmus with their daughters Kassie and Belinda.* Kathy took a deep breath as she tried to take in what she had just read. She checked the man in the photograph again. A flashback left her more convinced than ever. He was the man she saw kill her brother.

She rushed to the lounge, excitedly waving the paper at Rick.

'Look at this, lovey.'

She bounced up and down, impatiently waiting for his reaction.

'Do you recognise him, Rick?' she blurted.

Her eyes glowed with anticipation.

'It's the man we saw at Tuin kafee, look at it properly.'

He examined it closely.

'I think you could be right, Kath.'

'Of course, I'm right!'

Frances heard the commotion and joined them. Kathy passed her the article. 'Look at this photo, Mum. The man's name is Robert Erasmus and his wife was found dead at the bottom of a cliff.'

'*Who's,* wife?' she asked.

'Robert Erasmus, *that's* his name.'

Frances looked mystified.

'I don't *know* a Robert Erasmus, Kathy, but what a tragedy for this beautiful young mother to fall to her death.'

She had missed the point, which annoyed her excited daughter.

'*Yes,* Mum,' Kathy pointed at the family photograph. 'But look at this man... he's the man from my *sketch*!'

Frances took a closer look.

'He does look a bit like your sketch, sweetie, but remember, you have no proof. It's a lovely family photo though – and he looks like a nice man.'

Kathy simmered. She *thinks he looks nice. He's the man who killed her son.* She swallowed a biting comment.

At the mention of Kathy's sketch, Frances changed the subject.

'Captain Botha hasn't contacted us in nearly three months.'

She turned to her daughter, 'Can *you* go and see him in the morning, Kath?'

Neither Rick nor Frances could take time off work, so Kathy visited the police station on her own the following day.

'Hello, Mrs Barron.' Salamina Brits greeted her as she entered the station.

'Please call me Kathy... Mrs Barron makes me sound ancient.'

'Only if you call me Sally,' Mrs Brits responded.

When Kathy entered Captain Botha's office, she found him even more approachable than when she first met him. He was reclining in his chair with a copy of Trevor Parker's homicide docket on the desk in front of him.

'I'm sorry, I haven't contacted you, Mrs Barron, I've been on two weeks leave, and we're short-staffed.'

Kathy accepted his apology, mainly because he had apologised and seemed genuine.

'You have a remarkable memory, Mrs Barron. Amazing that you could draw such a detailed sketch after fifteen years.'

She ignored his flattery.

'That's why I came to see you, Captain Botha. I now know the name of the man in my sketch.'

She handed him the newspaper clipping.

'This photograph is from yesterday's newspaper. It's the tragic story of a young mother falling to her death off Morgan Bay cliffs.'

She gave him time to respond.

When he didn't, she continued, 'I'm sure you're already aware of this incident. The man in that photograph is the same man I saw at Tuin Kafee. He's the one who killed my brother.'

Captain Botha stiffened and glared at her.

'Mrs Barron! You cannot accuse *this* man or any other for that matter, of killing your brother, without proof. You were six years old and you only saw the killer briefly in poor light.'

His brown eyes lost their lustre.

'Please allow our homicide squad to do the detective work.'

Suddenly, Kathy was fed-up with being told she was too young to know what she saw.

'I'm not *six* years old any more, Captain Botha. My brother's murder left my parents shattered. Have you any idea what it must have felt like to return to Rhodesia, leaving their sixteen-year-old son's body lying on a slab in the East London mortuary? For eighteen years the police have made no progress, but now *my* memory has returned.'

She did her best to control the quiver in her voice.

'I gave the police my eyewitness account and all they have done is make excuses and cast doubts on my statement. What motive could I have to accuse an innocent man?'

The quiver developed into a tremble of frustration and she burst into tears.

'Mrs Brits!' Botha bellowed. 'Come here, quickly.'

Sally Brits rushed to Kathy's side and handed her a tissue, patting her back to comfort her.

'Are you okay, Kathy? Would you like to come with me to the ladies room?'

'No thanks.'

Kathy straightened and scrubbed at her tears.

'Thanks, Sally, I'm fine now… I won't be much longer.' She knew her outburst was due to being pregnant. She was not usually so emotional.

'Call me if you need me,' Sally glared at Captain Botha as if he was a monster.

'Leave the door open!' he called after Mrs Brits, as she left the room.

'You can relax, Captain Botha. I promise not to cry again.'

Kathy sat up straight and rolled her shoulders to release the tension.

'It's no secret that I have little faith in the police. You promised to contact us when you received Trevor's homicide docket; that was *three months* ago. You ask me not to interfere in a police investigation. What police investigation?'

She folded her arms defiantly, holding his gaze.

'I understand your frustration, Mrs Barron. Eye witness accounts usually stand up well in court; however, in your case, there are credibility issues. I've already mentioned your age, a fifteen-year memory lapse and poor lighting. We need evidence in addition to your statement.'

He glanced at the newspaper clipping.

'I suggest you speak to your husband; he's a lawyer and can explain this to you.'

This patronising remark riled her.

'My husband and I have spoken at length about my brother's murder, Captain Botha. Are you saying that because I have no proof, the police will no longer pursue this line of enquiry?'

She shifted forward in her seat.

'Did the police even question Robert Erasmus?'

'We have spoken to someone who resembles your sketch. I cannot mention names or go into detail. I'm asking you, please do *not* contact anyone you think looks like your brother's killer. You will be breaking the law.'

Although annoyed, she didn't want to offend the captain.

'I'll do as you ask and I won't contact Mr Erasmus, but I'm not making any promises about anything else. In return, I ask, that you keep in touch with us and advise us on the progress in this police investigation.'

He scribbled something into a small green notebook.

'I have made a note and will contact you every two months.'

Kathy had her doubts that they would hear from Botha again, especially when he closed the door a little too quickly behind her.

Chapter 12

Rhodesia had lifted its financial restrictions slightly, allowing funds to trickle through to the family bank account. With Rick and Frances in full-time employment and the housing markets fairly stable, the family had an opportunity to buy their own house.

They settled on a Dutch-gable corrugated-iron roofed house on the outskirts of the city. The property was structurally sound, and with a fresh coat of paint and a little modernising, it could be restored to its former glory. A pair of majestic rusted iron-gates secured the entrance to the large property and on the far side of the garage stood a two-bedroomed cottage. A two-metre-high brick wall surrounded both the residences.

This gave Frances a home of her own, yet she would live only a few metres from the rest of the family. The owner was eager to sell and accepted their offer. There were tenants in the house and they could only take occupancy on the 1st of September; the same day Kathy's baby was due. The timing was out, but Kathy assured her family that she would have everything packed-up in time for the move.

Charlotte arrived for a three-week holiday in July. The news she brought from Rhodesia was disturbing.

'You left at the right time, Kath. Frances got a good price for her house. Now there's a glut of houses and property prices have hit rock bottom, but there are still many Rhodesians who believe a solution is possible and the Rhodesian spirit is strong.'

Kathy was wistful.

'I still miss home, Char. If things come right, I would return home tomorrow.'

She still longed for her life in Rhodesia, even after living in South Africa for eight months.

Charlotte hand-delivered a letter to Rick from Clive Adair.

Dear Rick,

Just a quick catch up. Alice is pregnant and the baby is due in September. We have sold the house in Salisbury and will be moving to Durban next month. I have a few interviews lined up. I did unfortunately, lose my foot, but I am one of the lucky ones; I often think of Zach and the great times we had together, as I am sure you do. I have a prosthetic foot and am back on my feet (excuse the pun). I will write as soon as we have settled. I would hate to lose contact. Our love to Kathy and the twins. Your friend, Clive.

Rick was pleased to hear from his friend and wrote back giving his own news and their new address.

Kathy was thrilled to have Charlotte staying for a few weeks. They talked non-stop late into the night and spent every spare moment together. Charlotte accompanied Kathy when she dropped Ben and Becky at nursery school. Instead of turning for home, she drove into an industrial area.

Charlotte gave her a questioning look.

'Where are we going, Kath?'

'I want to check on something and I need your help.'

Kathy drove in through large gates and parked at the front entrance to a warehouse. Written across the top of the building was **Erasmus Furniture Supplies and Removal** in orange letters. Charlotte read the name out loud.

'Oh, I see. *Y*ou want to get a quote to move your furniture.'

'Something *like* that,' Kathy winked, 'I want *you* to ask about a removal quote. The owner of this business is Robert Erasmus – he's the man I saw at Tuin kafee and I believe he murdered Trevor.' She remained solemn. 'I promised Captain Botha I wouldn't talk to him, but I want to get a closer look at him, and fortunately, *you* didn't make any promises.'

Charlotte giggled.

'You've been scheming, Kath, girl! This captain fellow has no idea how crafty you are.'

'So, you'll help me?'

'Of course, I will… what's our plan of action?'

Charlotte was already bouncing on the seat, eager to go.

'If Mr E is there, I want you be your flirty self and do all the talking, while I make myself scarce.'

'What's the code word?'

'Ladies toilet! Same as always.'

They laughed and slapped hands.

As they walked towards the front entrance, Charlotte whispered, 'Promise me, you won't interfere, Kath.'

Kathy poked her tongue out and grinned.

Charlotte's high heels clip-clopped across the parquet floor towards the furniture showroom reception.

'Hello, my name's Charlotte; we're here to get a household removals quote.'

The receptionist greeted them and wrote Kathy's details on top of a quotation form.

'I'll have to check Mr Napier's appointment book to see when he can visit you, Mrs Barron.'

'Thank you.'

Charlotte smiled sweetly.

'Would it be okay if my friend used the ladies' toilet?'

Charlotte signalled to Kathy with a hand movement, indicating she should take her time.

When Kathy reappeared, Charlotte was standing in the middle of the showroom talking to Robert Erasmus. She was smiling flirtatiously at him and then spun on her high heels, her skirt flaring.

'Oh, there you are, Kath; you've been *ages,* are you okay?'

She made the introductions.

'Kathy, this is Robby, he's the owner, and he's given us this form to complete.'

She raised her eyebrows in a signal.

'Ahh, you poor thing, you look *awful,* we must get *you* home!'

She flashed a gleaming smile at Erasmus and hurried Kathy out the building.

Kathy was puffing by the time she flopped into the driver's seat.

'What are you doing, Char? I'm eight months pregnant, you know… you can't go dragging me around like an express train!'

Charlotte was indignant.

'I was just making sure you kept your promise and didn't speak to Robby. Gosh, Kath, he's nothing *like* I thought he'd be. He's *very* good looking, isn't he? Are you *sure* he killed your brother?'

Her eyes turned dreamy.

'I wouldn't mind going on a *date* with him.'

Kathy looked stormy.

'He's *not* a nice man, Char. His wife is *barely* cold in her grave and he's hitting on you.'

'No, Kathy, I was the one doing the flirting, and it was your idea. Poor Robby didn't know what hit him.'

Kathy lost her sense of humour.

'Poor Robby. That's just great, I can't even rely on *you*.'

She started the engine.

'Rick and the police think I've identified the wrong man, my mum thinks he looks *nice* and my best friend has the hots for him.'

Charlotte caught Kathy by the arm.

'Hold it right there, Missy. You asked me to flirt with him, I simply said he was good looking... and *you* go off on a tangent.'

While they were arguing, Robert Erasmus climbed into a golden Mercedes Benz and drove out the gates.

'I'm sorry, Char, you're right. I'm being oversensitive.'

Kathy's eyes followed Erasmus's vehicle.

'Anyway, Robby has gone. Would you like to see our new house?'

They left the property shortly after Erasmus, driving in the same direction. He was a few cars ahead of them and turned into the same residential area where they were going.

'I hope he doesn't think we're following him. Oops, I might have turned too soon.'

Just then Erasmus pulled over under a row of naked Jacaranda trees.

'Get down!' Kathy yelled as they drove on past him.

She turned right at the T-junction and pulled over onto the verge.

'Okay, Char, you can sit up; he's parked over there and I can see the gold bonnet behind that hedge. We need to check the map-book to find our house.'

'Duck!'

They both crouched as Robert Erasmus walked around the corner and down the opposite side of the street. Kathy watched him over the dashboard. He stopped and looked around before he opened the gate and hurried down a driveway, out of view.

'What do you think he's up to, Char?' Kathy whispered as she checked the name of the street. 'Williams Street, he's gone into number sixty-eight.'

'Why are we whispering, Kath?'

She sat up and lifted her voice.

'Because I don't want him to know we are here. He might think we've followed him. There's something very strange about someone who parks on a different street and walks when there's plenty of parking outside the house he's visiting. I bet he's having an affair.'

They spent several minutes speculating about the reason for his strange behaviour. Charlotte checked her wristwatch.

'How long are we going to sit here? If he's visiting a lady friend, he could be hours.'

Kathy knew her friend was right. They had *no idea* why he was there or how long he would be.

'We'll check the telephone directory and see who lives there.'

Kathy was about to start the engine when a postman came cycling into view. Charlotte had a better idea.

'Postmen have a wealth of information about the people on their runs. Let me talk to him, Kath.'

She was already starting to get out of the car.

'You'd better keep the engine running – just in case we need to make a speedy getaway.' she giggled as she scurried towards the postie.

The poor man didn't stand a chance. Charlotte flashed him her winning smile and he told her everything she wanted to know. He then continued on his rounds.

Charlotte was about to cross the road, when Robert Erasmus opened the gate. He appeared distracted and fortunately, didn't look around. She hurriedly plastered herself against a Hibiscus bush and waited as he hurried up the road walking purposely back towards his car. Kathy watched Erasmus do a u-turn and return the way he had come.

She then beckoned to Charlotte who ran back and jumped into the car.

'Let's go, Kath. I've got the scandal… sixty-eight Williams Street belongs to Jean Schmidt. She's a nurse and works in the maternity ward at the same *hospital* where you worked. Do you know her?'

Kathy thought for a moment.

'It's a big hospital, Char, but I did meet a nurse called Jean in the cafeteria once. She was a small-boned lady in her forties and she worked in maternity. It could be her.'

'Well,' Charlotte continued, 'she's a widow, with a seventeen-year-old daughter who is doing a secretarial course at the Technikon.'

'Okay, let's call in at the hospital to check which shift Jean Schmidt is working, but let's have a look at our new house first.

'Kathy pulled over outside their future home.

'There are still occupants in the house, so we can only look in through the gates.'

A large dog barked forcing them to move on.

'At least you saw the size of the property. There's a fair amount of work to be done, but it's got five bedrooms and two bathrooms – which we need with a growing family. Then, there's the two bedroomed, cottage for mum. What do you think?'

'It's a great buy, Kathy. I'd like to rent a room in the cottage when I emigrate if Frances is okay with that. I'll speak to her about it before I go back to Rhodesia.'

On the way home Kathy pulled into the hospital parking lot.

'So, do you still think Robby is a *nice* man, Char? You realise, he's having an affair with a teenage girl.'

Charlotte wrinkled her nose.

'Aren't we getting ahead of ourselves, Kath? If he's having an affair, then he's unbelievably speedy – he barely had time to unzip his fly.'

Kathy giggled. Her friend was incorrigible.

'Come with me, Char. We'll check the duty roster and find out when Nurse Schmidt is working. It's time I did a tour of that maternity ward.

Two nights later Charlotte and Kathy visited the hospital. Kathy recognised Jean as the same petite lady she had met a few months earlier. Her grey eyes were slightly sunken behind a nose too large for her face. She wasn't beautiful, but she was attractive and had a bubbly personality.

'Hello, nurse. Oh!'

Kathy feigned her surprise.

'You're Jean, aren't you? Didn't we meet in the canteen some time ago? I'm Kathy Barron and this is my friend Charlotte Pistorius.'

'Yes, I remember you from the woman's ward.'

She glanced at Kathy's belly.

'I can see why I haven't seen you around; when is your baby due?'

'First of September, that's why I'm here. I hope you don't mind me visiting at night. I have three-and-a-half-year-old twins and it's the only time I can get mum to babysit.'

Jean obligingly showed them around the facilities and then joined them in the cafeteria during her tea break.

'What's the news from Rhodesia?' Jean asked Charlotte.

Like most South Africans, she was genuinely interested in what was happening across the border. Charlotte began to update her on the deteriorating situation.

Kathy found their talk about Rhodesia upsetting and changed the subject, telling them amusing incidents about their journey to South Africa, travelling by car for three days with unhappy twins. They laughed together and Jean felt comfortable enough to open up a little, talking about her husband's death seven years earlier, and her daughter Jolanda.

'My daughter Jolanda started becoming secretive about a year ago. All my friends tell me that isn't unusual for teenagers.'

She gave a dismissive shrug.

'But I don't know… this big honk of mine has a keen sense of smell.'

She tapped her nose.

'Some mornings when I got home from night-shift, I could smell a stranger had been in my house. I wouldn't spy on my daughter, but I kept hoping she'd tell me who he is, or was. I think it's over now– I haven't smelt any strangers lately.' She lifted her nose and he eyes twinkled.

Kathy couldn't waste the opportunity.

'How old is your daughter, Jean?'

'She's seventeen and she's a beautiful girl. Like all teenagers she's complex, but hopefully we'll be close again one day.'

Kathy tried to keep the conversation upbeat by sharing a little about herself as a young girl.

'It's a challenging age; does Jolanda have a boyfriend?'

'She should have them lining up for her, but she hasn't introduced me to *anyone*. I suspect she's been seeing someone I would not approve of.'

'Maybe she's suffering from a broken heart,' was Charlotte's contribution. Jean checked her watch.

'I have to go, ladies. I'll see you in a few weeks, Kathy when baby arrives.

Chapter 13

Charlotte was great fun as a guest and the twins adored their Aunt Charlie. Frances suggested they all visit the beach before Charlotte returned to Rhodesia.

'The beach and estuary at Kleinemonde are perfect for small children. It's twenty years since I visited, but I'm sure it hasn't changed that much. There's a slip road down to the beach which only locals know about.'

Charlotte and Frances shared the back seat with Ben and Becky while Kathy and her baby bump, sat in the front passenger's seat. Frances remembered everything about their journey to the cottage even though it had been twenty years since she last visited.

'Oh gosh, look, there's a new cottage and new sheds. We used to have to open and shut gates but now they have cattle grids to drive over.'

The faded signpost with Travellers Joy was barely visible.

'Do you want to stop at the cottage?' Rick asked Frances as they approached the rectangular, single-story residence.

It was smaller than Kathy remembered, but she recognised the large trees she had climbed so many times with her brother.

'Could we stop, for just a minute, Rick? Not all my memories of our holiday here are unhappy ones. We won't get out of the car.'

He switched off the engine and even the children stopped their chatter while they sat in silence.

An elderly Xhosa man appeared from behind a hedge of Natal plums. He bowed his head in the traditional greeting, and moved slowly towards their car.

'Dear, Lord!' Frances exclaimed. 'It's *Lundi*; I cannot believe he is still alive he must be ninety years old.

She hurried from the car towards the old man.

He hesitated and pointed to his chest.

'Me Lundi.'

He was squinting through screwed-up eyes, leaning forward, trying to clear the haze.

'Lundi, it's me… Missy Parker.'

He covered his mouth with his hand.

'Ow it you, Missy Parker, you back!'

He beamed a toothless grin as he recognised the striking redhead.

Frances gave the customary Xhosa handshake, her hands clasping both of his and vice versa.

'Lundi, this is my daughter Kathy. Do you remember her? She was only tiny like this.'

She indicated with her hand out flat.

Kathy asked after his wife.

'Hello, Lundi, I remember you. Where's Bongani?'

'Bongani!' he shouted.

He pointed to his ears, demonstrating she was deaf and then walked back towards the hedge, shouting her name. An elderly African lady bent and using two walking sticks, hobbled towards them. She was almost blind and her husband led her gently by the hand, guiding her towards Frances. Lundi spoke directly into her ear, reminding her who Frances was. Her deeply lined face suddenly smiled in recognition and the frail silver-haired couple, probably now in their nineties, bowed as it was their tradition.

'Sorry, Master Treva.'

Lundi was expressing sympathy over the death of her son, Trevor. Tears welled in France's eyes, in appreciation of their kindness. Had she known they were still alive and living there, she would have bought a box of fresh produce for them and her old reading glasses would be useful for Lundi. The unused crutches standing in their store-room would have been a great help to Bongani too. She went back to the car and raided the picnic basket to give them whatever she could.

The twins were complaining, eager to get to the sea, so Rick suggested he and Charlotte go ahead.

'Kathy, can you and Frances walk to the beach after you've finished talking to Lundi and Bongani?'

Frances took Bongani's hand and lead her to a stool under one of the trees.

'I'm sorry to see you're having problems with your back and legs, Bongani.'

Frances pointed to her own back and legs to indicate what she was saying. Bongani looked puzzled. She spoke little English and possibly couldn't see Frances's actions. There was little point in trying to communicate, but she sat with the old lady out of respect.

Kathy stayed with Lundi.

'It's good to see you, Lundi. Trevor and I loved those little cakes you used to make with the curly icing on top. Do you remember?'

She curled one hand into the shape of a cup-cake and twirled her finger to indicate the icing.

'Uwathanda[15] cakes.'

Lundi beamed with pleasure.

Kathy knew that Lundi understood her actions more than her words. Being back here at Travellers Joy made her tearful and she wiped away a tear.

'Did you hear anything the night Trevor was killed? She held her ears then stabbed her stomach with her fist to indicate someone being stabbed.

Lundi bowed his head.

'Night, Treva kubulawa[16].'

He pointed to his ears.

'Isithuthi[17] Brrrrrrrrrrm.'

He moved his fist across his flat hand as he made the sound.

'You heard…'

She indicated her ears.

'A vehicle, Brrrrrrrrm. The night Trevor died.'

She closed her eyes and lowered her head to indicate a dead person.

'Ewe[18].'

Kathy knew this meant, yes.

'Thank you, Lundi. Did you tell the police?'

'Ewe."

She didn't understand most of what he said, but she would check if a vehicle was heard that night.

---

[15] Uwathanda:-   he loves them

[16] Kubulawa:-   killed

[17] Isithuthi:-   transport

[18] Ewe :-   yes

As they walked towards the sea, Kathy asked her mother, 'Did the police take a statement from Lundi and Bongani after Trevor was killed?'

'I don't *know,* Kath. I was too upset at the time to keep track of *what* they were doing. I presume so, why do you ask?'

'I don't presume *anything* when it comes to this police investigation, mum.' Her tone was biting.

'What are you getting at, Kath?'

'I've just asked Lundi if he heard anything the night Trevor died. He made this sound like a vehicle. Bbbrrrrrrrm – that sound means the same in any language. You can't hear the main road traffic from here, so he must have heard a vehicle on the road leading to the cottage that night.

'Mmm, I don't recall anything about a vehicle being heard that night. We should ask Captain Botha about that.'

Kathy joined Charlotte and the twins at the water's edge where they were making sandcastles while Frances prepared their picnic lunch.

They left for home as the sun was going down. Kathy had had too much sun and that night she was restless. She dream about climbing a tree at the back of Travellers Joy cottage. She was on a high branch, peering down at Robert Erasmus who was dressed in his business suit. Two policemen accompanied him and they were holding a large saw. "Climb down from that tree you, naughty girl… or we'll cut it down." In her dream, she refused. She was terrified of the man in the business suit.

'Wake up, Kathy.'

Rick shook her hard.

'You're having a nightmare. It's okay, lovey, calm down.'

She was shivering with fear.

He gathered her in his arms. 'We shouldn't have visited Travellers Joy. It's upset you and brought back bad memories.

Three days later, they waved goodbye to Charlotte when she boarded the plane. Kathy and the children would miss their Aunt Charlie, but she assured them she would be back at Christmas, this time for good.

Kathy sat alone across the road from sixty-eight Williams Street determined to continue what she *had* started. Her patience eventually paid off when an attractive brunette opened the gate. She wore a mini skirt and long boots. The young girl reversed her small red Volkswagen beetle down the driveway and then closed the gates behind her. Kathy knew it was Jolanda; she was right and her suspicions confirmed. Erasmus could be implicated in his wife's death, should anyone find out about his affair with a teenage girl. A small red car had been seen near the cliffs according to the newspaper article. Kathy felt sick to her stomach. *Have I stumbled onto more than I bargained for?*

The day before her baby was due, Kathy was restless and felt the need to visit the police station. She wanted to tell Captain Botha about Lundi having heard a car the night of her brother's murder, and give him their new home address.

Captain Botha could only see her for a few minutes. She placed a slip of paper with their new contact details on his desk and flopped heavily onto the chair.

'Captain Botha, you remember you told me we needed evidence to convict my brother's killer? I might have found something.'

She wriggled uncomfortably on the chair.

'My family visited Travellers Joy cottage a few weeks ago and I discovered that Lundi, the old caretaker still lives there. He heard a vehicle on the night Trevor was murdered and says he told the police. I don't remember seeing anything of a statement from Lundi in the original docket?'

The captain pushed back his chair and stood up.

'I'll check into it for you.'

She stubbornly remained seated.

'Thank you, Captain Botha, I'd appreciate you letting me know the result,' she rested both hands on her pregnant belly.

'Captain Oberholster asked me how the killer got to the cottage. Well, now we have the answer. He drove there.'

The captain reluctantly sat down again.

'I also wanted to tell you something that happened when I visited Erasmus removals – to get a furniture removal quote.'

His jaw dropped, but she quickly assured him she hadn't broken her word.

'Charlotte did all the talking while I went to the ladies' toilet. I didn't even speak to Erasmus.'

She rushed on, wanting him to know what happened.

'We followed Mr Erasmus and when he stopped near Williams Street…'

The captain's eyes widened, and he shot bolt upright.

'Mrs Barron,' he groaned, 'you cannot stalk members of the public… it's a serious offence!'

She switched to damage control.

'Oh, no. That came out wrong. We weren't following him. We were going to see our new house and he was driving in the same direction in front of us. He pulled over and we carried on and then stopped to check the map book. The strange part is that he walked around the corner and down the road to a house with plenty of parking outside.'

She blinked her big eyes innocently.

'I wondered if he was having an affair.'

'Mrs Barron, why are you telling me this? I cannot listen to scandal.'

His fingers gripped the arms of his chair in exasperation.

'I'm a very busy man and you're wasting my time.'

He stood up. Kathy suddenly clutched her stomach, doubled over and cried out in pain – her water had broken.

Wendy Frances Barron lay cradled in her mother's arms. The new-born was exercising healthy lungs when Jean Schmidt greeted them.

'Hello, Kathy, congratulations! I hear you caused quite a ruckus at the police station today.'

She checked Kathy's pulse.

'Sally Brits is a friend of mine and she was asking after you. She tells me Captain Botha was in a panic when he thought he was going to have to deliver your baby.'

She pushed a thermometer into Kathy's mouth.

'Sally adores you. She remembers your altercation with Captain Oberholster all those years ago. She detested the man and overheard Commandant Marais ask Captain Oberholster why your statement had been translated from English into Afrikaans. She thinks it was because of you that Captain Oberholster was transferred shortly afterwards, and she's eternally grateful.'

Kathy chuckled, nearly choking on the thermometer. *Mum must have laid a complaint against Captain Oberholster when she visited Commandant Marais in Pretoria. I'll have to remember to thank her.*

Frances and Rick visited Captain Botha with a bottle of whisky to thank him for taking care of Kathy. To his credit, he had stayed by her side until the ambulance arrived. He was a teetotaller and would not accept alcohol, but he was pleased they had visited. He wanted to discuss something with them.

'Do either of you know why Mrs Barron came to see me yesterday?'

'No,' Frances admitted.

'Mrs Barron claims that a local businessman killed her brother. I asked her not to *make* unsubstantiated accusations.'

He folded his arms.

'Together with a friend, she visited Erasmus furniture removals and then followed Mr Erasmus in his car. Unbelievable. Mr Barron, you're an attorney – you *know,* I cannot be associated with members of the public who break the law. Please speak to your wife and explain that what she is doing is *illegal.*'

Rick and Frances looked at each other in wide-eyed bewilderment.

'When did she visit Erasmus furniture removals?' her mother asked.

'A few weeks ago. She didn't give me a date.'

'*Charlotte!*' Frances exclaimed. 'Sometimes, I worry that the girl has too much influence over my daughter.'

'Mrs Barron claims her friend did all the talking while she sat in the toilet which exonerates her from any collusion.'

The captain's lips twitched.

Rick stifled a laugh.

'I'm sorry, Captain Botha, I didn't even know my wife and Charlotte had visited Erasmus Removals. I *will* speak to her. She's very strong-willed as you know, and has possibly been bored while waiting for the baby to arrive.'

Captain Botha's tension appeared to diminish as he relaxed into his chair. 'I'm pleased Mrs Barron and the baby are well.'

'Thank you, Captain, we just dropped in to thank you for taking care of her yesterday and to let you know we've named our little girl, Wendy.'

October had arrived before Frances broached the subject of her daughter's visit to Captain Botha.

'Why didn't you tell us that you and Charlotte visited Erasmus Removals, Kathy?'

'There was no reason to tell you, Mum. I received removal quotes from several companies and we chose the cheapest.'

She cradled Wendy to her breast, preparing to breast-feed, but Frances wasn't going to be fobbed off.

'If you're *right* about this man being Trevor's killer, he could be dangerous! I don't want to lose another child. Promise me, you'll keep away from him and let the murder and robbery squad do their job.'

Kathy was miffed.

'I suppose it was Captain Botha who told you about my visit to Erasmus furniture removals?'

'Yes, he was very annoyed. It's illegal to tail people and make accusations or interfere in police business.'

'I wasn't tailing him. He was driving in front of us and pulled over a few streets away from the house we've just bought. I drove past him. I suppose you agree with Captain Botha.'

'Yes, I do, Kathy… let the police do their job.'

'Mum, if you can tell me *anything* the homicide squad has done during the past twenty years, I'll *happily* back off.'

She cuddled Wendy.

'I only remembered about Trevor four years ago and in that time, I've given birth to three children, changed countries and moved house twice!'

Her eyes flashed a warning.

'I know the name of the man who killed my brother, where he works and lives. I also know about his wife's accidental death *and* there's a possibility he's having an affair. Then I discover that Lundi heard a *vehicle* on the night of Trevor's death.'

She pursed her lips.

'I know you're just trying to protect me, mum, but someone needs to keep this investigation alive. I'll let you and Rick know what's going on before I visit Captain Botha next time. For now, I have a baby to feed. Can we talk about this some other time?'

Frances had done her best, now it was up to Rick.

Rick took a different approach. He waited a few days and spoke to her when they were getting ready for bed.

'Kathy, Captain Botha doesn't want you to visit him without another member of the family. You have to remember that Trevor's homicide is an ongoing inquiry.'

'Ahh, you as well, Rick. Did Captain Botha tell you to say that?'

'Yes.'

'Hmmph. What *ongoing* inquiry?'

116

Rick frowned.

'Be reasonable, Kath. You know, it would be unprofessional for Captain Botha to listen to scandal. I'm asking you to talk to your mother or me *before* you go to the police.'

Kathy agreed to do as he asked.

Chapter 14

Kathy had found her favourite blooms, the flame lily flowering in the front garden and picked them to fill a vase on the mantelpiece. She had always regretted not giving 66 Bakestone Street a name, so she varnished a large plank of wood, painted the words Flame Lily Villa and then added a spray of flame lilies to one side. Rick attached it to the outside wall near the gate.

A coat of light grey paint coated the walls of their new house and cottage. The rusty roof and gates were restored to their former glory with a coat of black paint. Their furniture suited the old house and although there was still plenty of work to be done, the veranda was ready for a house warming barbecue. Rick, Kathy and Frances invited their friends.

Twenty guests attended the barbecue, including some of Rick and Frances's work friends. Kathy had invited Jean, Jolanda, Sally Brits and her husband. Sally and Jean soon gravitated towards each other, which allowed Kathy time to speak with Jolanda on her own.

'Rick was my first and only love... I nearly lost him when I stripped to swim in a city fountain with my best friend, Charlotte.'

She giggled.

'He's such a prude, but I love him dearly.'

She told Jolanda about some of her teenage antics, hoping the young girl would relax and share her own experiences.

'You're very attractive, Jolanda; you must have plenty of guys chasing after you?'

The girl appeared bashful, peering out from beneath her long fringe.

'No. I haven't. But thanks for the compliment anyway. I *was* seeing someone much older than me, but that's all over.'

She stiffened.

'Oh, Kathy... please *don't* tell my mum. I shouldn't have said anything about it.

Kathy feigned a bewildered look.

'What *don't* you want me to tell her?'

'That I *was* seeing an older man.'

'Oh, okay. Didn't your mum *know* you were seeing him?'

She pretended to be disinterested.

'Don't worry. I won't tell anyone. Were you in love with him?'

'I thought I was, but we broke up months ago. It's over now. It's just that I don't want my mum to know.'

'I won't tell her. I give you my word, Jolanda. Is he married or something?'

'Yes… that's why I don't want *mum* to know.'

'I'm sorry. You must be going through a tough time.'

Kathy remembered how hurt she had been when she quarrelled with Rick and they had parted company.

Jean and Sally joined them, bringing their private conversation to an end. Kathy guessed the older man was Erasmus, which is what she wanted to know.

Frances suggested another visit to Kleinemonde as she wanted photographs of the children playing on the beach for one of her publications and it was also a perfect opportunity to deliver supplies to Lundi and Bongani. She knew they were getting too old to walk to the nearest shop. They had their own vegetable garden and a few chickens, but they relied on their children and grandchildren to bring them supplies. This time, Kathy opted to stay at home – a whole day of sea, sand and sun with a two-month-old did not sound like fun.

The family arrived home from Kleinemonde exhausted after a long day and it was only after the children were asleep that Rick and Frances could tell Kathy about their day.

Frances was pleased with herself.

'I adjusted those crutches for Bongani, but she's so frail and bent I couldn't get them down low enough. They were also a bit heavy for her. I don't know if she'll use them, but Lundi was thrilled with my old reading glasses. He claims to be able to see better than he had for years. The supplies should last them sometime.'

Rick quizzed his wife.

'You'll know something about this Kath – Lundi says he told you about hearing a vehicle the night Trevor died.'

Kathy looked interested.

'Well, he had a visit from a Xhosa speaking policeman wanting to know more about what he'd heard.'

'Aha! So, Captain Botha *did* listen to something I said,' Kathy gloated.

Rick didn't want to encourage her, but he was curious.

'Captain Botha didn't mention anything about a vehicle when we last spoke to him.'

'Isn't that interesting? Twenty years later the police finally interview the staff – even though Lundi says he did tell the policeman.'

She was pleased that she was being taken seriously.

Rick was starting to have doubts about the thoroughness of the original police investigation. He had rechecked the docket and found no mention of a vehicle. He thought back to when he first heard that Kathy's brother had been murdered. *I took Kathy to the police station to give a statement; then I backed off, believing the police would follow through.* There was no comparison between the police investigation and Kathy's bulldog-like tenacity. Her methods were unorthodox, but since they had arrived in East London, she had searched tirelessly for evidence to help convict the man she claimed killed her brother. It had taken courage to stand up to a bully like Captain Oberholster. *What if Kathy's right and she has identified the right man?*

He decided it was time to revisit the police station. He needed to know more.

'Your wife mentioned the native staff had heard a motor vehicle. We investigate all new information, so I sent someone out to follow up on that.'

Rick adjusted his glasses.

'Lundi said he gave the police this information during the original investigation; surely, that's *old* information not *new* information.

Captain Botha shifted uncomfortably.

'This is an ongoing investigation, Mr Barron. The homicide squad may have checked for a vehicle, but dismissed it for some reason or the results may have been misfiled. We take all leads seriously, which is why I sent someone out to interview the witness *again.*'

'Did Lundi reveal anything else of importance, captain?'

'No, it was just routine. The caretaker confirmed he had heard a vehicle that night.'

'Captain Botha, I know my wife has ruffled some feathers, and I spoke to her about interfering in a police investigation. Her comment was, "*What* investigation?" Surely hearing a vehicle near the scene of a crime is vital evidence.'

He mentally weighed up the significance before continuing.

'Travellers Joy is isolated, so the vehicle must have been in the vicinity of the cottage. The police would have used resources to check for tyre tracks or visited neighbouring properties to find out if they heard or saw anything. There must be something recorded somewhere.'

It was Rick, the lawyer asking these questions.

'As I said, Mr Barron, I know nothing about the original investigation, but I'll ask Mrs Brits to make further enquiries. We may have missed something.'

'Thank you, Captain Botha. I feel I should be up front and tell you that I'm going to do a record search of the archives. If another crime was committed on or around the same day my brother-in-law was murdered, the evidence could be there.'

'I'm on your side, Mr Barron. By all means, you're a lawyer and have access to these files. If you find anything of interest, please come and see me. In the meantime, I'll check for any other details relating to the original docket.'

Tim was eager to see Frances. When he heard that Charlotte was emigrating from Rhodesia and travelling to East London in her Peugeot, packed with her worldly belongings, he offered to travel with her and share the driving.

In leaving Rhodesia, Charlotte was leaving behind the medical team she considered her extended family. They had worked tirelessly, side by side for seven years saving the lives of hundreds of patients passing through the biggest emergency department in the country.

She shared her feeling with Tim.

'When I received confirmation that I'd been accepted by the East London General Hospital I nearly turned down the offer.' Charlotte admitted. 'I hadn't realised until then, how difficult it would be to leave the country where I was born and grew up. It was my promise to Kathy that kept me on track.'

'Believe me, Charlotte, I know what you mean. My daughters and their families are settling in Durban and want me to move with them. It's difficult enough moving country without having split loyalties. I'm in love with Frances and I'm going to ask her to marry me, so my intention is to live in East London. You're the only person I've told, so it's our secret.'

Charlotte was delighted.

'Oh, Tim, I'm so pleased.'

By the time they reached East London, they were firm friends, having shared many of their innermost thoughts.'

It was a relief to drive up the driveway at Flame Lily Villa. Frances, Kathy, Rick and the children were there to welcome them. Frances had prepared the spare room in her cottage for Charlotte. Tim would stay three weeks, returning to Rhodesia after Christmas.

Christmas Eve was a festive occasion at the Van Wyk's home. Turkey with the traditional trimmings, ham and roast potatoes. The evening ended with Maria playing the piano and Rick his guitar while family and friends sang Christmas carols.

'Aah, we aren't tired, mummy, do we *have* to go?' the children pleaded when Kathy tried to round them up.

'We haven't put out the mince pies for Santa and carrots for his reindeer,' Kathy reminded them, 'and Santa only comes when you're asleep.'

All of a sudden, they couldn't wait to get home.

Rick climbed into the car with Tim.

'Can you and Frances take the children home, Kath? We have some last-minute shopping to do.'

'But all the shops are closed,' Kathy thought it a little odd.

'I've arranged to meet Santa. This gift isn't from the shops.'

The children were asleep when Rick and Tim arrived home. Rick was carrying a red drawstring bag. Whatever was inside was wriggling.

'Merry Christmas, Kath.'

He handed her the bag. She opened it cautiously and peered into the amber eyes of a Labrador puppy. She pulled the pup into her arms and cuddled the wriggling bundle of joy, receiving a thousand licks.

'Ooh, she's beautiful, why didn't you tell me we were getting a puppy?'

'Because she's *your* surprise Christmas present. Happy Christmas, my darling.

Rick grinned sheepishly.

'I took a chance you would fall in love with her.'

'Aaaah! She's mine. I love her. Thank you, my love, what should we call her?'

'She's yours, Kathy. Call her whatever you like.'

'Huchi… no… Honey,' Kathy grinned, 'we'll call her Honey.'

The family's first Christmas day at Flame Lily Villa was a happy and chaotic occasion. Honey introduced herself to the twins at the crack of dawn and was an instant hit.

Tim proposed to Frances on New Year's Day. Of course, she said, "Yes".

Kathy hugged her mother. 'Congratulations Mum, Tim's lovely, and I know he makes you happy.'

Her previous prejudice against him, now long forgotten.

'Will it be a long engagement?' she asked the same question her mother had asked her.

Frances smiled.

'We've been apart for a year and it could be another year, so yes, a very long engagement.'

A few weeks later, when they waved goodbye to Tim at the airport, Frances and Tim had still not announced their wedding date.

Now that Charlotte was living in East London permanently, Kathy arranged for Jean and Jolanda to join them for drinks in the ladies' lounge at a local hotel. She arrived early to find Jolanda had already downed a few drinks and was a little drunk.

'Are you okay, Jolanda?'

'I can't sleep, Kathy, I'm having nightmares.'

Jolanda put a finger to her lips in a shush sign.

'No one must ever know… remember, you promised?'

'What's going on, Jolanda? I thought you were over this man.'

Kathy studies her. She had accepted the girl's comment that the affair was over.

'Oh no! I don't *miss* him; it's, the other thing.'

Jolanda burst into tears and Kathy guided her to the ladies' room.

'You're in a bad way, Jolanda. We can't talk now; you've had a bit too much to drink and your mum and Charlotte are about to arrive. Can we meet for lunch tomorrow in the tea garden next door?'

Jolanda agreed and Kathy moved to get her sober before the others arrived.

'I'll order you a strong coffee and I suggest you stick to coffee.' Jean and Charlotte were waiting for them when they returned to the ladies' bar.

The following day, Kathy found a private booth in the tea-garden where she had arranged to meet Jolanda. Wendy lay asleep in the stroller next to her mother.

Yolanda raced in. 'Sorry I'm late, Kathy. I didn't want Mum to know I was meeting you and I nearly didn't make it,' she looked flushed as if she'd been running.

After they had ordered, Kathy asked. 'What's been keeping you awake at night , Jolanda?'

'Kathy, I trust you, but I need you to promise you won't tell anyone what I'm about to tell you. Not even your husband, because I'm breaking a promise by telling you.'

Kathy thought she was overdramatising, but wanted to hear what she had to say.

'It's up to you, Jolanda, but I'm not comfortable with knowing something I cannot share with my husband. We always tell each other everything.'

The girl bit her bottom lip.

'I guess I have to trust someone. Your husband's a lawyer, isn't he?'

'Yes, he is and he wouldn't repeat anything I ask him not to.'

'Okay, you can tell your husband, but *no one* else.'

Jolanda dropped her voice to just above a whisper.

'I was on the cliffs at Morgan Bay when Joan Erasmus fell to her death.'

She fidgeted with the edge of her blouse.

'I'm such a fool. I drove all that way to talk to her about my affair with her husband. Then I didn't have the courage to do it.'

She looked around as though afraid someone might hear her.

'I went for a walk along the top of the cliffs to clear my head before I drove back home. I saw Joan balancing on a ledge about a metre down the cliff and when she saw me, she waved? It all happened so quickly. A bird... it wasn't a very big bird, but it was screeching, flapping its wings and clawing at her face. She tried to swat it away with her hands!'

Jolanda's voice was barely audible now.

'Oh, Kathy, it was awful, she lost her balance... she fell over the cliff... I can still hear her screams as she fell onto the rocks below.'

Jolanda crumpled, hugging herself, battling to control her sobs. Someone had arrived in the booth behind them, so Kathy moved closer and hugged her, speaking gently.

'It's okay, Jolanda… it's okay, sweetie. It wasn't your fault. I'm so sorry you're unhappy, please don't carry on if it's too upsetting, we can talk another time.'

Wendy woke up and started crying too. Kathy rocked the stroller and held the dummy in her baby's mouth until she went back to sleep.

Jolanda sat up and swallowed convulsively.

'No! Please let me finish… this is why I have these nightmares.'

'Jolanda, listen to me, sweetie. This wasn't your fault.'

'But I feel so *guilty* – if I hadn't been there, Joan wouldn't have waved to me and disturbed the bird. She wouldn't have fallen. I looked over the cliff and saw her body lying there broken and lifeless on the rocks below.'

Kathy wrapped her arms around the unhappy girl.

'No wonder you're so upset; you've been blaming yourself for something you didn't do. Why didn't you phone the police?'

'I wanted to. I drove home as fast as I could and phoned Robby. He told me I mustn't tell anyone because if the police knew I was there and found out about our affair, they might think I *pushed* her.'

Kathy thought for a moment. *He's possibly right. It was an accident and telling the police wouldn't bring his wife back. But now Jolanda's guilt-ridden.*'

You're the only person I've ever told, Kathy. I had to talk to someone. *Now,* do you understand why I can't tell my mum? She would want me to go straight to the police.'

'Jolanda, please listen to me, you've done nothing wrong. You witnessed a lady fall to her death after a bird attacked her on the cliffs. You reported the incident to her husband and *he* failed to report it to the police. There is nothing I can do to help you… I still think you should tell your mother.'

'*No, never.* Mum is the last person I will ever tell.'

Wendy was fidgeting now and Kathy realised It was time to leave.

Chapter 15

Four months later, Tim had sold his home in Salisbury and arranged to have his belongings transported to East London by rail. Like most Rhodesians, it was with a heavy heart he left the country where he had lived most of his life. He arrived at the East London airport towards the end of May, eager to be reunited with Frances, the woman he loved and was soon to marry.

A wedding reception on the veranda at Flame Lily Villa was all the couple wanted. Fairy-lights wound around newly painted pillars and baskets of flowers hanging from the rafters. Twenty guests attended the candlelit dinner, speeches and good wishes accompanied the clinking of champagne glasses.

Kathy was seated next to Tim. 'Thank you, Kathy, for welcoming me into the family. I realise that no one could take the place of your father, but I'd like to think of you as my daughter.'

The back of her neck tensed. She would accept Tim as her mother's husband, but could never be his daughter. She smiled at him and then noticed Wendy crawling amongst the guest's legs.

'Please excuse me, Tim. I must see to my baby; she is about to be stood on.'

Kathy tucked Wendy into her cot and sat on the rocker watching her fall asleep. Tim's words rang in her ears; *I'd like to think of you as a daughter.* She pictured her father's tall figure, his laughing eyes and recalled his wonderful sense of humour. He was the most honourable man she had ever known.

'I miss you, daddy,' she whispered.

The net curtain at the French doors floated up on a breeze and she shivered before realising the doors were closed. Her brother stood before her for the first time in a long time. Her lips quivered. 'Trevor, are you here because mum has married Tim?' She knew he was a figment of her imagination, but to her, he seemed so real.

A voice whispered in her mind, '*Kathy... go back to Travellers Joy.*'

'*Why Trevor? I've already been there. What am I looking for?*

'Go inside.'

The curtain settled and she cried out.

'No, Trevor, don't go; tell me *what* to look for?' She closed her eyes, allowing the motion of the rocker to send her to sleep.

Rick woke her up some time later.

'Are you okay, lovey? We were wondering where you got to?'

'I fell asleep. It must be the champagne.'

She stretched.

'Rick, I need to tell you something.'

'Go ahead, lovey.'

She could smell alcohol on his breath and decided it could wait.

'It's nothing... don't worry, let's go and enjoy the reception, we can talk tomorrow.'

Tim and Frances joined the family the following morning for breakfast before leaving on a two-week honeymoon in Durban where they would visit Tim's daughters and grandchildren.

'Have a wonderful holiday, the two of you. I'm told the road along the Transkei Wild Coast is beautiful. We look forward to seeing you in a few weeks.'

The family waved them goodbye.

The following evening Rick and Kathy sat alone on the veranda. Kathy broke the silence.

'Rick, I need to speak to you about something that happened last night.'

'Sure, is it important?'

He settled back into the solid wooden Morris-chair to give her his full attention.

'It's important to me. I know you'll be sceptical, but please hear me out. I believe I received a message from Trevor last night.'

She was half expecting a dismissive sigh.

'I want to re-visit Travellers Joy cottage to re-enact what I saw in the kitchen that night. Will you come with me, Rick?'

He leaned forward and took her hand.

'Of course, I will. I admire the way you've never given up on finding your brother's killer. I'll contact Captain Botha and make an appointment to see him.'

Kathy was relieved when Captain Botha was open to her idea.

'Of course, we'll need the owner's consent and you'll need to complete the forms explaining why you want to enter a private premises, but I'll certainly give the application my full support.'

It was midweek before Rick received a phone call confirming they could visit the cottage that evening. Captain Botha had arranged for Constable Heinz, who spoke fluent Xhosa, to accompany them.

He was waiting for them outside the station. A handsome young man immaculate in his starched uniform and highly polished boots.

They travelled on the open road towards Kleinemonde, making good time. Rick and Heinz sat in the front, alternating between Afrikaans and English.

Kathy sat quietly in the back, watching through the car window as the clouds played peekaboo with a full moon.

She pictured the events of that fateful night when Trevor died.

Daddy, you're back. She recalled the relief at knowing he was safe. The waves crashed and the four of them knelt on the sand hugging each other. They were laughing; they laughed a lot as a family.

"So, what do you think of my huge fish?" he beamed with pride.

"It's a monster, dad. What bait did you use? What kind of fish is it? How long did it take to land?' Trevor asked excitedly.

"I was on the rocks and it nearly got away. I'm told it's a muscle cracker and it's thanks to one of the Indian fishermen, that I landed it."

The fish weighed more than Kathy did and the moon lit their way as her parents shared the weighty load, dragging the fish towards the cottage.

"Mum, dad, I'm going ahead to light the lamp. I'll cover the kitchen table with plastic so we can fillet the fish," Trevor called as he ran off.

His long legs leaped effortlessly up the steps towards the cottage and he disappeared through the front door.

"Can I go too?" Kathy's little voice asked.

"No, you stay with us until we're closer, sweetie." her mother insisted.

Eventually, she was allowed to run ahead, her short legs worked extra hard to clamber that same steep cliff. She felt a sense of relief on reaching the top step and sat down to catch her breath.

'Kath, pass the sandwiches please,' Rick's voice brought her back to the present.

They had left home before dinner and she had packed ham sandwiches and a flask of tea.

They turned off the main tarred road and drove for some distance over a rough dirt road. Cattle grids divided paddocks, and their progress was hindered on one occasion when a large Afrikander[19] bull stood stubbornly in the middle of the road.

Constable Heinze climbed out the vehicle.

'Git, git.' he shouted.

The bull put his head down and moved forward - horns facing the nervous young man who quickly jumped back into the car. They laughed, then breathed a sigh of relief as it moved over.

On arriving at Travellers Joy, Lundi appeared from behind a hedge, a paraffin lantern in hand. He had heard their vehicle coming and hurried to see who it was.

'Hello, Inkosi[20].'

His aged face creased to a smile when he recognised them. He was wearing the reading glasses Frances had given him and courteously accepted the box of produce Kathy handed him.

Constable Heinz spoke to him in Xhosa, explaining why they had come. Lundi peered at the document shown to him, then admitted he couldn't read or write.

Kathy asked Lundi to light the gas lamp she had bought with her. It was similar to the one used that fateful night twenty years ago. She asked if she could enter the holiday cottage through the front door.

'I'd like to be left alone in the cottage, if that's okay with everyone,' she asked quietly.

The veranda was bare of furniture and used only as a passageway. She made her way to the kitchen where she placed the lamp on the table and then stood back to allow time for her eyes to adjust. She drew open a pair of blue and white curtains on either side of the window above the sink, allowing the moonlight into the room. Then she pinned the back the door and studied the interior. It had changed from the yellow she remembered. The walls and cupboards were now a light shade of blue trimmed with white. The wood stove and sink hadn't changed; the fridge was old but different from the one she remembered and the concrete

---

[19] Afrikander bull :-   breed of cattle

[20] Inkosi :-   Master

floor was covered with brown vinyl. In the middle of the room stood the original rectangular wooden table with its six matching chairs.

She returned to sit on the front step. In her mind, she recalled hearing the two voices; her brother and the other, a stranger. She walked to the kitchen archway and dropped to her knees trying to bring everything into proportion from the eyes of a six-year-old. *I wish Trevor had told me what to look for.*

Robert Erasmus, or his identical twin, stood with his back against the sink, while her brother leant on the centre table facing him.

Why had Trevor's spirit told her to go inside the cottage? There must be a reason. She went over every detail in her mind as she had done so many times before. She visualised Erasmus leaning forward and seizing Trevor's shirt collar. *There was a sound...a pinging sound.* Something had hit the cupboard.

Her knees were beginning to hurt so she rolled onto her hip. *That's what it was...now I remember. It was the sound of Trevor's Saint Christopher medallion hitting something. I must ask mum what happened to it.* Her head ached and she massaged her throbbing temple. She was hot, yet shivering. She clearly remembered the hollow look on Trevor's face. The way his body slid under the table into the shadows. Blood-soaked visions left her distressed and she curled into a foetal position. Totally drained she must have dozed off and had no idea know how long she lay there.

'Kathy, are you okay?' Rick was kneeling beside her.

'Please take me home,' she whispered.

He walked her out to the car and helped her into the back seat.

'I love you, darling,' he whispered as he placed a rug over her and a cushion under her head. She slept all the way home.

The next morning, Rick woke her as he slipped Wendy into the bed next to her.

'Charlotte has fed the kids and I'll drop the twins at nursery school. Try to get some rest during the day, Kath.' She was pleased to have time to herself.

Frances phoned from Durban at lunchtime and Kathy told her about their visit to Travellers Joy.

'It was all a waste of time. I learned nothing new. Tell me mum, have you still got Trevor's St Christopher medallion?'

Frances took her time before she answered.

'I'd forgotten about that, Kath. I found it the morning after Trevor... it was on the floor near one of the cupboards.'

'That's what I *thought* must have happened. I presume the police didn't find any fingerprints on it?'

Again, Frances hesitated.

'I didn't give it to the police. I'd already lost so much and I was afraid they wouldn't give it back to me. It was the last gift we ever gave Trevor.'

'I know it has huge sentimental value, mum, but where is it?'

'It's in a small black box in my jewellery case.'

'It could be evidence. I remember seeing the killer snap the chain when he grabbed Trevor's collar. The killer might have touched the medallion and it could have his fingerprints on it.'

'I didn't think about it at the time, Kath. If you think the police might find fingerprints on it after all these years, you can give it to them, but make sure I get it back.'

Chapter 16

Rick's respect for his wife's tenacity continued to grow. She refused to give up on trying to solve her brother's murder and clung to her theory.

"I believe the reason Trevor was killed was to protect the killer's alibi for another crime committed earlier the same day." Her words, and a few other inconsistencies prompted Rick to investigate other crimes in the area, around the same date.

He requisitioned five dockets from police records at the archives, all referencing crimes committed in the East London area.

'Keep dinner for me, Kath. I'll be home late tonight. I want to check through these dockets I've just received.'

The index on the first page of each docket helped him eliminate three cases immediately and there were two possibilities. In the end, only one of them ticked enough boxes to be of interest.

Rick didn't look very positive when he arrived home. 'I'll tell you what I found after supper, Kath. While he ate, Kathy filled him in on the conversation she had with her mother.

'Mum didn't give Trevor's Saint Christopher medallion to the police because she was afraid, she wouldn't get it back. Poor mum, she must have been in such a state.'

Kathy was now more understanding about how her mother must have felt.

'I've found the medallion so I'll take it to Captain Botha on Monday.'

She shrugged.

'I doubt they'll find anything after twenty years, but it's worth a try.'

Rick agreed there was little chance of a print surviving after so long.

He opened his briefcase and handed Kathy his rough notes on the only docket he felt might have a vague connection to Trevor's homicide.

'It's a long shot, Kath. This crime was discovered three days after Trevor's murder, but the estimated time of death is the same night Trevor died.'

Name of deceased: Rudy Sutton. Date of Birth: 10/01/1938 Age 20

Date of crime: 28th of April 1958 approximately (body found three days after the crime was committed). Cause of death: skull crushed by a heavy object – body placed in vehicle and burned.

Crime: VW Kombi, doused with petrol then set alight: Victim possibly already dead.

Scene of the crime: 23 miles North of East London in remote coastal bushland.

Pathology report: Blunt force trauma to skull, resulting in death.

Accused: Dawie Grobler: Found guilty, 18 years prison sentence.

Kathy pushed a strand of hair back from her face.

'I don't see any similarity, Rick. They found the killer – he's in prison.'

She couldn't hide her disappointment.

'These are rough notes I've jotted down, Kath. The police are not fools. They will have checked for similarities and because the modus operandi is so different, they possibly rejected any connection between these two crimes.'

He didn't want to raise her hopes too high.

'If your theory is right, there may be something that's *not* obvious. We have to keep an open mind. Grobler was convicted on *circumstantial* evidence. I want to take a closer look at this docket first, before I reject it.'

Kathy was doubtful.

'Thanks for checking, Rick. I appreciate you're taking the time to investigate this for me.'

They now had several reasons to visit the police station the following day.

'Thank you for arranging our visit to Travellers Joy last week, Captain Botha,' Kathy stopped bouncing Wendy on her knee and made eyes contact with him. 'I was asleep when we dropped Constable Heinz off at the station; please thank him for me, he was extremely helpful.'

The captain agreed and she continued, 'I explored the cottage and retraced my steps. There was only one piece of new evidence, *if* I can call it that. I remembered that my brother's silver chain snapped when the killer grabbed his shirt.'

Kathy sheepishly pulled a small black box from her bag.

'Is there any chance that your forensics team would find a *fingerprint* after twenty years?'

Captain Botha took the box.

'I don't know, Mrs Barron, but I doubt they would find a print on something as thin as a chain anyway.'

Kathy shook her head realising she hadn't explained herself adequately.

'Not the chain, the Saint Christopher medallion hanging on the chain.'

'Aah, now that could make a difference. I believe the type of surface is important for fingerprints. There's only one way to find out – we'll ask our forensic team.'

'Thank you, Captain Botha. This was the last gift my parents gave my brother. Please make sure my mum gets it back as it has tremendous sentimental value to her.'

Captain Botha placed the box in his top desk drawer and locked it.

Rick then took over.

'Captain Botha, have you ever heard of the Rudy Sutton case?'

He looked doubtful.

'No, what happened?'

'Well,' Rick answered him bluntly, 'someone bludgeoned Rudy Sutton to death, then set him and his vehicle alight. He was discovered on the outskirts of East London three days later. The modus operandi is completely different from the Trevor Parker homicide, except that both crimes were committed on the same day.'

Captain Botha's fingers drummed the arms of his chair.

'Mr Barron, I know nothing about this um…Sutton case. Was anyone convicted of the crime?'

'Yes, his name is Dawie Grobler, and he's due for release shortly.'

'I see. I've only been the officer in charge of East London for four years, so I'm not familiar with that case. I'm making a note to read up about it, but we must presume the murder and robbery squad checked for similarities.'

Kathy couldn't help herself.

'I wouldn't *presume* anything, Captain Botha. The police didn't even investigate the *vehicle* that was heard the night Trevor died.'

Rick intervened, not wanting to raise Kathy's hopes or criticise the police force.

'Let's just take one step at a time and not get ahead of ourselves. I intend to visit Dawie Grobler in prison to see if he can tell me anything of interest.'

'You may need an interpreter.' the captain suggested.

Rick grinned.

'My Afrikaans is pretty good now, but thanks for your suggestion.'

'One more thing, Mr Barron,' the captain warned, 'this Dawie Grobler was sent to prison because he was found guilty of murder by a jury, but you can expect him to swear he's innocent... most offenders do.'

'Thank you, Captain, I deal with criminal cases daily, but to be *fair,* juries are known to get it wrong.

Kathy was not surprised to receive a phone call from her mother that night. Frances was not taking any chances.

'I phoned Commandant Marais at Pretoria police headquarters to make sure the police returned Trevor's medallion to me after they've checked for fingerprints. He couldn't confirm that the prints would have survived twenty years, but he's going to contact Captain Botha.'

'That's good to hear. How is your holiday going, mum?'

'We're having a marvellous time in Durban, the weather is perfect, but I'm missing you all and it's a long journey back.'

Kathy had a hunch her mother would return home early, and her prediction proved correct.

Frances and Tim arrived back in East London two days earlier than expected. This meant that Frances could join Rick and Kathy when they visited the police station to hear the results from the forensics team.

To their amazement they found Commandant Marais in Captain Botha's office when they arrived. He was out of uniform, wearing civilian clothes and it took Frances a moment to realise who he was.

'Commandant Marais, how wonderful to see you again.'

He clasped her extended hand in both his, smiling warmly.

'It's good to see you, Mrs Parker, eh, Frances. I'm visiting a family member in East London and Captain Botha invited me to join the briefing.'

He motioned for the captain to proceed.

'I have the results of the forensic examination of the Saint Christopher medallion.'

He glanced down at the sheet of paper.

'It's written in Afrikaans, so I will translate for you. A partial print was found on the surface of the silver Saint Christopher medallion. No match was found to Mr or Mrs Parker or Trevor Parker, and no match is recorded in their current records.'

He cleared his throat.

'There is also a summary here, er… it says that "due to ongoing forensic advancement, all prints are kept on record, pending further results".

Kathy beamed.

'This is so much more than I'd hoped for,' she was excited. She felt there was a ray of hope at last. 'I didn't hold out much hope, but now I believe that one day this print might help prove who killed my brother.

Commandant Marais gave a rare smile.

'Time will tell, young lady. A partial print is difficult to match unless there's a complete print to compare with, but great advances are being made in fingerprint forensics.'

Captain Botha returned the medallion to Frances.

'The item I'm returning to you is police evidence. You can thank Commandant Marais for pulling a few strings to make sure you got it back, Mrs Parker.'

Commandant Marais intervened.

'I was involved with the original homicide squad when we investigated the Trevor Parker homicide. I want to assure you, Frances, that this case is still open, pending further investigation.'

Kathy remembered him from when he'd tried to question her as a little girl at Travellers Joy. Now it was *her* turn to ask *him* a question.

'I remember you, Commandant Marais. I was six when you asked me if I had seen anything. I couldn't answer you back then.' her eyes met his inquiringly. 'I believe you've read my statement, so you now know *what* I saw, but you think I've identified the *wrong man.*'

She didn't allow him time to comment.

'When Captain Oberholster saw my sketch, he *also* said I was mistaken. His comment was, "How would this man get to an isolated cottage and why would he have killed your brother?"'

She held the commandant's gaze.

'Well, thanks to Constable Heinz, who spoke to the caretaker at Travellers Joy, we now know a vehicle was heard the night of Trevor's death. Can you tell us what follow-up action was taken by the original homicide squad? We couldn't find anything in the docket notes.'

Captain Botha looked uneasy. Kathy guessed it was because she was asking his superior officer a question. The commandant smoothed his moustache while holding her gaze.

'Well, I see you've *got* your *voice* back, young lady.'

He gave the hint of a smile.

'An interpreter assisted us with the statements taken from the caretaker staff and they should be in the docket. I'm on leave for another week, but when I get back to Pretoria, I'll make enquires. Captain Botha, can you check the docket again and see if there's anything there.'

Kathy looked ready to ask more questions, but Rick gave a discouraging squeeze of her hand. The commandant gave Captain Botha a questioning look to which he responded.

'I arranged for Constable Heinz who is fluent in Xhosa to interview the caretaker, Lundi…he claims he *did* hear a vehicle that night. I'll give you a copy of his report, sir.'

Commandant Marais had the last word. 'It was nice to see you again, Frances. I'm sorry the fingerprint result wasn't more positive, but we will keep you informed.'

That evening Charlotte joined Kathy on the house veranda where they waited for Rick to return from work. Charlotte was dating Burt Rossouw, a good looking, orthopaedic surgeon who worked at the hospital. When Charlotte had first met him, she had vowed to never go out with him.

'He's *too* good looking, Kathy. Every nurse in the hospital is in love with him and he's in love with *himself.* You know *me*, I have to be numero uno.'

Burt had not given up and continued to pursue Charlotte until she eventually agreed to a dinner date. The couple had been an item ever since.

'I think I've fallen in love with him, Kath. I haven't felt this way about a man since I was dating Zach back in high school.'

Kathy patiently listened to Charlotte talking about the new love in her life, but she was bursting to share her own news about the partial fingerprint on the medallion and cut in as soon as she could.

'It's amazing after all these years that forensics found a partial print. They know the print doesn't belong to mum, dad or Trevor, but I'm convinced one day it will prove who killed my brother. Commandant Marais said forensics are making great strides which gives me hope.'

Wendy woke, calling for her mother. Kathy went to attend to her, leaving Charlotte sitting alone on the veranda.

'Where's Kathy?' Asked Rick when he arrived home.'

'She went to check on Wendy,' Charlotte looked thoughtful, 'I feel sorry for Kathy, Rick; she's tried so hard to find evidence to put her brother's murderer behind bars. The problem is, she's *convinced* its Robert Erasmus, but he comes across as such a decent fellow. He visited the hospital yesterday with his little girl and I watched him, he's a wonderful father.'

'Are you implying that he's not *capable* of murder? Tell me, what do you think a killer looks like, Charlotte?'

She laughed.

'Good point, Rick; you're a criminal lawyer and have probably seen it all.'

'You're right, Char, I have. You'd be amazed at how devious offenders can be. I wish I'd been more supportive of Kathy while she's been methodically gathering information to solve her brother's murder. We now know there *was* a vehicle in the vicinity that night. Kathy's claims are not only possible, but probable. I wouldn't write off Erasmus just yet.'

He removed his glasses to rub his tired eyes.

'I'm seeing Grobler in prison next week. It'll be interesting to hear his side of the story.'

He glanced around to make sure Kathy wasn't within earshot.

'I haven't told Kathy, but the police questioned Robert Erasmus about the Sutton murder. He had an alibi from holidaymakers at the campsite where he was staying. But they only found the burnt-out vehicle three days later and these campers were just acquaintances and not friends. Holiday-makers seldom keep track of dates or time. I have my doubts they would remember Erasmus's exact whereabouts on the night in question.'

Charlotte looked at him quizzically.

'Are you saying, *you* think it was Erasmus who killed Kathy's brother?'

'No, I'm not. But I'm keeping an open mind. If Erasmus *was* involved in the Sutton murder, he'd have had to drive past Kleinemonde to get back to the camp site in Port Alfred.'

He put a finger to his lips.

'Not a word to Kathy about this… she's already having nightmares.'

Chapter 17

Rick could see that Kathy and Charlotte were eager to know what had happened when he returned from visiting the prison.

'Dawie Grobler is nothing like I thought he'd be. Not only does he speak English, he *is* English. He emigrated from England when he was nine and his real name is David Lewis. He changed David to the Afrikaans equivalent Dawie. Then after his father's death, he took on his mother's Afrikaans surname, Grobler. He found that having an Afrikaans name helped to stop the bullying at school. He's very good with figures and has been studying while in prison. He's now a qualified accountant.'

'Does he *look* anything like Robert Erasmus?' Kathy blurted out impatiently.

Rick bristled.

'Can I talk without being interrupted, please, Kath? I'm trying to tell you about the man himself. I'll get to that later.'

She promised not to interrupt again.

'Grobler swears he's innocent. He says Sutton had several enemies and was a nasty piece of work.'

Charlotte and Kathy's eyes brightened inquisitively.

'To answer your question, Kathy. No… Grobler doesn't look anything like Robert Erasmus. He's about five foot nine, stocky with red hair and a freckled complexion.'

Kathy looked crestfallen as he continued.

'He claims the homicide squad stitched him up just to get a conviction. The prosecution presented his motorbike tyre tracks as evidence, but he claims to have ridden his bike all around that coastal area, and there hadn't been rain for months.

'Do you believe him?' Charlotte asked.

His lips tightened.

'There's no easy answer to that one, Charlotte. After eighteen years in prison, he'll be a convincing liar and very few cons admit to their crimes. Then again.' He shrugged his shoulders. 'He could have been set up… or in the *wrong* place at the *wrong* time. It makes no difference; a jury found him guilty and he's served his sentence.'

'Did he mention Robert Erasmus?'

Kathy had waited patiently to ask this question.

'No, he didn't. Grobler claims there were several of his school friends who could have committed the crime. He rattled off a few names but not Erasmus. The poor guy has got a chip on his shoulder; can't say I blame him.'

Kathy slumped with disappointment.

'I had hoped he'd have volunteered more information than that. When is he due for release?'

'He's only got two weeks left in prison. Had I known that, I'd have waited until he was a free man. He's found a temporary job and he's going to move in with his mother and grandparents, here, in East London.'

Kathy fixed her eyes on her husband.

'Do you think he's guilty, Rick?'

'I've told you all I know, Kath. He's the only person who can answer that question.'

Rick had warned her it was a long shot, but she had hoped for some kind of a breakthrough. She was disheartened. Perhaps, it was time she returned to work to take her mind off finding her brother's killer.

As Frances still had a week of leave due to her, she asked Tim to book them into a hotel in the Hogsback Mountains. They would be away for several days which meant that Kathy would have to drop the twins at nursery school. Something Frances usually did on her way to work.

One morning when Kathy returned home after nursery school drop off, she noticed a golden Mercedes Benz was parked on the other side of the road opposite their gates. She glanced at the driver who wore a cap and dark glasses. Erasmus drove a similar vehicle and she mentally recorded the vehicle registration number, before opening the gates and driving into the yard. When she returned to close the gates, the vehicle was still there. She was about to cross the road to speak to the driver, when he sped off.

She didn't give this incident much thought, but mentioned it to Charlotte that evening.

'I didn't get a very good look at him, but I took the registration number in case the vehicle belongs to Robert Erasmus.'

Charlotte looked exasperated and sighed loudly. Kathy challenged her.

'What's your problem, Charlotte?'

'Ah, *come on* Kath, aren't you being a bit *melodramatic?* Lots of people park on the side of the road and there's more than *one* gold Mercedes Benz in town.'

She had hurt Kathy's feelings, but not wanting to argue, Kathy changed the subject.

That night Rick suggested they let Honey sleep in their bedroom. She was now seven months old and usually slept in her dog bed on the veranda. But she had thrown up her supper that night and her gums were pale.

'She's very quiet and doesn't look well, Kath. Let her sleep in our bedroom where we can keep a close eye on her.'

Kathy happily agreed.

In the early hours of the morning, Honey growled and then barked excitedly. Rick unlocked the gun safe and loaded his 9mm pistol whilst Kathy did her best to calm Honey. She mustn't be allowed to wake the children.

When Rick opened the French doors, Honey rushed from the bedroom toward the cottage barking frantically. Rick moved in the shadow of the wall, pistol cocked and ready for any intruder. Kathy could see very little through the French doors as they disappeared into the dark. She waited patiently until Rick returned with Honey by his side.

'There's nothing there that I could find. It's strange; Honey seldom barks for no reason. Someone might have tried to climb the wall, but it's all clear now.'

He unloaded the weapon and locked it away. They eventually settled and slept through the rest of the right.

The following morning was a Saturday and the whole family was home having breakfast when Charlotte knocked at the kitchen door.

'Can I borrow your car, Kath? I left my lights on all night and the battery's flat.'

Kathy handed her the car keys and obligingly opened and closed the gates for her. She then stripped the beds in the cottage and reloaded the washing machine, taking her time before returning to the kitchen.

Rick was on the phone in the hallway and the children were making a noise running amok in the kitchen.

'Shush! Daddy's on the phone.'

She tried to calm them and listen to his conversation at the same time.

'Are you sure you're, okay? Do you want me to come and fetch you? Well, if you change your mind just call me.'

He replaced the receiver and was about to explain, when the phone rang again.

'Hello, Rick Barron speaking.'

Kathy was eager to know what was happening, but peels of mischievous laughter sent her rushing back to check on the children in the kitchen.

'Put that down, Ben!'

She took his fire engine away and lifted Wendy down from the high chair where she was shrieking with delight at her brother's antics. Finally, Kathy was able to get back to Rick.

'What's going on, Rick…who was that on the phone?'

'Charlotte has had an accident in your car, Kath. The brakes failed at the intersection of Fourie and West Street. She says the pedal went right to the floorboards and she drove straight through a red traffic light. Luckily, she didn't hit anyone, but the car ended up in a pile of building sand on a building site.

Kathy rushed to the key rack and searched for her keys.

'We must go to her,' she cried. 'Is she okay… where is she? Where are my car keys?'

Rick caught her hand.

'She's okay. Calm down, Kath. She was driving *your* car, remember.

He hugged her.

'She's at the hospital with Burt… she needed a couple of stitches in her forehead, there are no broken bones and she says she is fine.'

He kissed Kathy gently on the forehead and then lifted her chin.

'Oh, God, Kathy… I'm so relieved you and the kids weren't in that car.'

Kathy was still flustered.

'What happened? Why did the brakes fail? Who was the second call from?'

'It was Constable Heinz. He witnessed the accident and pulled over to help. He wanted us to know your car has been impounded. The police mechanic is going to check the brakes on Monday.'

Kathy kept her thoughts to herself. Charlotte had already accused her of being melodramatic for recording the registration number of a gold Mercedes. She reprimanded herself, *don't be silly. It's all a coincidence, this has nothing to do with Robert Erasmus. The gold Mercedes could belong to anyone, and Honey has been known to bark at shadows more than once. Perhaps Charlotte put her foot on the clutch instead of the brakes.*

Charlotte did not return to the cottage over the weekend and with Tim and Frances still on holiday, they only had one vehicle, so Rick dropped the twins at nursery school on his way to work.

Kathy contacted Maria Van Wyk who kindly drove her to the police station on Monday morning.

'I'll take Wendy to the park while you're speaking to Captain Botha,' Maria offered.

Captain Botha appeared genuinely concerned about Charlotte's accident.

'Yes, she's okay,' Kathy assured him. 'Thank, the Lord. She's a tough lady, that one… she went back to work a few hours later. Fortunately, she only has a few stitches in her forehead and some bruising.'

The captain asked Sally Brits to phone the Police Automobile Division to get the test results for Kathy's car.

While they were waiting, Captain Botha mentioned he had received a report from Commandant Marias about Lundi's statement. I will translate it into English for you.

'A statement was taken from the caretaker and he did mention that he heard a vehicle the night of Trevor Parkers murder, ' he hesitated. 'They didn't pursue this line of enquiry because the car stopped some distance from the cottage. Most of the tracks had already been destroyed by other vehicles driving back and forth over the road, Fishermen often park on that road and then walk to the beach to fish off the rocks. Even if they had discovered unusual tracks there was nothing to compare them with.'

Kathy closed her eyes and shook her head.

'That was a mistake on their part, but it answers Captain Oberholster's question. The killer parked his vehicle some distance from the cottage and walked – that's *how* he got there!'

'You could be right. I guess we'll never know, Mrs Barron.'

Kathy felt a little self-righteous. *For once the police agree with me.*

The arrival of Sally Brits brought their discussion to an end.

'The mechanic is still working on the damaged car at the automobile workshop.' she advised them.

'Thanks, Sally; where is the workshop?'

'It's just behind the police station,' the captain told her.

'Can I walk there and have a look? I'd like to see the damage for myself.'

Before she left, she handed Captain Botha the vehicle registration number of the gold Mercedes Benz.

'It's possibly nothing, but please can you find out who owns this vehicle? It was parked outside our house the day before Charlotte's accident. Thank you for everything, Captain Botha, I appreciate your help.'

The mechanic was lying under the car when Kathy arrived at the workshop. She circled the vehicle, examining the damage. Apart from a dent on the front bumper, it looked perfectly okay.

'I'm so pleased to see there isn't much damage.'

She smiled hopefully at the man in overalls who had just wheeled himself out from under the car.

He appeared amused by her comment.

'You must be, Mrs Barron? I won't shake your hand.'

He smiled holding up his dirty hands.

'Tell me, Mrs Barron, have you ever heard the old saying, don't judge a book by it's cover?'

He didn't wait for an answer, but pointed towards the vehicle instead.

'Well, this is a perfect example... the damage is all *under* the bonnet. Your friend's lucky that pile of sand was in the right place to stop her from crashing into something more solid.

'I agree, she was lucky. Do you know why the brakes failed?' Kathy sounded hopeful.

A pair of keen eyes examined her through safety goggles.

'When did you buy this car, Mrs Barron?'

'My husband bought it for me about a year ago. It was a private sale and he told me he was impressed by its excellent condition and low mileage. I only use it locally to drive the children to nursery school or do the shopping.'

He eyed her quizzically.

'Hmmm, so you didn't have it checked or serviced?'

His tone gave her reason for concern.

'*Why?* Is there a *problem*?'

'Yes, there is, I can hear you're not a South African. How long have you lived here, Mrs Barron?'

'We've been here about eighteen months.'

He scrubbed his greasy hand on a piece of mutton cloth.

'I'm sorry to tell you this, lady, but your husband was sold a lemon.

He looked sympathetic.

'You'll soon learn that not all the sharks live in the sea – the speedometer has been turned back. I'd estimate this vehicle has done three times the mileage on the clock and has possibly been in an accident. It's been given a spray paint to spruce it up, but everything under the bonnet is badly worn. I'm sorry, this vehicle is *not* road-worthy.'

Kathy was appalled.

'Are you telling me, the brakes failed because they were worn out?'

'That's a possibility. You're lucky there were no children in the car when it happened. I suggest you tell your husband to buy from a reputable second-hand dealer in future.'

Kathy knew Rick would be furious with himself when she told him he had bought a dud car. It would wound his pride, especially as they would receive only a pittance for their scrapped vehicle.

She was right; Rick did take it personally and was furious when she gave him the mechanics report.

'I'll never buy another second-hand vehicle. We will have to manage with one car and save the deposit for a *new c*ar.'

The following day, Captain Botha phoned to tell Kathy that the Gold Mercedes belonged to an estate agent who was checking on properties in the area. Kathy felt foolish. Charlotte was right, she was behaving irrationally.

It was midweek before Burt brought Charlotte back home to Flame Lily Villa. She held her fringe back to show Kathy her stitches, but all Kathy could see was the enormous diamond on her finger.

'Ouch,' Kathy jumped back playfully.

'Careful, you'll get a shoulder injury lifting that *rock*. Congratulations, Char,' Kathy hugged her. 'Does this mean you're officially engaged?'

She examined her friend's enormous engagement ring with a touch of envy. Charlotte glowed with, happiness her car accident already forgotten.

Wendy called out during the night and Kathy hurried to comfort her. She sat on the rocker waiting for her daughter to fall asleep again. In the silence of the night, she gave herself a good talking to. *My life changed the day my memory returned. My children have never known the carefree girl their father married. I must put Trevor out of my thoughts and focus on my children's future. Charlotte's right. I've become a neurotic nutter, relating everything no matter how remote, to my brother's murder.* She decided that from that moment on, she would concentrate on the future and positive thoughts.

At twenty-six, Kathy's ambition had changed. She wanted to be *more* than a nurse. She had noticed the respect her friend Doctor Charlotte Pistorius received whenever she mentioned she was a medical doctor. *I want that kind of respect too.* Since her own amnesia experience, her interest in psychology and psychiatry had grown. She had read numerous books and contacted the nurses she met on honeymoon. Indi and Fron worked at Groote Schuur University hospital in Cape Town where she was making enquiries about further studies in psychology.

But try as she may, her thoughts kept returning to her brother's murder. *Perhaps, the police will take me more seriously when I have letters after my name. I'm putting you on the backburner, Mr Erasmus, but don't kid yourself, I haven't forgotten, I'll be back.*

Chapter 18

Frances and Tim returned from their week's holiday at Hogsback hotel and expressed their concern about the car accident.

'It's lucky that Charlotte wasn't badly hurt in the accident; are you going to buy another second-hand car?'

'No, Mum. Our car is a write-off, so we won't get much from the scrap dealer. Rick insists we save up and put a deposit down on a new car.'

Tim had been listening and offered what he hoped would be a solution.

'I'm visiting the Nissan dealership tomorrow to buy a Nissan utility. You're welcome to drive it any time, Kathy. It won't be much good for collecting the twins from nursery school, but it's ideal for you to go shopping or visiting your friends.

An opportunity to use the vehicle arose sooner than she anticipated. Her nursing friend, Jean Schmidt, had left a message on the answering machine for her, but when Kathy tried to phone her back there was no reply. She called the hospital who told her Jean was on leave, so she continued trying to phone the house. Finally, Jean answered.

'Oh, Jean, I'm so relieved I've reached you at last. I've been trying to phone you all day.'

Jean didn't sound her usual bubbly self.

'Is everything all right?'

'Thanks for phoning back, Kathy… something awful happened last night.'

'I can hear you're upset, what's wrong?'

'Jolanda tried to kill herself. If I hadn't come home early, I don't know what would have happened.

Her voice dropped to a murmur.

'She took sleeping pills and I couldn't wake her,' she hurried on. 'She's okay now. But she's furious with me and won't allow me to visit her in hospital.'

'Oh, Thank God she's okay! I'm coming to see you right away.'

Kathy didn't wait for an invitation. She borrowed Tim's utility and drove to sixty-eight Williams Street, where she found her friend, more concerned than tearful.

'I've taken a week off work, Kathy. My nursing friends would want to know what happened to Jolanda and I can't face them just yet. Thanks for coming, I really need someone to talk to.' she sighed. 'I came home early and found Jolanda lying on her bed. I couldn't wake her. For one *awful* moment, I thought she was dead!'

Jean looked visibly distressed now.

'The ambulance arrived within minutes and we rushed her to emergency where they pumped her stomach. They're keeping her under observation in a private ward for another night.'

She clutched at the gold chain around her neck.

'Jolanda blames me for over-reacting and won't even talk to me.

Together, they tried to examine why a young girl would do such a thing. Kathy knew of two reasons. *I know Jolanda regrets her affair with Robert Erasmus and feels partly responsible for Joan Erasmus having fallen to her death, but I doubt she'd try to kill herself.* She couldn't mention this to Jean as she had promised Jolanda she would not repeat what she knew.

'I don't know, Jean, but would it be okay if I visited Jolanda at the hospital tonight?'

'I think she'd see *you*, Kathy; she *likes* you. We've been getting along better and she's even started to see her old school friends again. Maybe she'll open up and tell *you* what's worrying her.'

'Perhaps.'

Kathy felt a twinge of guilt for not sharing what she already knew.

Jean made a pot of tea and they continued their chat.

'I know I'm overprotective of my daughter, Kathy, and I dread the day she turns twenty-one and I have to tell her the truth about her father.'

Kathy didn't hold back her opinion.

'I *detest* secrets, Jean. I know from personal experience that hiding the truth can cause so much unnecessary pain. My mother was going to tell me about what had happened to my brother when I turned twenty-one and then I found out on my own. I wouldn't wish *that* on Jolanda or anyone else.

'I don't know what happened to your brother, Kathy, but I know it will crush Jolanda when I tell her the truth about her father.'

Jean's eyes dulled

'I'll tell you what happened. I was seventeen and had just started nursing when a group of friends asked me to join them for a beach party one night.'

She twisted her chain around her finger.

'During the evening, I wandered off behind a sand-dune to have a pee. I was only going to be gone for a few minutes, so I didn't ask anyone to come with me.'

Her eyes lifted to meet Kathy's.

'That night, I was attacked and raped. I tried to fight him off, but I've always been small-boned and wasn't strong enough. I could smell the woodsmoke on is skin and stank of beer; I know he was one of the men from the party.'

She gave an involuntary shudder.

'My late husband Greg used to get angry with me when I said it was *partly* my own fault because I should have asked someone to come with me. He would say, "You did *nothing* wrong, Jean, whoever raped you was a bastard and a coward."'

Kathy was beginning to realise how little she knew about her friend.

'It was too awful. Can you imagine the reaction when I insisted that one of the men from the party had raped me?'

She gave a cynical scowl.

'My so-called, friends said *I* was mistaken and just trying to cause trouble. Of course, *they* stuck *together* and gave each other alibis. I've never got over the whole experience. Then six weeks later, I discovered I was pregnant. I thought my life was over.'

Her derisive smile expressed her angry thoughts.

'I decided to put my baby up for adoption and would have gone through with it, had she not been such a kicker.'

She sat back in her chair and relaxed her shoulders.

'I *just couldn't* give her up! I didn't know if it was a boy or girl, but I already loved my baby,' she sighed resignedly. 'I had a boyfriend who wanted to marry me. He didn't care that I was carrying another man's child. He was happy to raise her as his own and I agreed that after the baby was born, I would give him an answer. We never did marry, but that's another story.'

Kathy's respect for Jean had grown as she listened to her story. She knew it took strength of character to keep a baby out of wedlock during the 1950s when society treated unmarried mothers with utter disdain.

'I'm *so* sorry, Jean. I had no idea that you had raised Jolanda on your own. You must have gone through hell, not knowing who her father was – then having to contend with bigoted people talking about you behind your back, did you grow up here, in East London?'

'Yes, I was born and raised here. And you're right, Kathy, it wasn't easy being known as *the unmarried* mother.'

All of a sudden, her eyes lit up.

'But that all changed when I married Greg. Suddenly, Jolanda and I were *respectable*.'

Kathy poured another cup of tea and took a long approving look at her friend.

'Fortunately, people are more tolerant these days. When did you return to nursing?'

'My parents were wonderful. I'm an only child, so they were excited about having a grandchild. Mum took care of Jolanda from when she was three months old so I could return to nursing.'

Her whole face shone.

'That's where I met Greg; he was one of my patients and we fell in love and married when Jolanda was a year old. She believes he's her father, and *he* loved *her* as if she was his own. The three of us had nine wonderful years together before he died of testicular cancer. Now you know *why* I'm waiting until Jolanda is twenty-one before I tell her, that the man she adores, is not her *real* father.'

Kathy remembered the bond between herself and her own father.

'I'm so sorry you've had such a rough time, Jean. Cancer is an awful disease. I saw my father deteriorate and die from a melanoma.'

Kathy felt sympathetic, but this didn't change *her stance* on keeping secrets.

'I do understand your dilemma and I know it won't be easy to tell Jolanda about her real father, but imagine if someone *else* told her *first*. Jolanda is stronger than you think... and if you open up with *your* secret, she may tell you *hers*.'

Jean didn't want to talk about *her* secret any longer.

'What did your mother hide from *you*, Kathy?'

'It's a long story. I saw my brother murdered when I was only six and I was so traumatised that I blocked him from my memory for fifteen years.'

She explained briefly, just enough to give Jean the gist of her story, leaving out dates and places.

Kathy looked at her watch. 'We've been talking for hours.'

'It's been good to catch up with you, Jean. I must dash. I want to get home and make the children's supper, so that I can visit Jolanda at the hospital during visiting hours.'

At the hospital, Jolanda was pleased to see Kathy and started to unload almost immediately.

'I'm furious with my mother; she completely overreacted. I took one sleeping pill to get some sleep and you won't believe this. She had emergency staff *pump* my stomach.'

'Yes, she told me they had to do that because *you* took an overdose of sleeping pills.'

'I did *not*.

She was furious.

'I only took that one sleeping pill because I still occasionally have nightmares about Joan's screams.'

She caught Kathy's hand.

'I hope you kept your promise and didn't tell my mum anything, Kathy?'

'You don't need to worry… I *won't* break my promise.'

'I've moved on now and I'm seeing my old friends again. I don't even think about Robby anymore.'

She let go of Kathy's hand and smoothed the bed sheet.

'Your mother loves you, Jolanda. Perhaps, she *did* overreact, but someone as young as you shouldn't be taking such strong sleeping tablets. Don't you think it's time to tell her *why* you aren't sleeping?'

Her eyes blazed.

'You *know* why I can't tell her… she'll insist I go to the police. After *they* start snooping, they'll find out about Robby and me. Oh… I shouldn't have told you.

She turned her back on Kathy.

'You *promised* you wouldn't tell.'

Kathy looked taken aback by the young girl's, tantrum.

'I've already told you I've kept my promise to you.'

Jolanda turned to face her again.

'I don't think you realise how *complicated* this is, Kathy. Mum trusts Robby completely. He is one of her *best* friends… she would never forgive either of us if she ever found out about our affair.'

Kathy's cheeks flushed as if she'd been slapped. *Jean and Robert Erasmus are friends.*

'You didn't tell me they were *friends*'

'They lived next door to each other and have been friends all their lives.'

Kathy was still trying to take in what she had just heard when the matron appeared.

'Time's up, Mrs Barron, this young lady needs her rest.'

As Kathy drove home, her mind was in a whirl. She tried to recall what she had told Jean about her brother's death. *I'm sure I didn't mention Trevor by name... or where the murder happened. She's got no reason to tell Robby Erasmus. I must get a grip of myself – I'm behaving neurotically again.*

The following Sunday, Kathy, together with Becky and Wendy attended church down the road, and as always, they sat in the back pew. The service had just started when Robert Erasmus and his daughters walked to the front accompanied by an elderly couple. Kathy felt uneasy and was tempted to take her children and leave. She could not concentrate during the church service, knowing that Erasmus was worshiping at the same church. She left as soon as they had sung the final hymn. He irritated her for many reasons, but the final straw was after church, when he climbed into a flashy new Red Mercedes Benz and waved like royalty as he drove off. She was surprised by her own anger. *I can't worship at a church where my heart is full of hate.*

Her mood had not improved; and her head was aching by the time she arrived home. Rick took the three children for an ice-cream at the Dairy-Den, so Kathy could have peace and quiet. She tried to lie down, but her mind was overactive. Suddenly her anger reached boiling point. She borrowed Tim's utility and drove to Robert Erasmus's house where she parked on the opposite side of the road.

Her thoughts were rampant. She wanted to get out the car and confront him, but couldn't find the courage. In her mind, she visualised herself crossing the road and opening the gate, her head held high as she strode up the pathway, then pressed the doorbell and waited. Erasmus opened the door and looked her up and down, suggestively. She held his gaze, with malice in her eyes.

'Hello, can I help you?' he sounded self-assured.

'You don't remember me, do you, Mr Erasmus?'

'I'm sure I would remember someone as pretty as you if we'd met before.'

His flirtatious behaviour repulsed her.

'I was the little girl standing in the shadows when you kill my brother.'

She snapped out of her reverie. It was all wishful thinking. She hadn't even got out of the car. She had tried to put Trevor's murder out of her mind, but the pompous way Erasmus sauntered into church and then drove off in his new Mercedes left her fuming. She started the engine and drove back home.

When she opened the front door, it was quiet.

'Where are the children, Rick?'

'They're having lunch with granny. Your mum thought we should have some time together. You looked unhappy when you got home from church and then drove off in a huff.'

'I've just been to Robert Erasmus's house.'

'Aah, Kath, I wish you hadn't done that, what happened?'

'Nothing. I didn't have the courage to get out the car. I had rehearsed exactly what I was going to say... then I chickened out and drove home. I have to find another church. I *cannot* worship there anymore.'

'It's okay, lovey, you'll find something.'

He cuddled her.

'I love you and we'll work through this together.'

She nestled into his shoulder.

'I've made some silly mistakes. One of them was to encourage us to move to East London. Ever since we arrived here, I've been too focused on solving my brother's murder instead caring for our family.'

She pulled back from him and looked into his green eyes.

'I want to talk to you *about* something, Rick... I didn't say anything earlier, because I wanted to be sure before I suggested we uproot our whole family and move again. Please hear me out; it's important I share my thoughts with you and I think the time is right.'

He looked uneasy as she rushed on.

'Do you remember those sisters, Indigo and Saffron, who we met at Ocean-View Hotel when we were on our honeymoon?'

He cocked his head to acknowledge he did.

'Then you might recall they both work at Groote Schuur Hospital in Cape Town, as nurses.'

'Yes, I remember, Kath.'

'Well, I've been corresponding with them... about doing a medical degree in psychology. I haven't spoken to you about it, because I didn't know if the university would accept my qualifications.'

She gauged his reaction before continuing.

'I heard back from the university on Friday. They sent me the application forms for next year's psychology intake, I'll only fill them in and send them off if I have your support.'

He looked puzzled.

'What does a psychologist nurse do, Kath?'

'Not a nurse... a *doctor*. That's why I didn't say anything to you sooner. It'll mean completing four years as a psychology undergraduate, and another three or four years as a graduate. The focus is on emotional and mental suffering.'

Keep to the fact's, she reminded herself.

'I know it's a big ask. I'll be a student and won't contribute much to the family finances for at least four years, although, I could do part-time work at the hospital.'

He looked somewhat taken aback.

'This is very sudden, Kath. How long have you been thinking about this?'

She ignored the question, determined to push the positives.

'Our biggest challenge is moving the family to Cape Town.' She sensed his hesitation and hurried on. 'Please, let me finish. You're wasting *your* legal skills in East London. When we met, you were ambitious. I can see you're frustrated working for a small law firm who don't have the resources to support your ideas. If we moved to Cape Town, you'd have the opportunities you want and deserve.'

She listed the positives.

'Your parents are moving to live in Cape Town, so we'll see more of *them*. We should get a good *price* for Flame Lily Villa after the improvements we've made and the twins are starting school next year. The timing is perfect for a move.'

Rick looked astounded.

'Wow! You've got it all worked out haven't you, Kath? I've been worried about you thinking there was something seriously wrong. Now I discover it's nothing more than you're *scheming* about a new career and moving the *whole family* to Cape Town.'

He shook his head in bewilderment. His response was better than she had dared to hope.

'It's just an option; all I'm asking, is that, you give it some thought. Please, Rick.'

'Is there anything else I should know, Kath?'

She kissed him.

'I realise I'm asking for a lot, lovey... but after I'm qualified, I'll be earning really good money and helping people who are going through the sort of mental trauma I experienced.'

'You're impossible, but you're *right* about one thing.'

He kissed her.

'I'm *not* happy in my job. A move could benefit both of our careers – I'll give it some serious thought; but for now, let's send your forms off and see if you get a *place* in the next psychology intake. When we know, we can make a final decision.'

Over the next few weeks Rick and Kathy discussed the pros and cons of moving to live in Cape Town. Kathy and the children would need to be there by mid-January for the start of the school year. Rick started checking positions vacant in the Cape Town Times and contacted several employment agencies.

Nothing would happen unless Kathy's application was accepted or Rick found a suitable job. The distraction was good for Kathy, she was sleeping better and tried not to think about her brother.

She found a new church on the other side of town. Rick drove her and the girls there in time for the morning service. The men in the family did not attend church, so Rick took Ben across the road to a park and kicked a football.

After church, Kathy and the girls found a third person playing ball with Rick and Ben. He was showing Ben passing and kicking techniques. They stopped playing as Kathy approached and Rick called out to her.

'Hi Kathy, this is Dawie Grobler, he's waiting for his mother and grandparents, they also go to this church.'

Kathy realised she was staring and quickly recovered.

'Hello, Dawie. Have you found a job yet?' She had spoken without thinking, he looked surprised and glanced questioningly at Rick, who answered quickly,

'My wife knows who you are, Dawie. We tell each other everything.'

Kathy felt bad.

'I'm sorry... I didn't mean to pry; it's just that, I wish you all the best. It can't be easy starting over again after so long.'

He bounced back with a smile.

'Not at all, thanks for asking. I've found a temporary position in the administrative department at the hospital.'

He stretched to shake her hand.

'It's good to meet you, Mrs Barron,' He was distracted by someone calling his name and he waved at her, 'There's mum, I must go. Perhaps I'll see you again.'

Two weeks later, while Kathy was waiting for Charlotte in the hospital canteen, she saw Dawie standing in the lunch queue. She greeted him as he walked towards her.

'Sit for a minute, Dawie. I'm waiting for my friend, she's always late,' She pointed at an empty seat.

He peered into the stroller where Wendy lay sleeping and slipped into the seat.

'It's good to see you, Mrs Barron. What are you doing here?'

'I'm meeting my friend Charlotte for lunch. She's one of the doctors here.'

'Then I'll only stop for a minute.'

He dropped his voice.

'I wanted to ask you to not mention anything about my past to the people who work here. They don't know I've been in prison.'

She thought how difficult it must be for him to integrate back into society after so many years.

'I wouldn't do that, Dawie. I'm the *one* person who believes you didn't kill anyone.'

His brows knitted in a bewildered frown.

'What do you mean?'

She regretted her words the moment she spoke them. *Rick told me not to presume Dawie was innocent just because he said he was.*

'I shouldn't have said anything. It's nothing really,' she countered.

His eyes widened.

'You can't make a statement like that and then say it*'s nothing.* Why are you so *sure* I'm innocent?'

She couldn't retract her words and leave him hanging so she would tread carefully.

156

'It's just a theory I have that the same person who killed my brother also killed Sutton. I saw the man who killed my brother and it wasn't you.

He stared at her.

'Do you know something about the Sutton murder that can *help* me?'

'*No,* I was six when I saw my brother murdered and the only link between the two murders is that they happened on the same night. I'm sorry, it's just a silly idea, there's probably no connection. I shouldn't have said anything.'

Their conversation was cut short by the arrival of Charlotte.

'Hi, Kath, sorry I'm late.'

She shot a questioning look at Dawie who picked up his tray.

Kathy rushed in to save him embarrassment.

'Charlotte, this is Dawie. He's a friend of Rick's. He's working in the administrative department here at the hospital.'

He nodded a greeting to Charlotte and then quickly moved away to find another table.

'Where do you know *him* from, Kath?'

'I thought you might have recognised his name. That's Dawie Grobler; the guy Rick visited in prison. I feel sorry for him, Char. He asked me not to tell anyone that he's an ex-con; he's trying to start a new life. Charlotte's expression said it all.

'I can see you disapprove, Charlotte, but please greet him if you see him.'

Chapter 19

It was some weeks before Kathy met Jean again. It was good to see her back to her bubbly self and she couldn't wait to tell Kathy how Charlotte and Burt's engagement had rocked the hospital.

'Everyone is talking about our two most eligible doctors announcing their engagement. It's so romantic.

She hugged herself.

'Jolanda's much better; she's going out with a group of lovely young people she knows from school… and we're getting on famously. We have put her overdose incident, behind us.'

Kathy said all the right things, and they happily chatted away until Jean mentioned Robert Erasmus.

'I told my friend Robby Erasmus how helpful you had been when *Jolanda* was at her lowest. I'm sure *you* know what's troubling her.' She brushed this statement aside and continued. 'Robby wanted to know where I'd met you, so I explained that we nursed together, and how you nearly gave birth to Wendy at the police station.

Kathy forced a laugh.

'When I mentioned you had twins, he said he thought he knew you from church.'

Kathy wasn't happy about Jean discussing her with Erasmus, especially when *he* was asking the questions.

She joked in an attempt to hide her sense of discomfort.

'I hope you didn't tell him the colour of my underwear?'

'Oh no. He was more interested in your friendship with *Jolanda.* He's always been fond of her in a fatherly way, especially since Greg died.'

Kathy stifled a cough and quickly changed the subject.

'Did I tell you that I'm thinking of studying psychology, Jean?'

They talked for some time and agreed they should meet up for cocktails again soon

Charlotte and Burt were the only people, other than immediate family, who knew that Rick and Kathy were exploring the possibility of moving to live in Cape Town. Rick didn't want his employer to know.

Flame Lily Villa was in disarray. Tim was re-tiling the bathrooms, workmen were replacing kitchen cupboards and counters, and Ben and Becky were driving them crazy by touching and moving their equipment. Honey chewed a piece of new skirting board while Wendy teetered on chubby legs tipping over a tin of paint. Kathy was relieved to drop all three children off at nursery school. She then drove Rick to work, before returning home to continue renovating.

In the afternoon, she returned to collect the children. Wendy was waiting for her, but the twins weren't there.

'I think their father collected them, Mrs Barron,' Nancy the relief teacher told her.

'He *couldn't* have. He hasn't got a car. I'm on my way to pick him up from work after I collect the children.'

'Well, I *thought* he said he was their father.'

'Did they go with him willingly?'

'I *think* so… so many children were being collected at the same time that I didn't really notice.'

'What did their father look like?'

'Umm, gosh I don't remember.

She ruffled her hair and considered the question.

'He was medium height with light brown hair, I think.'

Kathy choked with fear. *Erasmus said he knew I had twins.*

'Oh, my God. I need to use the phone, please, Nancy.'

She tried to calm her muddled thoughts. The phone where Rick worked just kept ringing. *He's probably waiting in the car park. S*he phoned her mother's work number and was relieved when she answered.

'Mum, I'm at the nursery school. Wendy's with me, but someone's taken Ben and Becky. The nursery teacher says it was Rick, but *he* doesn't have the car. Can you collect Rick, he's probably waiting for me in the carpark where he works, and bring him straight here? I need you both.'

She couldn't hide the tremor in her voice.

'You must call the police immediately, Kathy. I'll collect Rick and be there in ten minutes.'

'Thanks, Mum. You always know what to do,' her thoughts again started to wander into dangerous territory. She took a deep breath and reprimanded herself severely. *Don't go there, Kathy.*

Sally Brits answered the phone at the police station.

'Stay where you are, my dear. Have you phoned your husband?'

Kathy explained what she had already done and held on while Sally spoke to Captain Botha.

'He's leaving for the school right now, Kathy. Don't panic. There'll be a simple explanation.'

While she waited for the police, Kathy tried to get some sense out of the relief teacher.

'Do you remember what the man who collected the twins was wearing?'

'I'm trying to remember, Mrs Barron. He had on a white shirt, and long grey trousers. I think that's right.'

Rick usually wears light blue, but he does have a white shirt. Kathy was sure he had on a blue shirt that morning.

When Captain Botha arrived, he questioned Nancy.

'Did the man leave a message?'

'No.'

'Did he have an accent?'

She didn't know.

Word of the missing children spread like wildfire amongst other parents collecting their children and a small group gathered outside the office.

Frances arrived and hurried towards her daughter.

'Rick wasn't there, Kathy. Maybe he borrowed someone else's car?'

That *was* a possibility, but why would he only collect the *twins?*

One little boy said he had seen the twins climb into a car.

'It was silver and the man got in the back seat with Ben and Becky. Another man was driving.'

He nodded his head solemnly.

'And there was a lady in the front seat.'

The four-year-old knew more about it than Nancy did.

Frances phoned Tim to let him know what was happening.

'No, Franny… the twins are at the *main house* with Rick. His parents are visiting from Cape Town and they must have collected Rick and the twins on their way home.'

Kathy dropped into the nearest chair and blinked away tears of relief. *How could he frighten me like that?'*

Her mother comforted her and the police alert was stood down.

When she arrived home, she needed to calm herself before speaking to Rick and followed Frances to her cottage. He came looking for her.

'I tried to phone you from work, Kath, but there was no answer. I presumed you had already left. I'd forgotten that Wendy went to nursery school today.'

Kathy knew his carelessness wasn't *deliberate,* but he was dismissive and hadn't even apologised.

'Why didn't you leave a message with Nancy… or phone the nursery school as soon as you got home, Rick?'

'Oh, *come on,* lovey! You're making a *mountain* out of a *molehill.'*

Kathy had been teetering on the edge. She let it rip. Her eyes blazed.

'A strange man in a silver car takes *our* children. *Nancy,* who can't tell her *arse* from her *elbow*, couldn't even tell me if the children went *willingly or were kicking and screaming.'*

Her eyes flickered.

'And you are of medium height and wearing a white shirt.'

She poked a finger at her tall husband's blue shirt.

'*My* children go missing from school and *you* have the audacity to say, I'm making a *mountain* out of a *molehill.'*

Tears were spilling from her eyes as she picked up the car keys and drove off.

When she calmed down, she returned home. Rick was apologetic now. Of course, she forgave him. She felt partly responsible for allowing her fixation with Robert Erasmus to affect her better judgement.

'I thought Robert Erasmus had taken our children, Rick. Jean mentioned that Robert Erasmus thought he knew me because of the twins. I'm so relieved they were with you, lovey. I have to stop being so neurotic. I've nearly accused Erasmus twice, for something he knows nothing about.'

Despite her words, Kathy still believed Erasmus was guilty of killing her brother. But for the sake of her sanity, she pushed him to the back of her mind and kept herself busy preparing the house for sale.

Flame Lily Villa had been transformed and was looking amazing. They were pleased when an estate agent told them they had bought their house at the right time and in the right area, so it should bring a reasonable price. They would contact the agent again when *Rick* gave the go-ahead to sell.

A week later, Kathy excitedly handed an envelope to Rick as soon as he walked through the door.

'Please have a look for me, lovey. It's from the university and I'm too nervous to open it myself.'

He assumed a deadly serious expression as he unfolded the letter and scanned the wording. He glanced at her

'Do you really want me to read this to you, Kath?'

He definitely looked despondent now. Her heart dropped.

'Go ahead… I've prepared myself for the worst.'

'Dear Mrs Barron… we wish to advise… I'm sorry, Kath.' he hung his head and then continued in a rush of words, 'you *have* been accepted to…'

He didn't finish. She flung her arms around him, squealing with delight.

'You're a horrible tease Rick Barron,' she beamed from ear to ear as she read the letter. 'Oh, Rick, I'm so thrilled. Now we can start making plans to move.'

Rick was happy for her although he knew the next few years would be financially challenging.

After congratulating her, he shared some other news.

'I had an unexpected visitor at work today. Dawie Grobler called in to ask me for a job reference. I explained I couldn't give a reference to someone I've only met twice.'

He frowned at her.

'I don't believe that was the reason for his visit… what did you tell him about your brother's murder, Kath?'

She felt like a naughty schoolgirl caught in the act of cutting class.

'I told him my brother was killed the same night as Rudy Sutton and I thought the same person might be responsible for both crimes.'

'Why did you do that, Kathy? After I asked you not to. A jury convicted this man of a brutal *murder*. Promise me, you'll keep away from Dawie Grobler *and* Robert Erasmus.'

She looked remorseful.

'I shouldn't have said anything. I know you're trying to protect me. It's just that I feel sorry for Dawie… I know how it feels when no one believes you.

He hugged her.

'*I* believe you, my love, but I don't want you mixing with convicted criminals, no matter *how* sorry you feel for them. Dawie asked me about the man you thought was responsible for killing your brother. You've raised his expectations now. He thinks you can help prove that he's innocent. It wasn't a smart move, my darling.'

Chapter 20

A few weeks later, Rick left early in the morning to travel to Cape Town to attend three interviews over the next two days. He planned to spend the night with his parents and return the following evening.

With the house and cottage now ready for sale, Tim and Kathy had turned their attention to trimming the garden shrubs and tidying the garage. All three children were away at nursery school.

Kathy ran up the stairs to answer the phone with Honey in hot pursuit. She was breathless as she answered.

'Hello... Kathy here.'

'Hello, Mrs Barron, is your husband there?'

'No, I'm sorry, he's not home.'

She couldn't place the voice.

'Who's speaking?'

'It's Dawie Grobler, Mrs Barron. I phoned his office, and they said he was on leave.'

'He is on leave, Dawie, but he's not home right now. Did the office give you this number?' on reflection she thought it to be unlikely.

'No, it was Mr Barron; he wrote it on the business card he gave me.'

She was curious enough to continue the conversation.

'He's away for the day, Dawie, but can *I* help you?'

'Not really. I wanted to arrange a meeting with him. I've thought of someone who might have had a motive to kill Rudy Sutton, but I'll contact Mr Barron later in the week.'

'He'll be phoning me this evening... do you want me to pass on a message?'

'I don't like talking over the phone, Mrs Barron. This phone is on a party-line, and there could be people listening. I'm going fishing at the dam later this morning if you want to meet me there, we could talk without being overheard.'

She had promised Rick she would *keep away* from Dawie Grobler, but her curiosity got the better of her and she wanted to prove she wasn't neurotic. *What harm can it do if I meet with him in a public place for a few minutes?*

'Which dam are you going to?'

Dawie gave her the details.

'I'll be there from ten o'clock onwards and I'll look out for you.'

'I *might* come, Dawie. It depends on whether I can borrow a vehicle.'

After she replaced the receiver, she gave it some thought. *I'll stay just long enough to find out who Dawie suspects. If I tell Tim where I'm going and who I'm meeting, I should be safe enough.*

Tim was happy to lend her his utility vehicle. She handed him the directions to the dam that Dawie had given her.

'The Stein Dam signpost is just over the rise, about a ten-minute drive, I shouldn't be more than thirty minutes, Tim.'

Honey jumped onto the front seat next to her.

'Out, Honey. You can't come with me.'

The puppy wagged her tail and refused to budge.

'Oh, all right,' she called to Tim, 'I'm taking Honey with me as a *guard dog.*'

She giggled as she wound down the window just enough for Honey to stick her head out.

At the Stein dam sign, Kathy turned onto a dirt track, drove through an open boom gate and then past a notice board that said, "Fishing licenses available at main office. Prohibited. No motorboats. No swimming. No DOGS."

'Drat! I'm not taking you back home, Honey – you can stay in the car.'

She turned left at a T junction and took the third right over the rise and into a clearing near the water.

Dawie sat on a bench attached to a rustic wooden table. He was sorting through his fishing tackle. Reels of fishing line and containers spread out in front of him. A faded green Morris Minor sedan sat parked in the shade of a tree. He was the only person there.

As the utility came to a halt, Honey squeezed herself through the half-open window and took off after a herd of Impala[21] along the shore line. Kathy called

---

[21] Impala:-   antelope

after her, but she was untrained and kept bounding after her target. Kathy laughed as she approached Dawie.

'Honey's only a puppy – those impala are in no danger.'

She noticed his rusty fishing box with rusty hooks and sinkers. *I wonder if his mother kept his tackle for him all these years while he's been in prison?* He was wearing casual clothing and looked relaxed.

'Hello, Mrs Barron. The rangers are very strict about dogs at the dam,' he warned.

'Sorry about that,' she explained. 'I intended to leave Honey in the utility, but she was too quick for me.'

Kathy slid onto the wooden bench opposite him.

'You've found a nice private fishing spot here, Dawie.'

Without any further small talk, she came straight to the point.

'Who's this person you think killed Rudy Sutton and could also be my brother's killer?'

Dawie put down the fishing reel and made eye contact with her.

'His name's Hansie Jost. He went to school with me and he had a foul temper. There were several punch-ups between him and Rudy Sutton. He was *lucky* – his mother gave him an alibi for the night of Sutton's murder. It's a pity *my* folks weren't home to give me one.

'What does Hansie look like?' she queried.

'Brown hair... a little taller than me, but narrower across the shoulders.'

'That description could be anyone.'

She laughed.

'What did he *sound* like?'

He looked puzzled.

'Like a guy, what do you *mean* – what did he *sound* like?'

'Well, for instance, did Hansie have a deep voice or a squeaky voice?'

'I wouldn't say it was deep. He had a bit of a lisp... couldn't say his r's and said yubbish instead of rubbish.'

'Thanks, Dawie, but it doesn't sound like the guy I heard. Where does he live?'

'I've just found out he was killed in an accident three years ago. That's what reminded me of him and I thought I would mention it to Mr Barron.'

'I guess if he's dead, we'll never know. Maybe if I saw a *photograph* of him, it might help?'

She referred to his earlier comment.

'Where were your parents that they couldn't give you an alibi?'

'They were away for the weekend and I was home alone.'

He looked down and started to wrap line around the fishing reel again. She heard footsteps. Someone was approaching the table from behind. Kathy turned to find Robert Erasmus standing a few metres behind her. He was wearing long trousers, a long-sleeved white shirt and a striped tie. Dawie looked as surprised as she did.

'Hello, Robby, you're very early. I thought you were joining me later this afternoon. Have you met Mrs Barron?'

'It's nice to meet you, Mrs Barron.'

He put out his hand. She pretended not to notice and turned to face Dawie.

'*What's he doing here?*' she asked herself, feeling annoyed.

Erasmus moved to the end of the bench, preventing her from leaving unless she turned in a tight space or slid across the rough bench to go the other way.

'Hello, eh.'

She couldn't bring herself to say his name but forced a smile and made brief eye contact.

'I've got to go. My dog has run off and I need to look for her.'

She indicated she wanted to leave, but he deliberately blocked her way.

'Don't leave on my account, Mrs Barron. I'm not staying long. I've just come to tell Dawie that I won't be joining him this afternoon because something has come up.' he smiled charmingly.

Dawie possibly noticed Kathy's body language.

'Have you met Robby before, Mrs Barron?'

'No, Dawie… but I know who he is.'

Her mind was racing. *Rick was right; they're all friends and I should have been more careful… all of them… Jean, Jolanda, Robby and Dawie.* She turned in the tight space between the table and bench, catching her calf on a wooden splinter.

'Ouch.'

She pulled a sliver of wood from her flesh, and wiped away the trickle of blood with a tissue. She was flustered, and in a hurry to get away.

Dawie spoke to Erasmus.

'Mrs Barron's brother was murdered the same night as Rudy Sutton… she saw his killer and thinks I'm innocent. This other man might have been responsible for both murders.'

Kathy caught the flicker in Erasmus's eyes, before he gave a smug grin.

'Who do *you* believe committed both crimes, Mrs Barron?'

She realised he was toying with her.

'Well, *Dawie* thinks it's someone called, Hansie Jost.'

His gaze intensified.

'I asked who *you* think killed them?'

She felt her cheeks flush.

'Please move out of my way, I need to look for my dog.'

'Of course, but first tell me who *you* think killed your brother?'

She huffed, turned her back on him and cautiously slid her way along the bench. After she was out on the other side, she walked purposely towards the utility.

'Honey!' she gave a pathetic whistle. 'Honey, come, here.'

Much to her relief, the puppy bounded into view, only to veer past her when she saw the two men. Erasmus caught her collar.

'Let her go, please.' Kathy snapped in an acid tone.

'You come and get her. I'm *holding* her for *you,*' he countered.

Reluctantly she made her way towards him.

'Thank you.'

She gripped Honey's collar and dragged the overgrown puppy back towards the utility. When she tried to open the door, it was locked. Her face reddened, and she fumbled through her shorts pocket. Honey continued wriggling and knocked her off balance. She gritted her teeth, found the key, shoved it into the lock and then looked guardedly up at Erasmus; His hands were in his pockets and self-confidence oozed from his pretentious smiling face. *Why should he get away with it?* Her emotions boiled over.

Enraged, she stepped away from the utility and faced him.

'It was *you* I saw. You're the *bastard* who killed my brother.'

She had *dreamed* of having the courage to say these words to his face and now she *had* said them. For a few seconds, she *felt* triumphant.

'You're wrong, Mrs Barron,' Dawie responded, 'I've known Robby most of my life. He wouldn't kill anyone.

Her anger overruled her reasoning. *I'm sick of people telling me how wonderful he is.* 'You don't know him, Dawie... decent men don't have affairs with teenage girls behind their wife's back. Ask Robby about *Jolanda!*' The words were out, before she stopped to think.

Dawie swung to face Erasmus.

'Not *Jolanda*! Robby. Tell me, you wouldn't *stoop that* low.'

Erasmus backed away.

'She's lying, Dawie. She's a liar.'

Dawie was white faced.

'I've always stood by you, Robby, but if you've laid a finger on that girl, I'll *kill* you with my bare hands.'

'Don't listen to her, Dawie. She's a bitch.'

Kathy's heart was racing.

'Why would I lie?'

'Yes, Robby... why *would* she lie? You're a filthy bastard; that girl could be your own daughter.'

As he circled the table. Erasmus backed away.

'That's bullshit. How could I be Jolanda's father? Jean's crazy about me. I wouldn't have had to *rape* her.'

Dawie stopped circling and appeared to be giving this comment some thought. He sat back down on the bench. They were now speaking in Afrikaans, but Kathy knew enough to get the gist of what they were saying.

'Hey, Dawie, let's *not* forget who *helped* you with Rudy Sutton,' Erasmus was on the defensive.

'Yeah, *right*. If I'd gone to the police like I *wanted a*nd told them it was self-defence, I wouldn't have done eighteen years,' he scowled. 'Anyway, I've done my time, so let's not bring that up. I've been thinking about that piece of junk you called a jeep. It could have overheated on the way back to Port Alfred that night... you could have been involved in both murders.'

'Don't talk shit Dawie,' Erasmus curled his lips.

'You may be my friend, Robby... but *beware if* I find you've been having sex with Jolanda,' He rose to his feet.

Robby smiled sardonically and Dawie took a swing at him. Erasmus saw it coming and ducked.

'Not a good move, Dawie.' Erasmus was the taller of the two; his long reach connected with Dawie's jaw sending him staggering backwards over Honey. He fell striking his head on the corner of the table.

Honey barked frantically.

'Shut that dog up,' Erasmus muttered.

Kathy stood mesmerised staring at Dawie as he lay in the shadow of the table, a trickle of blood seeping from his skull. She was reliving the nightmare of her brother's murder all over again. *I must get away from this monster,* her mind told her, but her feet remained glued to the ground. Erasmus had almost reached her before she came to her senses. She turned and frantically tried to open the door to the utility. Erasmus slammed it shut and pinned her against it. He twisted her arm up between her shoulder blades.

'Get away from me – let me go!' she screamed and kicked at him.

'Bitch!' he spat into her hair.

Kathy used all her strength to fight him, but he was too strong for her. He marched her towards the bench past Dawie who groaned and rubbed his head.

'What are you going to *do, Mr Erasmus*... kill *me* too?' she taunted him in defiance.

'Wait and see, *Mrs Barron.*'

He was amusing himself at her expense.

She kicked at his shins and continued to struggle. He forced her arm higher until she cried out in pain.

'Not so clever now, are you, *Mrs Barron*? The police visited me and said some woman had identified me as having killed her brother at a cottage in Kleinemonde. I've never killed anyone. You're going to stop telling lies about me. Or else.'

'You're the liar... let me go!'

A wave of panic tore through her. He continued to push her towards the tree line at the base of a steep hill. She was out of her depth. *He's going to kill me. I have to keep screaming.*

'Dawie, help me, he's going to kill me!'

Her arm hurt; she was no longer struggling.

'Let me go. You're hurting me. I won't tell anyone about you and Jolanda.'

She again attempted to pull free, but he tightened his grip, forcing her to walk on tiptoe in front of him.

'Pity you didn't mind your business a long time ago, Mrs Barron,' he whispered into her ear while continuing to push her deeper into the wooded area. 'I'm going to teach you a lesson… you've become a real nuisance.'

She wouldn't give him the pleasure of knowing how terrified she was.

She bravely shouted back at him, 'The police will *know* you're responsible if anything happens to me.'

He sniggered, keeping his voice low.

'I'm not even here. I walked down the hill from my business and no one knows I left the office. My staff will swear I was at my desk the whole time – I have the perfect alibi. It's Dawie Grobler you came to meet – remember? The police will accuse Dawie; they'll think you're his latest victim.'

Her fear lifted a notch and she was furious with herself for allowing this to happen. He was even more dangerous than she had imagined.

'Help me, Dawie! He's going to kill me and blame it on you.' she screamed.

Erasmus placed his hand over her mouth to keep her quiet, then frog-marched her to the base of the hill.

I mustn't give up. I must think clearly. She slumped her body becoming a dead weight to slow their progress.

Honey barked, rushing back and forth in front of them. *Good dog, Honey, keep barking, I need time to think.* She recalled the defence classes she'd taken during the Rhodesian bush war. *Keffas Mudzuri had chanted as he stamped his feet. "Remember these words, ladies. The element of **surprise is the key.** Knees, elbows and teeth are your weapons. Move from the feet. Find your inner core strength and strike when your attacker least expects it."*

'Shut up, dog!' Erasmus's boot missed its target and he stumbled.

Kathy planted her feet firmly, dragged in a deep breath and rammed her elbow into his ribs.

'Oomph.' the blow took his breath away and he loosened his grip over her mouth.

She sunk her teeth into his finger, biting to the bone and locking her jaw.

He flung her from him.

'You, bitch!' he gasped.

She was free at last, zigzagging through the trees, spitting flesh and blood as she screamed.

'Help me, Dawie, *help* me, Dawie… he's going to blame *you.*'

Erasmus was enraged. He tripped, regained his stride and started to gain on her. She glimpsed the water through the trees. Dawie was no longer lying next to the table and she heard a vehicle.

'Help me – help!' she continued screaming.

Surely someone would hear her. Just when she thought she was free, a hand muffled her screams. The taste of his blood was disgusting.

He wrenched her arm back up between her shoulder blades. She was semi-conscious as he dragged her deadweight further into the trees. He dropped her to the ground and tightened his hands around her throat.

Chapter 21

Her mind was hazy, her throat sore and dry and a shooting pain travelled through her shoulder.

'Go away, Honey.' she groaned as a rough tongue licked her face.

'Get that dog away from her.'

She recognised the voice. It was Captain Botha.

'It's okay, she belongs to me, Captain.'

She coughed and then flinched; the pain in her shoulder was excruciating.

'Don't move, Mrs Barron, the ambulance is on its way.'

He crouched beside her.

'You're safe now, my dear.'

He reached for a damp cloth, wiped her brow and then her face.

Honey barked furiously and he shouted, 'Someone put a *lead* on that dog.'

He then turned his attention back to her.

'I'm leaving you with Constable Heinz, Mrs Barron. Don't try to talk now. I'll see you at the hospital.'

'What's happening?' she whispered, but he had already gone.

'It's Constable Heinz here, Mrs Barron, rest your voice. We received a call from your stepfather who was worried about you.'

She squinted at him through pain-filled eyes and attempted a weak smile. Her immediate thoughts were for her children.

'How long have I been here? Has anyone collected my children from nursery school?'

'I'll check that for you, Mrs Barron.'

Honey barked frantically at the strange men carrying a stretcher towards to her mistress.

Two ambulance attendants lifted her onto the stretcher. She screamed in agony as one of them wrenched her torn shoulder. She almost passed out with the pain, sobbed and vomited into the dirt. She instinctively tried to protect her injury with her good hand.

'Don't touch my shoulder,' she gasped through clenched teeth, 'it feels like it's torn from the socket.'

The clumsy attendant appeared indifferent to the pain his incompetence had caused.

'Stop talking, miss. I'm sorry it's uncomfortable, but we need to get you to hospital as soon as possible.'

When Kathy woke up, she was in a private room, her shoulder bound and arm in a sling. The pain was under control, but her throat was sensitive each time she swallowed. She gazed at the dark green curtains tied back to allow the light in through small square window-panes.

'Aah, you're awake, Mrs Barron,' Nurse Venter's voice boomed as she crossed the room. 'You've had several visitors asking after you. I'll let Doctor Pistorius know you're awake.'

'What's the time, nurse?' she whispered.

'*No, no!* You mustn't *speak*, Mrs Barron.'

She shook a warning finger.

'Rest your voice. I'll give you a pen and paper for when you want to tell us something.'

Kathy grimaced and tried to push herself up using her good arm. Nurse Venter rushed to place a pillow behind her.

'Just ask if you need help.'

I thought I wasn't allowed to talk. As if she had read Kathy's mind, the nurse placed the pad and pencil on the pedestal beside her bed.

'Write down anything you want, Mrs Barron; we'll do our best to help you.'

Kathy balanced the writing pad on her lap and scrawled awkwardly with her left hand. *Has anyone collected my children from nursery school?*

Charlotte suddenly appeared, with a frown on her beautiful face and picked up the notebook.

'Your mother collected the children from nursery school, Kath.'

She pulled a chair up and hugged her friend.

'Thank, *God,* you're okay. I've been so worried about you, what *happened*?'

Charlotte didn't give Kathy time to write her answer.

'I've been hovering around outside your room, waiting for you to regain consciousness. The ambulance guy tells me they stretchered you in from a wooded area near the dam. What *on earth* were you doing *there?*'

Long story. Kathy wrote.

'I'm so angry with whoever did this to you,' she raged. 'I know you can't talk just yet, but when you *can*, I *want* to know *everything...* the police want to talk to you too.'

Charlotte was speaking too quickly now. This was something she did when trying to hide her feelings.

'It was Tim who phoned the police...why would you meet an *ex-con*, convicted of *murder*, in a remote area like that dam? Are you *crazy?*'

There was no stopping her.

'The ambulance guy told me that the park rangers were trying to catch Honey. He said she was leading them all on a *merry dance*,' she giggled and even Kathy smiled.

Kathy wrote. *Your ambo man nearly ripped my arm off. How bad is my shoulder?*

'I'm sorry, Kath, about his clumsiness, we have new trainees. I'll find out who he was and book him in for the next ambulance assistant training course.

Charlotte lay with her head on the pillow next to Kathy and hugged her.

'I love you, Kath; I don't know what I would do if I lost you. Don't worry about your shoulder. Burt was the surgeon who fixed you up. He'll come and see you later, but from the little he told me, you should make a full recovery... Kathy, you must tell me what happened as soon as you can.'

Long story – not allowed to talk. Kathy wrote. She then indicated she wanted to lie down flat to sleep.

Charlotte removed the pillows, made her comfortable and then left the room. As she lay there Kathy's thoughts drifted to something Charlotte had said earlier. *They think ex-con Dawie attacked me. If I had died, I wonder if Erasmus would have got away with murder again. I must tell someone the truth.*

The next time she woke, Rick and her mother greeted her with smiling faces. They packed pillows behind her to prop her up. She caught Ricks hand and shook it urgently, then hurriedly wrote. *Erasmus it was Erasmus who attacked me – Not Dawie.*

Rick read her note. 'Erasmus?' he looked puzzled. She nodded. 'Not Dawie? But it was Dawie you went to meet at the dam?'

Writing took too long, so she spoke in a whisper. 'Erasmus arrived unexpectedly – he attacked me.' She tore the sheet from the pad and insisted that Rick took it. 'I don't think the police know that, Kath.' His jaw bone tightened as he clenched his teeth. 'What a bastard. I'll let Captain Botha know.'

She felt a sense of relief now she had told someone.

'You're not meant to speak,' her mother reminded her. 'How are you feeling?'

Not too bad - how are my babies, she wrote.

Frances spoke at length about the children. It was comforting to have a loving family to take care of the children while she convalesced.

Her pen got busy again. *How did your interview go Rick?*

'I attended two of the interviews and postponed the third when I received a message about you being attacked.'

He looked at her searchingly.

'I know you can't talk, lovey…but I want to know everything that happened. Why was Erasmus there? did Dawie get you there under false pretence?'

Kathy shook her head.

'I'm so relieved you're okay, I'm going to sit in when Captain Botha speaks to you tomorrow.'

I will tell you everything, writing with her left hand was barely legible. *I need to sleep – see you tomorrow.*

Frances removed the pillows and hugged her gently.

'Don't worry about the children, sweetie. *We'll* take care of them. Tim made them spaghetti Bolognese for supper and Ben even asked for *more please,* but of course, they miss you… we're all looking forward to you coming home.'

Doctor Burt Rossouw visited Kathy later that night.

'Fortunately, there shouldn't be any permanent damage. It's a torn shoulder and will need plenty of rest., The *real* work will start when you visit physiotherapy. Your attacker tried to strangle you, possibly using his hands. I'm guessing he was disturbed, because the force didn't cause enough damage to block your airway long enough to kill you.'

He leant over her to check the sling was still doing its job and holding her arm in place.

'I'm told that Captain Botha gave you mouth to mouth resuscitation to get you breathing properly again. I expect you to make a full recovery, Kathy,' He held her gaze,

'You possibly noticed that your friend Charlotte is a nervous wreck. She's known as the *unflappable doctor* by the emergency staff…that's until *you* were admitted. She was so distraught… almost in a panic. None of the staff have ever seen her like that. She stayed by your side until you were in surgery, then she paced up and down outside the theatre and demanded a *full* debrief the *minute* you were wheeled out,' he smiled warmly. 'She considers you her sister and loves you dearly, Kathy.'

Kathy answered his smile with her own.

'I also consider her as my sister and I love her too.'

She swallowed, her voice sounded dry and croaky.

'Charlotte reacted like that because Zach died in the Salisbury emergency room. She couldn't save him and she's never got over it. He was her first love and I'm sure she will tell you about him one day. Thanks for everything, Burt.'

The following morning when Captain Botha visited Kathy, she was permitted to speak for ten minutes only and after that she would have to *write* her answers. Rick insisted on sitting in on the interview.

'Mrs Barron, can you tell me who attacked you?'

The captain's eyes betrayed a degree of sympathy.

'I was attacked by Robert Erasmus.'

Kathy stretched her neck to relieve the dull ache in her shoulder.

'Mrs Barron alleges it was Robert Erasmus who attacked her,' The captain recorded.

She stiffened. *Here we go again. A lowly woman accusing an important businessman.*

'It *was* Robert Erasmus. I am not *"alleging"*.'

She didn't hide her annoyance.

'Captain Botha, I'm choosing my words carefully, because I can only talk for ten minutes.'

She coughed, took a deep breath and then dropped her voice.

'If I *say* it was Robert Erasmus who attacked me, it *was* Robert Erasmus. I'm not *"alleging"*. I'm *one hundred percent* sure it was him.'

'I'm sorry, Mrs Barron. I wasn't questioning your answer. I was using a legal term. I have the park ranger's statements and they say they found two men fighting when they arrived at the crime scene. I was mentally comparing your answer with theirs.'

His explanation softened her prickly attitude. She remembered how he had wiped her face with a damp cloth and spoken kindly when she regained consciousness.

'I'm sorry, too, Captain Botha. I thought you might have assumed it was Dawie Grobler who attacked me, but it was *Erasmus!* Dawie was knocked out after Erasmus punched him. He fell back and hit his head on the table and he was coming around when we moved past him. Do you want me to make a statement or answer questions?'

'I'd like to ask you a few questions if you feel up to it. I'll take a full statement after you're back home and feeling better.'

She gave a thumbs up.

'Can you tell me why you were at the dam?'

She explained briefly, 'I was meeting Dawie Grobler. He claimed to know who was responsible for both my brother and the Sutton murder. I don't believe it was a *trap* or that he *enticed* me there under *false* pretences. It was only when *Robert Erasmus* arrived unexpectedly that everything started to go wrong.'

She had answered most of his questions when Nurse Venter returned to hand Kathy the pen and paper.

'That's enough talking for today, young lady. Write your answers from now on.'

Captain Botha could see she looked tired.

'Thank you, Mrs Barron, I've got enough information for now; let me know when you're back home and we'll arrange for you to visit the police station and give a full statement.'

He turned at the door.

'Just one more question; do you know *why* Robert Erasmus and Dawie Grobler were brawling?'

She wrote, *no, I don't*, and then held up the pad for him to see. He raised his brows and held her gaze for a second.

'Are you quite sure Mrs Baron?'

She nodded. She knew Jolanda was possibly the reason they had argued, but she didn't want to mention her name. Her intention was to keep the young girls name out of this sordid mess.

Kathy caught Rick's hand to stop him leaving and wrote, *Give my love to the children.*

He kissed her and whispered, 'I love you, my darling,' then he left the room.

When Kathy returned home the following day, she sat in her mother's wicker chair on their veranda. One by one, she cuddled her children.

'Come here, Becky, and give Mummy a hug,' she called.

Her little girl shook her head.

'I don't want to hurt you, Mummy.'

Kathy waved her good arm in the air.

'Look, darling. I can use this arm.'

Becky then climbed cautiously onto the chair and snuggled up to her.

'Like mother, like daughter,' Frances commented, making her way up the steps. 'One of *my* happiest memories is cuddling with *you* in that same wicker chair, Kathy.'

Over a cup of tea, Kathy explained to Rick, her mother and Tim how Erasmus had attacked her. She took this opportunity to thank Tim for contacting the police.

'If Captain Botha hadn't arrived when he did, I doubt I would be sitting here with you today, Pops.'

She didn't like to call him dad, but he seemed happy with being called pops. The children also now called him pops, instead of Uncle Tim.

'Charlotte tells me that the park rangers were also at the picnic site when the ambulance got there to collect me. I'd like to know what Dawie and Erasmus have said in their statements before I give mine. When you visit Captain Botha, tomorrow, Rick, could you find out as much as possible for me please?'

'I'll do my best, lovey. I want to know what happened after the captain found you unconscious. None of us knows those details yet.'

Kathy was having regrets about breaking her promise and telling Dawie about Erasmus and Jolanda's affair. If neither Dawie nor Erasmus mentioned Jolanda's name, she would do the same.

She continued telling Rick the little she remembered after regaining consciousness.

'Burt tells me that captain Botha gave me mouth to mouth resuscitation to get me breathing properly again.'

'That's interesting, so he may *also* have saved your life?'

'It appears *several* people played a part in saving my life. Perhaps you can ask Captain Botha about that too – and please thank him for his kindness.'

When Rick entered Captain Botha's office, he shook Rick's hand and asked after Kathy, before they got down to business.

'Fortunately, your wife had given detailed directions to your father-in-law, so we were able to drive directly to the picnic site at the dam. As we approached, a vehicle passed us going in the opposite direction. Constable Heinz took down its registration number and later we discovered the car belonged to Dawie Grobler's mother.'

Rick continued jotting down each point as the captain spoke.

'We noticed your father-in-law's utility was parked under a tree and joined the park rangers trying to catch the dog. She led us straight to Mrs Barron, who was lying on the ground in a thicket of trees. I gave your wife mouth-to-mouth resuscitation and she came around fairly quickly. Constable Heinz radioed for an ambulance and I left your wife in his care while I spoke to the park rangers.'

The captain pinched his chin. 'The rangers were there to catch a dog, The dam is a wildlife sanctuary, so dogs are not permitted. They heard raised voices coming from the foot of the hill and pulled apart two men who were having a fistfight. The rangers recognised Erasmus, he told them the dog wasn't his, then walked up the hill. Grobler was bleeding from a head wound and appeared disorientated and unsteady on his feet. The rangers helped him to a bench.'

Botha drummed his fingers on the chair armrests.

'They asked Grobler to wait while they caught the dog. When they returned, he had packed up his fishing tackle and driven off.'

Rick looked appalled. 'So, the rangers didn't even know Kathy was lying there injured?'

'No!'

The captain looked equally concerned.

'They would have eventually realised the dog belonged to whoever had driven the utility there, but it might have been too late by then.'

Rick was still piecing the story together.

'I see; I believe that Erasmus owns a furniture business on top of a ridge overlooking the dam?'

'That's right; there's a path leading from his business down the hill to the picnic site where your wife was attacked.'

'Was it thanks to *Tim* phoning, that you went to the dam and found Kathy?'

'That's right; we arrived not long after the rangers and it was that silly dog that took us to your wife.'

'And when did you visit Erasmus, Captain Botha?'

'When the ranger mentioned that he recognised one of the men was Robert Erasmus, I immediately thought about your wife's accusations against this man, so we visited him at his business.'

Captain Botha appeared mildly amused.

'The receptionist told us that Robert Erasmus was busy and could not see us, but we insisted. He kept us waiting. When he appeared, he had done quite a good job of tidying himself up, but he couldn't hide his split lip or the bruising on his left cheek. The receptionist supported his story, saying he hadn't left the premises all day. We reminded her of the penalty for giving false information and that unsettled her. She soon changed her story and told us about a back door to the business premises leading down to the dam. She admitted he could have left the building without her knowledge and agreed that the injuries to his face were not there when he arrived at work that morning.'

Captain Botha cleared his throat before he continued.

'Erasmus was wearing a blazer over his shirt. He must have washed the blood of his shirt collar – it was wet, but he'd missed a splatter of blood on the back of his collar. I asked what had happened to his freshly bandaged finger – he claimed to have cut it with a Swiss army knife when he was peeling an orange.'

The captain folded his arms with a satisfied look.

'When we told him that the rangers had identified him as being at the dam a few hours earlier, he changed his story. He claimed to be protecting an old school friend. Dawie Grobler had attacked him, but as he had recently been released from prison, he didn't want to get him into trouble.'

Rick underlined something in his notes.

'He appears pretty flexible with the truth. As soon as you disprove *one* fantasy, he creates *another*.'

'He's very persuasive, Mr Barron. He claimed to have no idea why Dawie Grobler attacked him, but insinuated Grobler might have been trying to hide something.'

'What did you tell him about Kathy?'

'Nothing. He claimed he didn't reach the picnic site, Grobler attacked him at the bottom of the hill. As far as he was concerned, there was no one else there. At that time, I wasn't sure who had attacked Mrs Barron, so thought it safer not to mention that she was in the hospital.'

'Thank you for putting her safety first, Captain. I guess we have no idea what a desperate man might do. When did you visit Grobler?'

'Later the same day. After we had established the other man was Grobler, we visited his home.'

There was a knock on the door; it was Mrs Brits.

'Would you and Mr Barron like a cup of tea? she asked.

The captain look up. 'Thank you, Mrs Brits.

'Yes, please milk and two sugars,' Rick asked politely.

'Right, I'll bring it through.'

Once she had left the room Captain Botha continued, 'Dawie Grobler's grandparents answered the door. His mother had taken him to the hospital; he'd been admitted for the night because of his concussion.

When I visited him, he appeared eager to tell his side of the story, up to and including how Erasmus punched him and he hit his head on the table. He claims that when he came to his senses, he heard Mrs Barron's screams. He found Erasmus kneeling next to her and pulled him off – the two of them started fighting and the park rangers pulled them apart. They helped him to the bench, he felt sick, so he packed his fishing gear and drove home.'

Mrs Brits interrupted and placed their cups of tea on the desk.

Captain Botha continued, 'When I mentioned Mrs Barron, he became anxious and blurted out, "I didn't kill her... it was Erasmus. I promise, I didn't lay a finger on her... I tried to save her."'

The captain adopted a softer tone.

'When I told him she was alive, he looked relieved. *His* statement was more factual and confirmed what Mrs Barron later told us. After we have recorded your wife's official statement, I'll be able to tell you more.'

Later that day, Rick repeated what Captain Botha had told him. Kathy was interested in what he *hadn't* said. There had been no mention of Jolanda. Since Dawie *hadn't* told the police about the love affair, she would do the same.

A few days later Rick and Frances accompanied Kathy to the police station to give her statement. After she had finished, she told Captain Botha she wanted to say something off the record.

'If it's not in your statement, we may not be able to present it in court,' he warned.

'I want to tell you something in confidence,' Kathy insisted.

Frances tried to persuade her. 'I think you should include it in your statement, sweetie.'

'No. What I have to say won't affect this case in any way. It's my word against theirs – two against one. They won't admit to what I'm about to tell you!'

Captain Botha gestured for her to go ahead.

'I should have listened to my husband; *he* was right... Dawie Grobler *did* kill Rudy Sutton, but it was self-defence and *not,* first-degree murder. *He* wanted to go to the police, but Erasmus talked him into setting fire to the vehicle to cover-up the crime.'

Captain Botha cut in.

'I read up on the Sutton case. The homicide squad suspected there was a second person involved.'

Kathy made her point clear. 'None of this makes *any* difference to me, except that it disproves Erasmus's alibi for the night of my brother's murder – he couldn't have helped Dawie *and* been in Port Alfred at the same time.'

She lifted her head. 'Erasmus owned a jeep, which according to Dawie, was a piece of junk. My *new* theory is that, on the way back to Port Alfred, after helping Dawie set fire to Sutton's vehicle, his jeep overheated and he turned off onto the side road to Travellers Joy. He parked the vehicle and walked to the cottage to get water from the kitchen. Trevor disturbed him and he panicked. His adrenaline levels were still high after covering up the previous crime and when he realised Trevor could disprove his alibi, he felt threatened and killed him. That's how Erasmus got away with *murder*.'

Her gaze remained fixed on the captain.

'Mrs Barron, your theory could be right, but without evidence, it would be difficult to prove.'

She knew the captain was being realistic.

'He may have got away with my brother's murder. The evidence is flimsy, a partial finger-print and the vague chance that Dawie Grobler will come clean and admit to Erasmus's involvement in the Sutton murder,' Kathy remained calm. 'But his attack on me will discredit his reputation. I'm relying on you, Captain Botha, to make *sure* the charges against Erasmus *stick* this time.'

Chapter 22

It had been a week since she was attacked at Stein dam and Kathy still looked pale. She wore no make-up and dark rings under her eyes told of restless nights spent sitting upright in the rocker in Wendy's room. Rick had taken the children to nursery school that morning and she was finding the day tedious; there was little she could do around the house, with one arm in a sling.

When she answered the phone, she didn't recognise the voice on the other end.

'Hello, Mrs Barron, my name is Kenny Theron. I'm a reporter with the East London News. We're a weekly independent publication. I would like to interview you about the incident last week at Stein Dam?'

He stopped and started when he spoke, as if he had rehearsed his words.

Kathy gave his request some thought. She had seen only one short article about her attack tucked away on the fifth page of the Daily Chronicle. Perhaps, it was time the locals knew the kind of man Robert Erasmus *really* was.

'I'd be happy to give you an interview, Kenny. I must warn you, there will be certain conditions. We can discuss them when you get here.'

She gave him her address and within the hour he was sitting opposite her on the veranda. Honey lay at Kathy's feet, eyeing the stranger with distrust.

'I want to tell you a little about the East London News, Mrs Barron. We're a small weekly newspaper circulated mid-week. We distribute to more than three thousand households within the East London Metro area.' He continued telling her about their policies and belief system and how they differed from other news outlets.

Again, she thought his words sounded rehearsed, but she gave him time to finish.

'I'll tell you everything that happened Kenny, but I want to see the article and sign off on it before it's printed.'

This was one of Kathy's conditions. Kenny agreed and she proceeded to tell him everything that had happened during the attack. The more she told him the more confident she became.

'This is my story; not a *statement* and I intend to tell you everything that happened to me without holding back.'

When she had finished, he asked a few questions and then put down his pen.

Over a cup of tea, Kathy gave a little more background on how she knew Erasmus and Grobler.

'I saw Erasmus in a café when I was on honeymoon here in East London, five and a half years ago. I identified him as the man I saw kill my brother. I was six years old when the murder happened and only remembered fifteen years later. That's one of the reasons the police claimed I'd identified the wrong man. I had no proof or evidence, so it was just my word against his.'

Kenny seemed genuinely interested, so she continued,

'I met Dawie Grobler by chance. I had this theory that the Sutton crime and my brother's murder were connected.'

She suddenly sensed something was wrong. Kenny was clenching and unclenching his fists.

'Is something wrong, Kenny?'

'I probably should have told you *this* when I made my introduction, Mrs Barron.'

He stilled his hands.

'I was at school with Erasmus and Grobler. I know them both well.'

Kathy was furious. *There's a nest of them… liars and cheats and they're in cahoots with each other.*

'Yes, you *should* have told me, Kenny! Why *didn't* you tell me you were friends?'

'Not *friends,* Mrs Barron.'

His eyes blazed.

'Quite the opposite in fact… I despised Erasmus. I felt sorry for Dawie, though. He was a smart kid who befriended Erasmus in return for protection from school bullies. Erasmus *exploited* that friendship and made Dawie do all his dirty work.'

'How long have they been friends?'

'Right back to junior school. Erasmus is a narcissist. He was captain of the rugby team, and he's charming in every way – *if* you're *wealthy* or well *connected*. He's done very well for himself by moving in the *right* circles.'

His mouth turned down with disgust.

'But, to ordinary people like me, he's just a calculating *bully!*'

A thought occurred to Kathy.

'Is this why you want to publish my story?'

'This is my job, Mrs Barron. I work for an honest newspaper – we write only the facts given to us. The story of you being attacked by Robert Erasmus will be our lead story in this week's publication. However, I must be honest – I have my *own* reasons for disliking Erasmus.'

Kathy didn't ask him to elaborate, but she liked the man and made a decision then and there.

'I'm going to *trust* you, Kenny. Phone me and read what you've written over the phone. If I like it, you can go ahead and publish my story. I don't need to sign off on a proof. Just remember the *conditions* I've requested.'

Once Kenny left, she felt emotionally drained and wondered if she had done the right thing in being so open and honest with a complete stranger. Perhaps, she should have contacted Rick to check on the legal implications or asked her mother to join them. *No. I did the right thing. I'm tired of being lectured to and told what I can and can't say. The police found my statement unreliable. Perhaps the public will be more supportive.*

She told Rick that night what she had done and he wasn't pleased.

'I wish you'd phoned me, Kath. I would have arranged time off work to join you. I hope you kept to the facts; don't forget you've just suffered a traumatic experience and you're still upset.'

'I'm an adult, Rick, and I have the right to make my own decisions.'

She wasn't sorry she had spoken to Kenny on her own.

'Rick, I want people to know what kind of man Robert Erasmus really is. It turns out that Kenny was at school with him. He detested the man – called him a narcissist. Anyway, the publication comes out the day after tomorrow. I'll contact Kenny and ask him to fax you a copy of what he intends to print. You can check for legal ramifications and ask him to make changes. We'll wait and see what happens after the publication has been distributed.'

At Captain Botha's request, Rick arranged to see him the following day and he collected Kathy from Flame Lily Villa during his lunch break.

'How are you doing, Mrs Barron?' he inquired.

'Better every day, thank you, Captain.'

She saw little point in complaining.

'I need to clarify a few facts if you're up to it?'

'Certainly, Captain Botha.' Kathy agreed.

'I now have Robert Erasmus's revised statement. His lawyer is claiming he's still grieving the death of his wife, and he snapped when you accused him of killing your brother but he swears he didn't touch you.'

Kathy was furious. *He's not getting away with it this time.*

'Lies all lies. So,' She clenched her fists. 'Tell me, Captain, who do you believe?'

'Mrs Barron, I'm not taking anyone's side. I'm just recording the facts and repeating what Erasmus said.'

'He's right. I *did* accuse him of killing my brother. Maybe he *is* grieving the death of his wife. Who cares? Either way, it doesn't give him the right to attack an innocent woman,' She heaved a sigh. 'By now, you must know that he's an accomplished liar who uses his good looks and charm to manipulate and deceive. My statement is accurate. Erasmus was responsible for all my injuries.'

Her eyes flashed dangerously.

'What did Dawie tell you about my attack?'

Rick caught her hand.

'Calm down, Lovey… don't get uppity with Captain Botha, he's just doing his job.'

Captain Botha folded his arms.

'Dawie Grobler claims what I told you before, that Erasmus punched him and he fell back hitting his head on the corner of the picnic table. He was knocked out and when he regained consciousness, he heard your screams. He got to his feet and found Erasmus bending over you. He pulled him away from you and they started fighting. The Park rangers pulled them apart. Does that sound right, Mrs Barron?'

'I don't know about Dawie pulling Erasmus away from me or the two men fighting. The last thing I remember is Robert Erasmus placing his hands around my throat.'

'Thank you, Mrs Barron. That is all I needed to ask you. Mr Erasmus still claims it was Dawie Grobler who attacked you.'

'What a gutless jerk! He's willing to throw his friend under the bus to save himself… if I hadn't survived, he might have got away with It. I bit his finger to the bone. Surely, you have identified his blood as part of the evidence. His blood was all over me.'

'Yes, there was blood on your face. I wiped it off with my wet handkerchief\ and we're waiting on the pathology results now. We've also got the doctor's statement that the injury to Erasmus's finger could be a human bite.' There's one piece of the puzzle that's missing. Do you know why Erasmus and Grobler were fighting, Mrs Barron? I've questioned them both and neither has given me an honest answer.'

'Maybe they were fighting over me,' Kathy chuckled over her own joke.

He shook his head.

'Mrs Barron, we both know that isn't true. I was hoping *you* would tell me the truth.'

'Huh. After all the lectures I've received about the police not accepting hearsay, you're asking for my unverified *opinion?* Sorry, Captain, I can't help you, I don't know what those two were thinking.

His expression suggested he didn't believe her. She guessed he was referring to something she had said several months earlier about Erasmus having an affair with a young girl. He had been furious with her at the time, saying he could not listen to her scandal. Now she was glad she had not mentioned Jolanda's name and she would continue to protect the young girl.

He looked hard at her.

'There has to be another reason, Mrs Barron?'

'Sorry… I can't help you, Captain Botha.'

Rick intervened.

'Captain Botha, what have you charged these men with?'

'Erasmus has been charged with attempted murder for the attack on Mrs Barron. His attorney pleaded stress and provocation to get him out on bail. We are very unhappy that he got bail at all.'

'Has Dawie Grobler been charged?'

'No. Erasmus has not laid a charge against him and neither has Mrs Barron. Grobler claims he stopped Erasmus from strangling Mrs Barron. If that's true, then he saved her life. We have nothing to charge him with.'

Kenny phoned Kathy the following day and read the article over the phone to her. She was pleased with what he had written and asked him to fax Rick a copy. A few changes were made for legal reasons, but this did not impact the important content of Kathy's story.

She checked the post box every hour until the newspaper arrived. Kenny had done an excellent job; the article in the weekly paper was everything she had hoped. He had complied with her three conditions. The headline read: "Prominent Business Man Accused of Attempted Murder." Robert Erasmus was mentioned by name in the first sentence, and her third request, Dawie Grobler, was referred to as *David Lewis*. Kenny had included everything from the sinister words Erasmus whispered in her ear, to sinking her teeth into his finger. It was a factual damaging article that would harm Erasmus's reputation. Kenny had produced a well-written piece that would achieve her objective and warn people about this dangerous man.

The following morning, an unexpected visitor buzzed the gate. It was Jean Schmidt. Kathy invited her in and they sat on the veranda.

'I'm sorry to hear what happened to you, Kathy. I can't believe Robby would harm anyone.'

They sat in silence for a time until Kathy spoke up.

'I'm sure he was always good to *you,* Jean. He's clever and surrounds himself with powerful people or friends he finds useful. If I had any doubts about him killing my brother, *before*, I certainly don't have *any now.*'

'He's still grieving his wife's death, Kathy. One article suggests he was possibly pushed over the edge, by *your* accusations.'

'He's your friend, Jean, so you're trying to make excuses for him, but *I* know he had every intention of *killing* me and then returning to his office. He boasted about it… he said, "No one knows I'm at the dam. I walked here and my staff think I'm in my office, so I've got the perfect alibi. Remember, Dawie Grobler's already been convicted of murder. Who do you think the police will believe when they find your body?" Those were *his* words. If I'd died, and the rangers hadn't recognised Erasmus, there's a good chance Dawie Grobler would be back in prison and Robert Erasmus would have got away with *another* murder.'

'I hadn't thought of it like that. That's not like poor Robby.'

Kathy's eyes flashed with anger. She was in no mood to hear about poor Robby.

'Have you seen Robert… or *Robby* as you *call* him?'

'No, I haven't. I'm too angry. Especially now that I know he intended to let Dawie take the blame.'

Her cheeks flushed.

'Robby and I have been friends, all our lives. There have been nasty accusations against him in the past, but I've always supported him. I believe people are jealous of his success.'

'Were you at school with Robby and Dawie Grobler?'

'Yes, Robby, Dawie and I were very good friends at school. My husband, Greg, didn't like Robby, so after we were married, I saw very little of him and nothing of Dawie, because he was in prison. It was only after Greg passed away that Robby started to visit us again. He was always very good to Jolanda.'

There was an awkward silence before Kathy spoke again.

'Robert has been lucky to have friends like you and Dawie, but his luck's run out. He's been exposed for who he *really* is.'

There was another awkward silence.

'It was Dawie who asked me to visit you, Kathy. He wanted to come himself, but after reading your article yesterday, he wasn't sure if he'd be welcome.'

She avoided eye contact.

'He agrees with everything you said and appreciates that you used his English name rather than the name most people know him by.'

Kathy was a matter of fact in her response.

'I asked the newspaper reporter to call him David Lewis to protect him. I believe he's done his time and deserves a chance. I'm told he stopped Erasmus from strangling me, so I thank him for that, but he drove away without telling anyone I was lying there. If Honey hadn't shown the police where I was, I could have died. It's possibly better if he doesn't visit me. I don't think Rick would like it.'

Jean was defensive.

'He saved your *life,* Kathy. When he regained consciousness, he helped you and fought Robby off. He was badly hurt and could hardly walk. He thought you were dead, remember, and the police would blame him.'

Kathy softened a little.

'I know he took a beating and I'm grateful he saved me, but Rick is still angry that he drove away and left me there.'

'He wasn't thinking right, Kathy; all he wanted to do was get away.'

Kathy took a deep breath and tried to think clearly.

'What you say makes sense. I'm truly grateful to Dawie.'

Suddenly the truth dawned on her – *Dawie has sent Jean to see me, because he wants to know if I've said anything about Jolanda and Erasmus.*

'How is Dawie?'

'He's got a few stitches in his head and on his face, but the doctor says he should make a full recovery. He's applying for other jobs.'

Kathy was feeling tired, hoping Jean would leave soon so she could have a sleep. Before she could mention this, Jean dropped a bombshell.

'There's another reason why I came to see you, Kathy… I wanted to find out exactly what happened at the dam. Dawie and I have been friends since we were ten years old and he's asked me to marry him.'

Kathy was stunned but did her best to hide her reaction.

'I've always cared deeply for Dawie and we would have married after Jolanda was born if he hadn't been charged with murder and sent to prison.'

Now Kathy understood more. This was why Dawie had been so outraged when she mentioned Erasmus's affair with Jolanda. She had touched a raw spot.

Jean looked thoughtful.

'His going to prison was a mixed blessing, really. I then married Greg and those were the happiest nine years of my life.'

Her face lit up when she mentioned Greg's name, then she knitted her fingers and looked a little tense.

'I've always known the truth about the Sutton murder. That bastard Rudy Sutton tried to *sodomise* Dawie. He found a tyre lever under the front seat and used it to fight him off; he didn't mean to kill him… it was self-defence.'

Jean looked agitated.

'Dawie wanted to go to the police, but when he got back to his parent's house, Robby was there. It was Robby who convinced him to set fire to the car and cover his tracks.'

She stared down at her hands.

'After they left the crime scene, Erasmus drove back to Port Alfred where he was camping to make sure he had an alibi from the other campers, while Dawie drove to my parent's house. He intended to use me as *his* alibi.'

She fiddled with the chain around her neck.

'He had no idea that I'd given birth to Jolanda that night. She arrived four weeks' early and my parents stayed with me at the hospital. Dawie fell asleep on the back porch, which meant no one could give him an alibi,' she sighed. 'When he told me what had happened, I asked him to go to the police and confess, but he wouldn't because it would have implicated Robby.'

Kathy gave a half-hearted shrug.

'As I said before, Robert Erasmus was lucky to have friends like you and Dawie. I didn't know the full story until now. You protected him from involvement in the Sutton homicide, and in doing so, you unwittingly colluded to give him a false alibi for my brother's murder. It's *not* going to happen *this* time.'

She knew she sounded bitter.

'If you'd told the truth in the first place, Erasmus might have faced justice for my brother's murder.'

Jeans features stiffened.

'It all happened a long time ago, Kathy. I've told *you* the *truth. N*ow please tell *me* what happened at Stein Dam. Was Dawie involved in the assault against you?'

'No, Dawie didn't hurt me in any way, Jean. You've just confirmed that he saved my life. I think you know that deep down he's a good man or you wouldn't be considering accepting his proposal.'

Kathy didn't have the energy to go over the whole story again.

'The article in the East London News is the full story. It's all there in black and white. I don't mean to be rude, Jean, but I'm having difficulty sleeping at night, so I try to get a few hours' rest during the day before the children come home.'

She walked Jean to her car.

'I wish you and Dawie all the best. He's served his time and you *both* deserve happiness. It might be easier though if you start your new life in another town.'

'Funny you should say that, Kathy. We've already discussed that option and we're thinking of moving to Port Elizabeth.'

Kathy chose her words carefully.

'While I was searching for evidence to bring my brother's killer to justice, I discovered secrets within secrets. You told me the truth about Jolanda's father. I'll never tell anyone, but I still think you should tell her the truth. She'll be hurt and shocked when she learns that Greg was not her birth father, but it's her right to know. East London is a small town – imagine how she would feel if someone *else* told her.'

'Thanks, Kathy, I know you're right. I have to tell her sometime, but it's such a difficult decision to make.'

Jean started the car engine.

Kathy spoke through the open car window.

'Please give Dawie a message from me. Tell him, we have an agreement, to tell the *truth* and nothing but the *truth.*'

She stepped back.

'Also, tell him, there is no reason to hurt the young and innocent.' Kathy continued. 'He'll understand what I mean.'

Chapter 23

Rick was at work when the switchboard put a call through from Captain Botha.

'I'd like to see you and Mrs Barron as soon as possible; can you come and see me this afternoon?'

'I'm working late tonight, could it wait until the morning, Captain?'

'I'm afraid not. I'll be here until six this evening; can you both be here by five-thirty?'

When Rick and Kathy arrived, in his office, Captain Botha shuffled uncomfortably in his seat.

'Thank you for coming, Mr and Mrs Barron, I have something to tell you.'

He hesitated as if searching for the right words.

'The article in the East London News weekly newspaper has resulted in two complainants laying charges against Robert Erasmus.'

Kathy felt a surge of excitement.

'What charges?'

The captain glanced at the dockets on his desk.

'Both are old complaints. One complainant claims to have lodged a sexual assault charge against Robert Erasmus. She withdrew the complaint after the police officer in charge, at the time, implied it was her own fault for wearing provocative clothes and flirting with a married man.'

He sighed and shook his head.

Kathy commented bluntly.

'The poor woman, I know the feeling… are the police taking her complaint seriously this time?'

'Yes, we're looking into it. We have a copy of her original complaint and the hospital records. She's determined to take her case to court this time.'

'Who was the second complainant?' asked Rick.

'A violent assault that took place several years ago. The man concerned withdrew the charge when Erasmus produced an alibi that proved he was in Cape Town at the time the assault took place.'

Rick folded his arms.

'Do you think these old complaints will stick after all this time, Captain Botha? We must remember that it was due to the time lapse between Kathy witnessing her brother's murder and her memory returning that caused doubts about her sketch of Erasmus.'

'There was also the age factor. Mrs Barron was very young. To answer your question, yes, we are taking both these reports very seriously. We have received a third report, but it would be premature to comment before we've checked it out.'

Kathy waited for the men to finish discussing the two new cases, before she had her say.

'When my mother visited Commandant Marais in Pretoria five years ago, she was told there was no reason to *suspect* Robert Erasmus. He had no priors and was an exemplary citizen. Why weren't these charges against him known back then?'

Captain Botha held Kathy's gaze.

'These charges were recorded, then withdrawn and filed away and appear to have been forgotten. I cannot answer your question, except to say we now have the original dockets and intend to check the cases thoroughly.'

Rick glanced at Kathy.

'Let's not harp on about the past, Lovey. I'm pleased these plaintiffs have come forward. I was concerned that your article might jeopardise this case, but it appears I was wrong.'

'Sorry lovey, but I can't accept such a vague explanation. When a complainant comes forward surely, it's recorded in... er,' she waved her arm in the air, 'a criminal register thingy. All the police had to do was check for the name Erasmus. Something isn't right. I get a feeling that these documents were deliberately misfiled.'

Captain Botha eyed her. 'Mrs Barron, I can't comment on that, but we are updating our systems, Mrs Brits has a team of ladies capturing data into computers and documents are being transferred onto microfiche. Hopefully with modern technology misfiling will become something of the past.'

Kathy guessed who she had to thank. It was probably Sally Brits who found the so-called misfiled information. I must thank her.

'Thank you, Captain Botha, for keeping us informed.'

'There is one more thing, Mrs Barron.' the captain added. 'We've heard from forensics. They have compared the partial print from your brother's pendant with Mr Erasmus's print. The result is inconclusive, but they have forwarded them to the USA for further comparison. It'll be several weeks before we hear the results.'

'Who knows, this may be the breakthrough on my brothers murder that we've been waiting for,'

Kathy sighed with relief as they left the police station.

'I was afraid Captain Botha was going to give me a lecture for giving my story to the newspaper. I didn't dream for one minute that my article would bring other complainants forward. Although... I *often wondered* if he had hurt other people. For the first time in years, I feel confident that Erasmus will face justice. Even if he gets away with my brother's murder, he still has to face an attempted murder and two other charges.'

Kathy kept the children home from nursery school the next day.

'My shoulder's so much better... I want to spend time with them. The twins are so cute and before I know it, they'll be at school; my three little ones are growing up too quickly.'

Rick was working long hours and arrived home very late the following night. The children were already asleep, so he gave each of them a kiss on the forehead before joining Kathy at the dining table. Whilst they dined, Rick told her about his day in court, defending a client in a complicated criminal case. Suddenly he remembered.

'I forgot to tell you, Kath, Captain Botha phoned. He wanted to see us. I explained my current workload and arranged to see him first thing in the morning, instead.'

'I wonder what he wants?' Kathy looked puzzled. 'We seem to be visiting him nearly every day. Why couldn't he just give you the information over the phone?'

Rick shrugged.

'He said it was important and confidential... perhaps he's received another complaint?' I said we would visit him in the morning.

Captain Botha looked glum. 'I promised to keep you informed on the progress in the Erasmus case.' His voice was controlled as his hands gripped the chair armrests.

'I visited Mr Erasmus at his home yesterday afternoon to question him about a third complaint lodged against him.'

The captain looked irritated.

'He wasn't there. He's broken his bail condition and his parents claim to have no idea where he's gone. If I hadn't visited when I did, he could have been out of the country, before we even knew he was *missing*.'

Kathy's jaw dropped in disbelief.

'I don't believe it!'

'I'm sorry, Mrs Barron. We opposed bail, as you know. I assure you we're doing all we can to apprehend him. We've set up roadblocks and all airports and border crossings have been alerted. He's withdrawn a substantial amount of cash from his bank account,' he hurried on. 'We've had the details of the vehicle he's driving broadcasted and we're confident he hasn't left the country.'

Kathy exploded.

'Unbelievable! You're telling me, he's heading for the border with a suitcase full of cash. He's been planning for this. You *do* realise; he's going to bribe his way out of the country.'

She was trembling with rage.

'Please tell me, the judge took away his passport.'

The captain looked at her steadily.

'We're doing all we can, Mrs Barron. We suspect he may have a second passport, but he'll have a problem getting through the border post.'

She closed her eyes and took a deep breath. *They didn't believe me when I said Robert Erasmus had killed my brother. Get proof, they said. I nearly gave my life proving how evil this man is and now they have let him get away!*

'Innocent men *don't* run, Captain Botha. Damn it… you *had* him and you let him go.'

She flung her good arm into the air. She was on her feet pacing – Rick didn't try to stop her.

Captain Botha didn't argue.

'Mrs Barron, I understand your frustration; you and the other complainants have every right to be angry.'

Rick intervened.

'I hate to inflame the situation, but Erasmus is a clever and charming man. He's good at covering his tracks and with four different country borders – five, if you include Swaziland – he could be travelling in *any* direction. If he leaves South Africa with a suitcase full of money, we'll never see him again.'

Kathy was struggling to control her emotions.

'I'm sorry about my outburst, Captain Botha, my anger isn't directed at you. I'll never forget how safe I felt when I heard your voice as I regained consciousness at Stein dam.'

She took a deep breath.

'I know you'll do your best to re-capture him.'

The moment she arrived home. Kathy phoned Kenny at the East London News

'Kenny, I need your help. Can you include an article on Robert Erasmus in the East London News next edition? Erasmus has broken bail, he's on the run.'

Kenny indicated he was eager to help.

'Let me speak to the editor, Mrs Barron. I've got a head-and-shoulders photograph of Erasmus and we could enlarge it, and print his name in bold, something like a Western movie wanted poster. The headline would read, "Breaking Bail" Leave it with me.'

Kathy thanked him, her hopes a little restored.

Frances and Tim joined her and Rick on their veranda that evening after the seven o'clock news. Police file had featured a photograph of Robert Erasmus and an appeal for information from the public.

Kathy seldom drank alcohol, but that night she *needed* a drink.

'You're very quiet, Kath, is everything okay?' her mother asked.

'Yes, Mum. I was just thinking about Erasmus's photograph on police-file. Who would have thought a respected businessman would have his face plastered on national TV as a wanted man?' she chuckled. 'Remember what happened when you visited Commandant Marais? He told you that I was mistaken because the man they interviewed had no priors and he had cooperated fully with them. Huh! He fooled them all.'

'You're right, sweetie. Over the last few weeks Erasmus has made a name for himself for all the wrong reasons.'

Frances stubbed out her cigarette.

'This is turning into a saga. We could write a book about our experiences with you as the lady detective, Kath.'

They all laughed but Kathy laughed the loudest.

'Oh, Mum, that's so funny. I think I'm getting my sense of humour back.' She felt a sense of well-being she hadn't felt for a long time.

'Thanks, Rick, I think I'll have another drink.'

Erasmus had tumbled from his elevated pedestal, but it was still important to Kathy that he faced justice. Her mother took the children to nursery school the next day and she busied herself, packing for their move to Cape Town. It was tedious work using only one arm.

When the phone rang, she didn't answer it immediately, but stood next to it and uttered a heartfelt prayer.

'Dear Lord, please let this call be from Rick to tell me that Erasmus has been arrested.'

She snatched up the receiver. It *was* Rick.

'I've just heard from Captain Botha, Kath… there's been a sighting of Erasmus's vehicle in the Nelspruit area. They think he might try to cross the border into Swaziland or Mozambique. Botha said he'd keep us advised.'

She jumped up and down, excited at the news.

'And, Kath, I've been asked to attend a final interview in Cape Town tomorrow afternoon regarding that position I'm keen on, so I've taken a day's leave.'

They were both excited at the prospect of him securing the job he really wanted. Rick left for Cape Town early that morning.

Frances took a day off work to drive Kathy to the doctor and physiotherapist. On returning to Flame Lilly Villa, they sat on the veranda, Frances in her old wicker chair while Kathy sat opposite. She loved her mother dearly and touched on the question she'd been afraid to ask.

'What have you and Tim decided to do about moving to Cape Town, Mum? We're hoping you'll come with us.'

'Of course, we're coming with you, Kathy. What did you think we were going to do?'

'Oh, Mum, I'm *so* thrilled.'

A broad smile crossed Kathy's face.

'I've been too afraid to ask. You're married to Tim now and he might not have wanted to move. I also thought you might want to stay because you love your job.'

'We didn't have any doubt, Sweetie. I can find *work* anywhere, but I only have one daughter and three grandchildren. Tim is my friend and companion, but you're my family. I'll always be where you are.'

Kathy protected her injured shoulder as she gingerly squeezed into the wicker chair with her mum and kissed her on the cheek.

'Thank you for being the best mum in the world. We'll find a house and cottage big enough for all of us to live together.'

The chair was cramped so Kathy moved back to the comfort of her own seat.

'I can't wait for Rick to get home. Just imagine – if he gets this job, we can move to Cape Town together as a family instead of me going ahead with the children on my own,' she chatted happily.

Frances eventually got a word in.

'Tim and I have discussed what we plan to do when we move to Cape Town. He's going to start an accounting business for small businesses. I'll help him and write short articles for magazines, like I did when we lived on the farm. I'm sure you'll be needing my help to transport and care for my grandchildren.'

'Yes, please, Mum. I'm *not* going to squeeze into that chair next to you again, it's too *awkward.* You'll just have to visualise me hugging you and saying a big thank you. I'm going to need all the help I can get.'

Rick arrived home late that night in high spirits.

'I've accepted the position, Kath. It's the job I was looking for.'

He shared details about the legal firm and the kind of work he would be doing.

'They want me to start in January.' This was what they had been waiting for and the final decision was made. Flame Lily Villa was put on the market the following day. It sold within days for the price they were asking.

Just before Christmas they packed their belongings and transferred them into storage pending their move to Cape Town. The whole family moved back in with Maria and Eric Van Wyk for the few days over the festive season.

There was still no news of Robert Erasmus and it had been five weeks since he broke bail. Captain Botha kept in touch, assuring Rick and Kathy that the police were following all leads and monitoring all border posts.

'We're convinced he's still in the country and someone is helping him. He's lying low in the Nelspruit area waiting for the right time to leave the country. We haven't had another sighting of the vehicle, but border security is on full alert over the Christmas rush.'

Rick was sceptical.

'We should have heard something by now, Kath. I wouldn't be surprised if he's in North Africa or Europe by now.'

Kathy was satisfied that Robert Erasmus's reputation had been ruined, but seeing him behind bars would be first prize.

'I've been so busy packing and sorting out the children that I haven't given Erasmus much thought, but Captain Botha could be right; he might try to slip out the country during the festive season.'

On Christmas morning there were squeals of delight from the children every time a gift was ripped open. Honey joined in the fun chewing on her toy bone.

Rick's parents travelled from Cape Town bringing Charlotte's mother Prudence who now also lived in cape town with them. Charlotte and Burt were there and Daniel Pistorius flew in from Pretoria.

Three tables pushed together into one long table made it a festive occasion for their Christmas midday meal.

Rick left the lunch table to answer the phone and when he returned, he tapped a spoon against a glass, requesting everyone's attention.

'That was Captain Botha on the phone. He asked me to wish you all a Merry Christmas.'

This message was met with a chorus of 'Merry Christmas Captain Botha.'

'That was kind of him.' Frances remarked.

'He also had news of Robert Erasmus.'

There was silence. Everyone looked at him expectantly.

'He's back behind bars.'

'Yes!' shrieked Kathy jumping to her feet. 'Tell us where they found him?'

'He tried to cross into Mozambique first thing this morning. He was found hidden behind a panel in a friend's vehicle. The police had a hunch he would try something like that and brought in reinforcements to search every vehicle.'

'Woohoo! Kathy was in high spirits.

Rick asked everyone to charge their glasses and stand for a toast.

'Ben and Becky, you hold Wendy's hands and lift them up. Please join me in raising your glasses in a toast to absent friends.'

A murmur of *"To absent friends"* and clinking glasses echoed through a moment's silence.

Kathy laughed and wiped away her tears at the same time.

'Are you okay, Kath?' her mother asked.

'I'm being silly, Mum. I'm happy that Erasmus is back behind bars but sad that Daddy and Trevor aren't with us.'

Frances left the room and reappeared with a large wrapped parcel.

'I commissioned a local artist to paint, *this* special gift to be opened after lunch.' She handed it to Kathy and kissed her on the cheek. '

'Merry Christmas, Kathy'

Kathy tore the paper from the large framed painting and stood transfixed.

From the corner of the frame, a beam of sunlight filtering through the branches of a flowering flamboyant tree. Huchi, their rambling old farm house took pride of place in the centre, with its chimney jutting from the rusty corrugated iron roof. A penny creeper climbed the exterior walls and the pillars of the deep veranda. Frances was sitting in her wicker chair with little Kathy on her knee. Trevor and her father were playing cricket on the front lawn while the two dogs Luger and Dallas chased a ball.

Kathy stared at the painting, her eyes sparkled with joy. The artist had captured every detail. The brass plaque read *"A Family Day at Huchi farm"*.

She wiped away a tear that trickled down her cheek and breathed softly.

'How wonderful.'

CPSIA information can be obtained
at www.ICGtesting.com
Printed in the USA
BVHW052225041021
618092BV00007B/491